Dare's voice
'Are you sur...
problems wi...
Addie?'

She brought her hands up to push against his chest, but he simply moved closer. 'No images to haunt?' The words were whispered so close that his lips brushed her skin as he spoke, and an involuntary shiver chased down her spine. 'No memories to rise?'

His mouth covered hers then, firm, a little bit angry, and a whole lot hungry. She tasted the demand on his lips and fought against it. But he was too close, and she felt a moment of panic when she realised that the moment she'd sworn never to repeat was playing out again.

Finally she opened her eyes, confused, vulnerable, in a way she rarely allowed herself to be.

'Ancient history, Addie?' Dare murmured again. 'Are you *sure* it's dead and buried...?'

Dear Reader,

Welcome to another sizzling selection of stupendous reads from Silhouette Sensation.

Marie Ferrarella brings us a new CHILDFINDERS, INC. book, *Heart of a Hero*, where a mother desperately needs help retrieving her kidnapped child, and Russell Andreini's the man she turns to in this crisis. Virginia Kantra's Jack Dalton is also the kind of man to have around when trouble is brewing, but this ex-navy SEAL is none too thrilled to be given a princess with attitude to guard in *Born To Protect*, the latest in the FIRST-BORN SONS series.

This Perfect Stranger by Barbara Ankrum, *A Husband By Any Other Name* from Cheryl St. John and *Cassidy and the Princess* by Patricia Potter are each fantastic stand-alone romances, with that extra dash of excitement to speed things along Sensation-style.

Last but not least comes *Hard To Resist* from Kylie Brant, one of her CHARMED AND DANGEROUS trilogy, and there's another one of these irresistible males—the last one—coming your way next month, too.

Enjoy!

The Editors

Hard To Resist

KYLIE BRANT

™ SILHOUETTE®
SENSATION™

First published in Great Britain 2002
Silhouette Books, Eton House, 18-24 Paradise Road,
Richmond, Surrey TW9 1SR

© Kimberly Bahnsen 2001

ISBN 0 373 27189 1

18-0902

Printed and bound in Spain
by Litografia Rosés S.A., Barcelona

KYLIE BRANT

lives with her husband and five children in Iowa. She works full-time as a teacher of learning-disabled students. Much of her free time is spent in her role as professional spectator at her kids' sporting events.

An avid reader, Kylie enjoys stories of love, mystery and suspense—and she insists on happy endings! When her youngest children, a set of twins, turned four, she decided to try her hand at writing. Now most weekends and all summer she can be found at the computer, spinning her own tales of romance and happily-ever-afters.

Kylie invites readers to write to her at PO Box 231, Charles City, IA 50616, USA.

Charmed and Dangerous

Hard To Handle – August 2002
Hard To Resist – September 2002
Hard To Tame – October 2002

For all our 'extra' kids—who fill our house,
empty our cupboards and enrich our lives.

Chapter 1

Addison Jacobs walked into her office and stopped short in the doorway. Six foot two inches of lean golden male was comfortably settled in her chair with his feet propped on her desk and crossed at the ankle. Her narrowed gaze followed that long, muscled line of jean-clad legs. The finely tailored linen shirt he wore covered a broad chest, flat stomach and was snugged in to the waistband at his narrow hips. The intensity of his electric-blue eyes was momentarily hidden behind closed lids. With the late afternoon sunlight haloing his bright-blond hair and outlining the chiseled perfection of his profile, a woman could be excused for believing she'd stumbled upon a dozing Greek god. Some might even go so far as to offer prayers of gratitude to the deity responsible for creating such a flawless specimen of manhood.

But not this woman.

She let the door slam behind her and watched with grim satisfaction as the man's eyes snapped open and the chair came upright with a start. "Get your ass out of my chair, McKay. And then keep it moving until it's out of my office."

The moment of surprise past, Dare McKay aimed a lop-sided smile at her. "Ah, Addie, as charming as ever. Good manners would dictate that you ask me politely to state my business. And I wouldn't turn down coffee if you're offering."

"It's A.J." Her tone was level enough, even though her jaw was clenched. "As you well know. And you gave up any right to polite behavior when you barged into my office and took up residence behind my desk."

"Your assistant said I should wait."

"I doubt very much Song meant for you to wait *in* my office." She approached the desk and set her maroon leather briefcase beside it, giving him a pointed look. He vacated her chair, but instead of moving to another seat, he leaned his hips against the desk close beside her. Much too close.

"Did you know there's a betting pool over which state's attorney is going to land the Delgado case?"

Comprehension dawned, and with it, a healthy dose of cynicism. Of course, the high-profile kidnapping/attempted murder case would bring a hotshot investigative reporter like McKay sniffing around. But if he thought he'd get information from her, he was dreaming.

He continued cheerfully, "I put ten on you, two-to-one odds. Mark Stanley was running just a bit ahead of you this morning, but I was betting on that cool-headed logic of yours to tip the scale in your favor. If Beardmore's instincts are better developed than his politics, he'll go with the best."

Deliberately looking at her watch, she ignored the flattery. "Doesn't the newspaper have you keeping regular hours anymore? Or does winning a Pulitzer entitle you to set your own schedule?''

Dare settled more comfortably against the desk and folded his arms across his chest. ''You wound me, Addie. Truly. I *am* working. I'm here to verify that you've been named lead prosecutor for the Delgado case.''

The sound of her teeth snapping together was audible. ''No comment.''

''C'mon, don't be like that. How about if I offer to split my winnings?''

''What part of my answer didn't you understand, McKay? The 'no' or the 'comment'?''

He grinned at that, his eyes dancing with amusement. ''Well, it was worth a try. Deadline's looming.''

''And we both know the lengths you'll go to for a story.'' The words were spoken with uncharacteristic impulsiveness, and A.J. regretted them even before Dare's eyes went cool, his smile fading.

''Or you think you do.'' Abruptly he pushed away from her desk. He went to the window and hooked the blinds with a finger, lifting them to look out at the view below. ''You know, I might be in a position to offer you some help with your case along the way.''

''Your offer is duly noted and rejected. I'm going to assume you remember the way out.''

He turned then, letting the blinds drop. ''Never give an inch, do you, Addie? You're going to be swimming with sharks in this particular case. Watch your back.''

Lifting her chin, she studied the man before her. He was convincing. She could almost believe that he was concerned about her safety. Dare McKay's entire career rested upon his ability to get people to trust him. But there was precious little Addison Jacobs trusted in life. This man would never make the short list.

Her voice tinged with sarcasm, she asked, ''Scare tactics,

McKay? Is this where I'm supposed to throw up my hands in horror and beg for your strong, manly protection?''

He cocked his head, pretended to give her question consideration. ''The image does hold a certain appeal.''

Snorting in derision, she said, ''Make sure to hold your breath until that day arrives.'' Rising, she strode to the door, pulled it open.

''A.J.'' The man poised before her doorway with his hand still raised to knock sent a considering look between her and McKay. ''Are you busy?''

''Dennis.'' A dull throb had started in her left temple, a normal enough occurrence when she was in McKay's company for any length of time. ''Am I late for our appointment?''

''You're not late. My schedule just filled up, and I thought we could move the meeting forward a bit.'' Cook County Senior Assistant State's Attorney Dennis Beardmore was a tall man, with a solid build just beginning to show the effects of too many rubber-chicken dinners consumed at political functions. He deliberately cultivated a theatrical look, wearing his wavy, prematurely white hair swept back from a broad forehead and left long enough in back to brush his shoulders. She doubted she was the only one who suspected Dennis dyed his hair for effect. At any rate, his appearance matched the deep, resonant voice he used to great advantage in the courtroom.

''Have a seat.'' She speared a glance at Dare, who was making no effort to leave. ''Mr. McKay was just on his way out.''

''McKay.'' Beardmore's voice held mild interest. ''I didn't expect to see you here. Congratulations on your latest Pulitzer. The second, isn't it?'' A.J.'s gaze shot to the reporter. She'd had no idea that the award was just his most recent. Beardmore continued, ''Had my office been fully apprised of just how far-reaching your exposé would turn out to be, perhaps we would have been a little more helpful when you approached us with questions.''

Dare's smile had cooled. ''Maybe next time.'' He turned to A.J. ''Ms. Jacobs. Always a pleasure.'' Exiting the inner office, he passed Song's desk and winked at her. ''Later, Ms. Wynn.''

The woman's audible sigh as the reporter left earned her a disgusted look from A.J. before she turned and followed Dennis into her office and closed the door. Slipping into one of the leather chairs facing her desk, she indicated for the man to do the same.

In his early fifties, Dennis Beardmore was a man with aspirations beyond his current position. Intelligent, driven and ambitious, he exuded charisma. Not the hot-and-cold-running charm of McKay, A.J. thought, but a more deliberate civility that he donned and shed as easily as his thousand-dollar suits, as the occasion demanded. Despite her personal distaste for his inner-office politics, she respected his expertise in the courtroom, where he used his genial and barracudalike qualities with equal effectiveness.

''How's the armed robbery case coming?''

A.J. proceeded to give him an update on the case that had kept her in court all morning, concluding, ''Judge Gaffney allowed the defendant's plea for an early recess. It'll drag out for another month at this rate.''

He nodded. ''That case is too advanced to consider someone else taking over for you now. But I've cleared the rest of your caseload.'' Ignoring her raised brows, he handed her a typewritten sheet of paper. ''This list details their reassignments. You'll want to meet with each of the attorneys, give them your notes and bring them up to speed.''

A.J. reached for the paper slowly. She couldn't remember another instance when Beardmore had considered one single assignment important enough to clear an attorney's calendar. Quite the opposite, in fact.

As if reading her thoughts, he fixed her with a shrewd gaze. "This is a big one, and I don't mind telling you, I want a win pretty badly." He handed her a thick file folder he carried. "Here's what we've got so far on the Delgado case. Most of it you already know, since you acted as charging attorney on the scene."

"Who's his defense attorney?"

"Joel Paquin."

Her stomach twisted. She should have known. She'd realized Dennis had to have ulterior motives for passing on a case that would be highly publicized. Paquin was potent motive. The man had the ethics of pond scum, but he was inarguably successful. And he'd beaten Beardmore three out of the last four cases they'd tried together. She was coming to a vague understanding of how the Christians had felt right before being thrown to the lions.

"I have faith in you, A.J. You beat Paquin the one time the two of you met, didn't you?"

The question was rhetorical so she didn't bother answering. Dennis was intimately acquainted with the records of every attorney working with him. She had no doubt that her win had been the deciding factor in her landing the case.

"I've named Stanley as secondary, so the two of you will be working closely together. That won't be a problem, will it?"

The quintessential professional, she kept her face impassive. "Not at all."

"Good. Secondary chair is usually reserved for less experienced prosecutors, but this case calls for stacking the deck a bit." Beardmore rose. "I'll want to be apprised of your progress every couple days."

The request didn't surprise her. The attorneys normally

gathered once a week to talk about the progress of their cases and to accept new assignments. But she'd already concluded that the Delgado case would be subject to more intense scrutiny.

"I've got a press conference planned for four-thirty, at which time I'll announce your assignment to this case. I'll expect you in my office at four-fifteen."

She followed him to the door. When he was out of earshot she speared a look at her assistant. "No maidenly sighs, Song?"

The woman shrugged. "So sue me. I'm a woman. And McKay is the kind of man who makes me really, really aware of it, you know?"

A.J. did. She counted herself lucky that she was immune. "If you want to take your chance with him, you'll have to stand in line. Women swarm around him like flies."

"An enticing picture." There was a speculative gleam in Song's exotic dark eyes. "Do you have any other information to share? Something acquired…firsthand, perhaps?"

"Well, let's see…" Enjoying the spark of interest on her secretary's face, she pretended to consider. "From my dealings with McKay I've found him to be deceitful, arrogant and downright nosy. A real dream man, all right." She allowed herself a little grin at Song's crestfallen expression.

"Here." She handed the woman the sheet Beardmore had given her. "Set up times I can meet with each of the attorneys on the list so I can bring them up to speed on the cases they're taking over for me."

Song took the sheet and glanced at it. "I heard you were named prosecutor. That's great news. Congratulations."

A.J. wasn't fooled. "How much did you win?"

Song looked startled, then smiled sheepishly. "Twenty. I was behind you all the way."

She'd need more than good wishes on this case, A.J.

thought, as she went back to her office and closed the door. She sank down into one of the chairs, leaned her head back and closed her eyes. The earlier excitement she'd felt at the assignment had long since faded. In its place was a mixture of determination and trepidation. With Paquin in the court-room, trials tended to take on a circuslike atmosphere. She could only hope they'd get a hard-line judge who wouldn't put up with any of the other lawyer's antics.

She rubbed her temples absently, her concentration fo-cused on the day's events. Two things already seemed cer-tain. Her superior had decided he'd rather sacrifice her to Paquin and the media rather than risk his future political career. And he'd assigned as secondary a fiercely compet-itive attorney who was going resent his position every min-ute of the trial.

As days went, this one couldn't get much worse.

Dare McKay tipped back the bottle of beer and drank appreciatively. "I'm surprised to see you out tonight. Thought that fiancée of yours had you pretty well tied up these days."

Rather than taking offense at the gibe, Detective Gabe Connally looked complacent. "Meghan and her nephew had an appointment. I'm picking them up in an hour."

"Got the wedding date set yet?"

"If I had my way it'd be tomorrow."

Dare marveled at the hint of disgruntlement in the other man's tone. Although he'd only recently come to know Connally better, the detective had always given the im-pression of a man wary of ties. Meghan Patterson had in-explicably changed that.

"She doesn't want anything big, but she does want to do the church thing, flowers, reception...all that." Gabe shrugged self-consciously. Not in a million years would he admit that the idea wasn't completely disagreeable. He'd take Meghan any way he could get her, and if he *had* to wait, maybe a church wedding wouldn't be so bad. It would, at least, lend a satisfying air of permanence to their vows. He cast a glance at the man seated across from him. "You can come."

Dare accepted the offhanded invitation graciously. "I wouldn't miss it."

Gabe gave him a wicked smile. "It's always good to have an unattached man to dance with the available ladies."

Squelching the quick spurt of panic the words elicited, Dare hastily added, "On the other hand, tell Meghan I'll be bringing a guest."

Mouth quirked in amusement the detective started to answer, before his attention was diverted. He nodded toward the front of the bar. "Actually, I'm here tonight to meet with her."

Dare turned in the direction of the man's gaze and saw Addie approaching the bar and placing an order with Jax, the giant bartender. From the looks of her, she'd just come from her office. She hadn't changed clothes, and he knew she often kept grueling hours.

Glancing at Gabe again, he asked, "Is this the first you've met with her since she's been named to the Delgado case?" As the arresting officer, the detective's testimony would no doubt become an integral part of Addie's case.

The other man nodded. "She called earlier, but Madison and I were working another investigation. We'll be tied up tomorrow, and I could tell she didn't want to wait, so…" He frowned a little. "How experienced is she? I don't want Delgado to walk away with a slap on the wrist because the prosecutor was a cream puff."

"Looks can be deceiving," Dare said dryly. "That madonna-like face is accompanied by a kick-you-in-the-teeth attitude."

A slow grin crossed Gabe's face. "That's right. You were going to give me the story on the two of you."

"Some other time, maybe." Ignoring the speculative note in the man's voice, Dare kept his eyes trained on the bottle in front of him. He knew what the other man saw when he looked at Addie. She was the kind of woman who looked as if she should be kept behind glass, where nothing dirty could sully her. Her hair was as blond as his own, her eyes a deep brown. Her striking looks had led more than one attorney to underestimate her skills. He'd witnessed the way she dismantled them in court, one argument at a time. He'd almost felt sorry for them. She was a tough prosecutor who didn't back down in the face of a challenge. At least, not in her professional life.

"I guess Beardmore had his reasons for naming her to this case. Is she a strict by-the-book type or is she going to be willing to listen to some theories?"

"Only one way to find out." Dare snagged his bottle with two fingers and rose. Ambling in Addie's direction, he accepted her cool look with equanimity. Although she was as impeccably groomed as ever, there was a hint of strain around her mouth that hadn't been there earlier today. The thought occurred that she worked too hard, but he banished the concern before it could form. She wouldn't welcome the emotion from anyone, especially him. He noted the way her spine straightened at his approach, as if she were physically arming herself to do battle. Then he passed by her, whistling tunelessly between his teeth. Continuing to the jukebox in the corner, he gave scrupulous attention to feeding quarters into the machine and choosing songs. When the strains of his first selection drifted through the smoke-filled air of the tavern, he retraced his steps through the bar. The Eagles were predicting a heartbreak tonight when he slowed beside Addie, who was chatting with some off-duty cops.

"Well, Addison Jacobs, as I live and breathe." Dare's eyes crinkled over the top of the bottle he brought to his lips. "Fancy seeing you twice in one day."

"I'm not in the mood for more of your babbling, Mc-Kay." She attempted to brush by him, but with a subtle shift of position he remained in her path. He saw her eyes narrow and hid a grin. No doubt she was considering a sharp elbow to his ribs. It certainly wouldn't be the first time. Despite her ethereal looks, she was about as helpless as a piranha.

"I hope you had some food sent in while you were working late. It isn't good to drink on an empty stomach."

Her voice was cool. "What makes you think I haven't just come from a restaurant?"

"You're still wearing that butt-ugly suit you had on earlier." He nodded toward her clothes, pretended he didn't notice her eyes go to smolder. "Figured you'd have changed if you had dinner plans. You might want to consider something more colorful the next time you're due to appear on the five-o'clock news. You looked a little washed out."

"A fashion critique from a man wearing a Hawaiian shirt, jeans and cowboy boots." She gave him a mocking smile. "You can't imagine what that means to me."

"Oh, I think I can." Dare rocked back on his heels and considered, not for the first time, what it was about this woman that made him continually bait her. No doubt it was a desire to draw some genuine emotion from her, even if it was negative. A juvenile objective, to be sure, but sometimes maturity was vastly overrated.

"You'll have to excuse me," she said with exaggerated patience. "I need to speak to someone."

"I know." He rubbed at the bottle's condensation with his thumb. "Detective Connally's waiting for you."

Her gaze traveled to the detective and then back to him.

"Am I going to be able to talk to him without you pressing your ear up against the table?"

Because he knew it would annoy her, he gave her a wink. "I've already published most of Connally's information. As a matter of fact, I actually provided him with some of it. But I guess it's time for you to catch up. Be my guest."

When he turned and sauntered away, she strode toward the detective, who'd risen. "Detective Connally." She reached out, shook his hand. "Good to see you again. I appreciate you meeting with me on such short notice." She sat down, setting her briefcase on the floor beside her.

"No problem. I'm as anxious as you are to see Delgado locked up for good."

She drew a legal pad out of the side pocket of her briefcase. "We went over the main points surrounding the arrest, after you took Delgado in custody. But I need to clear up some details so I can begin to prepare for the case." She consulted her notes on the pad. "Paul Delgado approached Meghan Patterson when she'd gone to The Children's Academy to pick up her nephew, is that right?" She waited for Gabe's nod before asking, "You've listed two witnesses who saw him get into her car. Are they both prepared to testify?"

Gabe nodded. "Chris O'Malley was across the street at the time, and recognized Meghan and her car. She saw a man approach her, but couldn't ID him for sure. The other woman, Lana Thul, was parked a ways ahead of Meghan. She got a clear view of Delgado with her."

"And then he drove her to 1510 Beck Street and kept her there for…how long?"

"It was about five hours before my partner and I arrived."

A.J.'s gaze dropped to her notes again. "In your attempt to rescue Miss Patterson, Delgado assaulted you with the same weapon he'd threatened the victim with, and you fought with him physically. Before you'd subdued him, the victim was stabbed and she was taken to the hospital.'' She looked at him. ''How badly was she hurt?'' The extent of her injuries could well prove to play a part in the case.

''It was a nasty wound. But she won't suffer any lasting damage. Her shoulder's still stiff, but she's regained the use of her arm.''

Detecting an odd note in the man's voice, she paused. ''You seem pretty familiar with her prognosis.''

His gaze was steady. ''Meghan Patterson is my fiancée.''

Sitting back in her chair, A.J. released a breath. ''I didn't know that.''

With a glint in his eye, Gabe said, ''Are you telling me that changes things?''

''It doesn't change the facts. But,'' she added honestly, ''it does give the defense a red herring to distract the jury with.''

''Meaning he'll try to prove my testimony is biased because of my relationship with Meghan.''

She nodded. ''Luckily your partner can back up your story. How far behind you was Madison? A few seconds? Several minutes?''

''He was at my back. Couldn't have been more than three seconds after me, tops.''

''Good. His testimony will corroborate yours.''

''There's no question about what happened in that room,'' Gabe said bluntly. ''Delgado tried to kill Meghan, and then me. I figure he snatched Meghan because he believed she could ID him. She and her nephew were just across the alley from the apartment of a perp I was investigating. Delgado was the last one to be seen with my suspect before the guy wound up dead. We were able to put together an artist sketch and posted copies all over the city.''

It could fit nicely, A.J. thought, when putting together a

motive for the kidnapping. If, as the detective claimed, Delgado had reason to fear identification, eliminating an eyewitness could be motivation for murder. "What was Delgado involved in? How'd he figure into your original investigation?"

"You've got a copy of his rap sheet and sentences?" At her nod, Gabe went on. "I have reason to believe that he's expanded his activities. Have you ever heard of Paulie the Knife?" The detective barely waited for her negative response. "He's a hired assassin, known for his ability with a blade. There's no picture of him on file. But his reputation is known by law enforcement agencies across the country. He's wanted for questioning in more than a dozen homicides in just the last few years. We had three bodies show up during my case that very well could be the result of his handiwork."

It took a second for A.J. to see where he was heading with the explanation. "You think Delgado is the hit man known as Paulie the Knife?" She sipped from her glass and considered the information. "Hired assassins don't come cheap. Whoever hired him would have to have connections. Money. Power."

"It didn't take him long to lawyer up," Gabe observed. "I understand that he never made any phone calls once he was in custody. Refused the offer, but Paquin showed up hours later, regardless. Makes me wonder if someone else sent him."

"Not necessarily. Paquin is a media junkie. He gets off on being in the limelight. It wouldn't be unusual for him to take this case pro bono just because of the exposure it's going to generate for him. He may well have approached Delgado and offered his services free of charge."

"How familiar are you with Paquin's career?"

She leaned back in her chair and studied the detective. "I've known him for about four years. Why?"

"Before that time, he defended a local scumbag named Victor Mannen, who was being charged with murder. The witnesses were in protective custody, but they, and the U.S. Marshals protecting them, were killed right before the trial was to begin. One got away, but disappeared."

"Interesting, but irrelevant." A.J. brought the glass to her lips and drank. "Paquin has built his career defending slugs like that. What does that have to do with this case?"

"In the course of our investigation we began to suspect that Delgado was working for Mannen. And Mannen's former lawyer is representing Delgado."

"Hardly a coincidence. Paquin is the most prominent defense attorney in the area. Did you discover any solid evidence connecting Delgado to this Paulie person?"

A muscle clenched in Gabe's jaw. "Not yet."

"Anything linking him to Mannen?"

"No." The word was clipped, as the man's frustration began to show. "But while he held Meghan, Delgado told her that he had a job to do on me, too. He was working for someone else, I'm certain of it. Right now I'm breathing down Mannen's neck, and having me out of the way eliminates a threat."

A.J. slipped her legal pad back into her briefcase. "I'm not saying it isn't possible. But you have to get me evidence to support that theory. For now I'm building a case based on the kidnapping and attempted murder of Meghan Patterson." She rose. "I'll be in touch soon. I'll want to speak to Meghan as soon as it can be arranged."

She walked by Dare's table on her way to the bar, not sparing him a glance. He watched her hand her glass to the bartender before she headed for the door. It was a curious habit she had. No one was ever allowed to buy her a drink, and she never left her glass on the table. She was an enigma, he thought, as she strode to the door with that brisk, no-nonsense walk of hers. At one time he'd thought

there was more to her than that composed professional facade she showed to the world. He'd been wrong.

He walked back to Gabe's table and slipped into the
chair she'd vacated. "You know, you're wearing an expression common to men who have recently had the pleasure of Ms. Jacobs's company."

The detective sent him a sour look. "God save me from
lawyers. They can't see anything unless it's in black-and-
white."

"Then we'll just have to find some hard evidence to
convince her."

"We?" Gabe reached for his bottle and drained it. "I
don't think so. Last I looked, my partner and I were named
investigators in this case."

Nodding, Dare said mildly, "I know. I also remember
how incredibly stingy you are with your information. But
don't worry. I'll still share whatever I uncover with you."
At the other man's muttered curse, he laughed.

"What's your stake in this, McKay?" Gabe's tone was
genuinely curious. "That information you gave us tying
Mannen to our investigation…that had to have taken
months to put together."

The guess fell far short of the truth, but Dare didn't correct the man. He raised his arm in the air to summon the
waitress. "My stake? The story of course." His gaze went
to the door Addie had just exited through and his smile
faded. "Just the story."

Her upcoming case was the furthest thing from A.J.'s
mind as she walked through the discreetly lettered doors of
St. Anne's Hospital. Recognizing the woman at the desk,
she smiled. "Good evening, Sister Katherine."

The nun beamed at her. "A.J. We were beginning to
think you wouldn't make it tonight."

"I know it's past visiting hours, but I thought if she was awake…"

Sister Katherine nodded. "I'm sure Mandy hasn't gone to bed yet. She's been having some trouble sleeping lately."

The reminder brought A.J. up short. "I know." She hovered in front of the desk with a hesitant air that was completely foreign to her. "Has she…is she any better?"

The nun's creased face settled into a mask of sympathy. "She's about the same. But the doctor is very encouraged by this new medication she's on. I'm sure there'll be progress soon."

Masking her disappointment, A.J. nodded before turning to walk the familiar path to room 118. She paused in the doorway of the spacious room, watched the figure move rhythmically in the rocking chair, crooning to the doll she held.

"Hi. You're up kind of late tonight, aren't you?" The cheerful note in her voice sounded forced, but it didn't matter. There was no response to her words. Heart sinking a little, she moved into the room and put her arm around the narrow shoulders, kissed the pale cheek.

"That's a pretty doll," she continued brightly. She reached out a finger to touch it, and it was yanked away, clutched against a frail chest.

"Mine!"

A.J.'s shoulders drooped a little, and her voice grew strained. The word was the only one she'd heard Mandy speak for two weeks. "Yes, I know it's yours. It's very pretty."

Silence filled the room, the kind that wove around the heart and squeezed tight. She took a deep breath and then released it slowly. She shouldn't have come tonight. The day had been too stressful to maintain her usual unshakable composure. But she could never manage to stay away.

She moved to the dresser and picked up the ornate hairbrush. "Shall I brush your hair for you?" Although there was no answer, she began, anyway, drawing the brush through Mandy's fine hair with long, soothing strokes. It was one of the few intimacies she would allow these days, and A.J. thought it seemed to soothe her. In truth, it soothed them both.

That was how Sister Katherine found them half an hour later. "I'm sorry to interrupt your visit, but we really should get Mandy to bed."

Nodding, she replaced the brush on the dresser and picked up her purse. The nun withdrew from the doorway, giving them a moment of privacy. "I'll try to come back tomorrow," she whispered. Even without a response, she couldn't stop trying to reach out. Couldn't stop hoping for some sort of miracle.

She bent, pressed her lips to the soft, blond hair and prayed for a divine intervention that wouldn't come. With an all-too-familiar heaviness in her heart she whispered, "Good night, Mama."

Chapter 2

A.J. was too used to sleepless nights to be slowed down by the one she'd just spent. She was in her office shortly after dawn, preparing for her morning in court. The armed robbery case she was trying was dragging on far longer than it needed to. But Gaffney was allowing the defense to bring up arguments ranging from his client's abusive childhood to the culpability of the gun manufacturers. As if, A.J. fumed, after the case had been recessed for the day, anyone other than the defendant had been in that liquor store firing the shots that had critically wounded the owner.

Her mood didn't improve appreciably when she strode into her office and found Mark Stanley lounging near Song's desk. "Mark." A.J.'s voice wasn't welcoming. "I thought we were meeting after lunch."

Stanley flashed his toothpaste-ad-bright smile and said smoothly, "I'm afraid I had to schedule another appointment for then. And I really didn't want to wait any longer to be brought up to speed on the Delgado case."

Mentally kissing away any chance of grabbing more than a stale sandwich at her desk later, she nodded. "Go on in."

While Mark entered her cramped office ahead of her, A.J. looked at Song and asked, "Did you have time to…"

Two copies of the notes from last night's meeting with Connally, freshly typed, appeared in the woman's hand. "Right here."

"That's why I keep you around, Song."

"Does it make up for letting McKay sneak into your office when my back was turned yesterday?"

Clutching the papers in one hand, she surveyed her assistant. "Sneaking is McKay's forte. Next time you'll be forewarned."

"Next time I won't take my eyes off him," Song promised solemnly. "Believe me, it will be no hardship."

Closing the door on the woman's giggle, A.J. concentrated on the man roaming her cramped office space. "Why don't you light somewhere, Mark, and we can get started?"

The man smoothed his perfectly groomed dark hair. "Maybe we should move this into my office. We'd have more room."

His words were something of an exaggeration, since they all occupied cubicles that looked claustrophobic with more than three people in them. But appearances were important enough to Mark that he'd equipped his office at his own personal expense. She knew he considered the trappings as a measure of his success, his stature in the department. Just as she knew that his ruthlessly combative streak was honed even sharper where she was concerned.

"Oh, I think we can manage here." Going to her briefcase and unlocking it, she withdrew the file Dennis had given her on the case and handed it to the other lawyer. While he skimmed through the items included in the file, she sat down at her desk and reread the notes Song had typed for her. She needed time to weave a strong connection between the victim and Delgado, but Connally had at least given her the foundation. Once she'd gotten home last night she'd jotted down a few more questions she wanted to ask the detective. One she hadn't noted, but still stuck in her mind, was the man's link to McKay. She couldn't help but wonder how the reporter had acquired the information he'd shared with Connally prior to Delgado's arrest. The most obvious solution would be to ask him. She'd rather chew glass.

Mark closed the file and looked up. "Is this all you've got?"

"Since I just acquired the case twenty-four hours ago, I don't have a whole lot of details yet," A.J. responded dryly.

"I heard we'll be facing off with Paquin." A flash of resentment shone in the man's dark eyes and then was gone. "There will be a lot of publicity on this one. He'll make sure of that."

Kicking her pumps off under her desk, she rubbed the arch of one foot. "I'm familiar with Paquin's tactics."

"That's right, you've argued against him, haven't you? Tough case."

"Which I won."

He went on as if he hadn't heard her reminder. "I can't help but think Beardmore should have used someone fresh on this one, someone Paquin hasn't gone up against." A.J.'s brows raised at the obvious reference to himself. "Are you afraid his familiarity with your style will give him an advantage?"

A wry smile twisted her lips. He was so slick and concerned, one would barely suspect that each statement was uttered with an intention to shred confidence, undermine determination. Fortunately she had an ample supply of both. "Actually, I think that my familiarity with his style might work to *my* advantage."

Mark pursed his lips. "You may be right." The words were shaded with just enough doubt to render his agreement meaningless. He slapped the closed file folder against his palm. "What strategy have you settled on? Have you talked to any of the primaries yet?"

"Last night." She switched her attention to her other foot. "Detective Connally updated me on the events leading up to Delgado's arrest."

"You didn't talk to the victim first?"

"No, Mark," she said with exaggerated patience. "I talked to the arresting officer."

"His involvement with the victim could be a problem, you know." Drumming his fingers against the folder, Mark surveyed her solemnly. "Defense is going to try and cast his testimony as emotional rather than objective."

"He'll try. But Connally's no rookie, he's not going to get shaken on the stand. And he wasn't working alone, at any rate." Growing weary of the man's game she decided to cut the meeting short. "I'll have Song make a copy of everything I've got so far so you can start your own file."

He nodded and rose, leaning to drop the folder on her desk. "I'll focus on the investigation end, shall I? It won't take me long to come up with a list of things we need from the CPD. And as you interview witnesses, of course you can add to that list."

His arrogance shouldn't have surprised her. Did he really expect her to hand over the most crucial part of the case to him while she spent her time on paperwork and briefs? "That won't be necessary," she said evenly. When his dark eyes narrowed in annoyance, she felt a flicker of satisfaction. "As primary I prefer to work closely with the investigator. I'll assign you duties as more information comes in."

The tic working under the man's eye was a more sincere

response than his words. "Of course. Just let me know what you need."

Turning, he strode from the office, his tall form rigid.

She watched him go, knowing she'd just made a bad situation worse, and found herself unable to care. There was a fine line between diplomacy and submissiveness, one A.J. found difficult to balance. Submissiveness meant weakness, and where one was weak one was vulnerable. She, better than anyone, knew how vulnerabilities could be exploited.

Her gaze dropped to the folder Mark had left on her desk. Despite the man's opinion, she hadn't been standing still on this case. Song was even now lining up appointments with the witnesses. And she intended to fill the time before her first meeting by familiarizing herself with the media accounts of the Delgado case. It would be like Paquin to start screaming for a change of venue if there had been more than a paragraph written about his client in the press.

She turned to the computer beside her desk and accessed the Internet, intent on bringing up recent newspaper articles dealing with the case. Making a face, she went to the *Register*'s site first. It sounded as if McKay had been in the thick of this investigation for some time. She didn't doubt that the most thorough coverage was going to carry his byline.

"This is bull, Creighton!" Dare speared his fingers through his hair to keep them from twining around the editor's neck. "This story is page one all the way. Below the fold, that's fine, but it's news. Why can't you see that?"

"Page eight, and cut it to one hundred words," Creighton Reetz replied. "Justice investigation or not, the story lacks any real connection for our readers. Sure, Golden Enterprises is a local corporation, but no one really knows who the owners are. The way those corporate blinds work, it could take years for Justice to untangle the people involved, much less prove wrongdoing on their part.''

Dare placed his fists on the man's desk and leaned forward. ''I know who one of the owners is.''

''You *think* you know. An important distinction in our line of work.'' Creighton met Dare's furious gaze calmly. At five foot five inches, the editor was a full nine inches shorter than the man before him, but this confrontation wouldn't be decided by size, but by position. ''When you have more than supposition linking Victor Mannen to Golden Enterprises, the story *might* have a chance of page one. But right now you really don't have jack, so it stays page eight.''

''This article could help flush out the owners, did you ever think of that?'' Driven to move, Dare circled the man's desk. ''Justice breathing down their necks, public attention to the whole thing…''

''You know what I think?''

Dare was all too aware of what Creighton thought. The man saw fit to tell him often enough.

''You're getting obsessed with the guy. You see him behind every crime, every underhanded scheme in the city. You have to question your objectivity, McKay. When it gets personal, it slants the news. You have to start wondering whether you're reporting it or creating it.''

''Are you saying my work has suffered, Creighton?'' Dare's voice was soft, deceptively so. ''Is that it? Just say the word. My resignation can be on your desk in five minutes.''

Reetz heaved a heavy sigh and cast his eyes upward. ''See, you're getting touchy, too. Did I say I was dissatisfied with your work? All I'm trying to say is that maybe you could use a little distance from this story. Hell, maybe you could use some distance, period. When's the last time you took a vacation?''

Dare considered for a moment. "In 1998. I was off for two weeks."

"You were in the *hospital,* for God sakes."

"Yeah, and I missed covering the midcity fire." The memory still rankled. Watching the biggest story of the year run in the *Register* with someone else's byline beneath it had been an frustrating ordeal, one he hadn't forgotten. He stopped in midstride, a thought striking him. "You know, Creighton, you may just be right."

With little difficulty the editor followed Dare's line of thought back to the present. "I am?"

"We'll bury this. It's better if the bastard thinks no one's paying attention. And then while Mannen and his cronies are focused on getting the government off their backs, I'll be establishing their link to Golden Enterprises." And, he thought grimly, proving the connection between Mannen and Delgado. He whirled, heading to the door.

"What about that vacation?" Creighton called after him.

"Try Cancun. I hear it's great this time of year."

A.J. checked the notes she'd made, running her finger down the page until she came to the last of the dates she'd jotted down. Then she replaced the newspaper she'd finished with and located the next one she needed. She went back to spread it out on the table where she'd been working and quickly flipped through the pages. McKay's name seemed to leap out from beneath the article she was searching for. Besides his twice-weekly column, he covered much of the major city news. And he'd written about the Patterson kidnapping extensively.

She would never admit aloud that she found his writing compelling. Not unlike the man himself, it was brutally frank at times and laced with wit. As one of the city's most respected journalists, he wielded his own kind of power. She'd seen for herself Dennis's reaction when Dare had been in her office. No doubt most politicians found it to their advantage to stay on congenial terms with the man. She doubted it did them any good. When it came to reporting the news, McKay wouldn't show favoritism. The story would be his only concern. Experience had taught her that.

"You know some people don't like coming down to the newspaper's archive room. Claim it's cold and sorta spooky. But damned if I don't always find the best surprises when I drop in."

At the first word her spine began to stiffen, one vertebra at a time. It still took more effort than it should have to force herself to turn and meet Dare's smile. "McKay. Somehow it's not surprising to find you where it's dark and damp."

His smile settled in his eyes. "You came clear across town to read my work?" Of course he would notice the page she had the newspaper turned to. "I can die happy now."

"That can be arranged." She turned back to fold up the paper and return it to its spot on the shelves.

He took a step back and propped himself against the wall. Folding his arms across his chest, he took a few moments to watch Addie tidy up the workspace she'd been using. It was no hardship. She moved with a quick lithe grace that elicited a healthy jolt of lust. He tucked it away with the ease of long familiarity.

"You know, the *Register*'s archives can be accessed on the Internet."

"Accessed, but not read," A.J. corrected him. "At least not past the headline and first paragraph. Anything more than that has to be paid for. Billing the office to skim a few paltry articles seems unreasonable."

He let the adjective pass without objection. "Nice to know at least one public servant who's frugal with the taxpayers' money.'' She tossed the legal pad she'd been writing on into her briefcase and closed the lid, securing it. ''Doing a little catch-up reading on the Delgado case? Did you find anything of interest in those 'paltry' articles?''

She faced him, both hands clutching the handle of the briefcase, holding it in front of her. ''As a matter of fact, one thing did interest me. It appears you were on the spot almost immediately when the arrest was made. How do you explain that?''

He gave a shrug and struggled for an expression of modesty. ''Just lucky, I guess.''

She pinned him with what he thought of as her prosecutor's stare, sharp and shrewd. ''You mentioned something about passing some details on to Connally before Delgado's arrest.''

His voice was mild. ''You wouldn't find those details in the news articles.'' As Creighton had reminded him, he didn't have all the facts he needed to lay it out for the public. Yet. ''If you had questions about those details, Addie, wouldn't it have been a lot easier to just call and ask me?''

Her next words sounded as though they physically pained her. ''I'm asking now.''

He considered her for a moment. ''I'm done for the day. Why don't we discuss this over dinner?''

''Forget it.'' She started forward, brushing by him. ''I can talk to Connally next week and save myself the aggravation.''

''Okay, okay.'' His agreement was hasty. The woman had a fast trigger, at least with him. ''Connally was chasing down a suspect in a money-laundering scheme. Delgado was seen with that suspect.''

She shifted her weight impatiently. ''I know that.''

He went on as if she hadn't spoken. ''The sink for the laundering operation was a big video chain. The chain is

one of numerous holdings in a huge conglomerate called
Golden Enterprises.'' He had her interest now. At least she
was listening.

"I think Golden Enterprises is a blind—a dummy cor-
poration. I was able to discover that local-sleazeball-
businessman Victor Mannen sold a full half dozen com-
panies a few years ago to none other than Golden
Enterprises.'' He waited, but her expression didn't change.
"I shared that information with Connally and his partner.
They started asking Mannen some questions shortly before
Meghan was snatched."

"You realize there's nothing tying Mannen to this
case?" She eased back, set her briefcase on the floor.

"Absolutely nothing,'' he acknowledged cheerfully.

"Do you have anything concrete linking him to Golden
Enterprises?''

"Not yet.''

She stared at him a moment longer, then shook her head.
"You have a gift for muddying the clearest of waters, Mc-
Kay. I've got a kidnapper, a live victim and three other
witnesses. I don't need conspiracy theories to win this case.
Juries deal better with straightforward facts.''

"You'll get your facts.''

It took her a moment to grasp his meaning. When she
did, her reaction was predictable. "Oh, no. You have nothing to do with this case. And don't even think about print-
ing any of that speculation. All I need is for Paquin to start
screaming about bias in the press.''

Resentment rose, was ruthlessly banked. "I know how
to do my job, Counselor.''

"So do I.'' She reached down for her case again and
straightened. "Let's agree to that, shall we? You let Connally do his job, let me do mine, and you continue what
you've always found most important—trampling people in

pursuit of a story. Just make sure that this time the story doesn't concern a case of mine.''

He was at her side in two quick steps, his temper on the rise. ''For someone always spouting off about facts, you never listened worth a damn to them two years ago.''

''Of course I did.'' Her chin angled with challenge, and her voice were brittle. ''Let's see, it was just coincidence that you released some critical information about the murder case I was trying just days after being in my apartment. Sheer coincidence that the information could have been found there in my briefcase.''

His words were precise, old fury barely reined in. ''Sleeping with you had nothing to do with that damn story.'' At her mocking smile the leash on his control slipped a little. ''Do you honestly believe I could have put that story together in the few days following our weekend together?''

''The whole thing? No. But the details you found by going through my briefcase sure rounded your article out nicely, didn't they?'' With that she moved past him and started up the stairs.

Before he could curb the impulse, he reached out, took her elbow and pulled her around. His face shoved close to hers, he gritted out, ''For the record, Addie, I don't need to sleep with women to get information. And you've obviously got a gift for revisionist history. You gave me my walking papers before that article ever ran.'' His own smile was brutal. ''After only two intoxicating nights, as I recall. So go ahead and believe what you want about my ethics. But don't try to pretend to yourself or to me that you kicked me out of your life over a story.''

''In hindsight, it appears that my instinct was fortuitous.'' She yanked her elbow free, the abrupt movement making her teeter on the stairs. Stumbling backward a step, she caught herself, but not before the awkward motion had snapped the heel cleanly off her left pump. Her eyes closed and she ground her teeth. "You'd better not be smiling."

He'd always had a well-developed sense of the ridiculous. The absurdity of the situation defused some of his anger. "I wouldn't think of it. C'mon. I'll give you a lift back to your office."

Those beautiful brown eyes opened, shot daggers. "I'll take my chances outrunning muggers."

He felt obliged to point out the obvious. "There's no way you're going to be able to walk like that, unless you fancy hobbling back to your car with one leg shorter than the other."

With quick, furious movements, she slipped off the other shoe and flung both, hitting him squarely in the chest. Her accompanying suggestion was neither ladylike nor anatomically possible. Then she wheeled around and stalked up the stairs.

Because it seemed a shame to waste the opportunity, he watched her retreating figure until it was out of sight, before returning his gaze to the shoes she'd hurled at him. His lips twitched. The analogy was obvious, but he'd be willing to bet that Prince Charming had never had to go through this.

A.J.'s first hot meal in two days went a ways toward soothing nerves that had been left edgy and raw from her encounter with McKay. She'd walked the block-and-a-half distance from her office to a cozy Italian restaurant in a new pair of taupe sandals. Being forced to buy shoes after she'd left the reporter was one more thing he had to answer for. She'd rather be beaten with a blunt instrument than shop, however briefly.

But there was nothing like carbohydrates, she mused, taking another bite of her fettuccine, to lower stress levels. She reached for her wineglass and sipped with genuine enjoyment.

"A.J. It's been too long."

Her newfound feeling of contentment abruptly dissipated. She pasted a polite smile on her face as the newcomer stopped beside her table. "Hello, Joel."

Some people shimmered wealth. Joel Paquin oozed it. From the tips of his thousand-dollar Italian leather shoes, to the cuffs of his Saville Row suit, there wasn't an inch of the man's stocky figure that wasn't tailored, buffed and polished. The sheen of gentility didn't extend to his personality. Beneath the surface lurked the instincts of a street brawler.

As if realizing an invitation wouldn't be extended, he pulled out the chair next to hers and sat. "You look incredible, as usual. When are you going to quit wasting your talents on your dreary little job and come work for me? I've got an office with your name on it."

"I'll bet that's discouraging for its occupant."

He smiled, a generous baring of perfect, capped teeth, but his eyes were intent. "You know I'm serious. You're throwing your life away on the system, A.J. What does it give back to you?"

"A sense of satisfaction. Dignity. Self-respect." She met his gaze coolly. "All qualities I fear I'd miss if I joined your firm."

He reached for a breadstick, snapped it in half. "The last time I checked, none of those qualities paid the bills."

Although his words hit their target, she was careful not to let it show. "Joel, your firm hires dozens of young hungry lawyers every year. I sincerely doubt that you need the services of one more."

"I want you." His blunt pronouncement shouldn't have had the power to chill her skin. "We'd work well together, A.J. And I could count on you to stand up to me, not just say what I want to hear."

"Well, you'll just have to be content with facing me in

court on occasion.'' Her gaze dropped to her plate, and she felt queasy. Her appetite had vanished at Paquin's appearance.

''I'm to have that pleasure soon.'' His smile was feral. ''I look forward to destroying the government's case against my client.''

''And I look forward to seeing what possible kind of spin you can put on it, when Delgado was caught in a criminal act.''

He shrugged. ''Who knows how a jury would interpret it? They may well see a pathetic loser with a crush on a woman who got carried away with a fantasy.''

She gave a laugh of disbelief. ''You're wasted on the law, Joel. You should be writing fiction.''

''And you should reconsider my proposition.'' He stood, preparing to rejoin his companions. ''It'll remain open. Even after I shred your case in court.''

She watched him cross the room, her interest in finishing her meal nonexistent. It was always incredibly easy to dismiss his job offers out of hand. She'd gone into law for the express purpose of acquiring a prosecutor position. The American system of justice wasn't perfect, but she believed implicitly in its principles.

Thoughts of her mother crept through her mind, like thieves in the night. There was no denying that a higher-paid position would go a long way toward paying Mandy's mounting medical expenses. So far A.J. had managed without relinquishing her standards. Somehow she'd continue to find a way to do so.

Darkness had long since fallen when she climbed her porch steps. In the glow of the security light, she fumbled for the correct key. The slam of a car door nearby didn't alarm her, but the sound of footsteps on her walk did. She whirled around, a key tucked between her fingers, jagged edge out, prepared for battle.

And then she closed her eyes in dismay, recognizing the man strolling toward her. "McKay, there has to be some sort of pest control ordinance you're violating."

He was wearing a particularly obnoxious shirt, this one with red and purple flowers rioting on an orange background. With a box tucked under his arm, hands shoved in his pockets, he looked for all the world like a fashion-impaired tourist out enjoying the tropical night air.

A slight smile played at his lips. "Is that thing loaded?"

It took a moment to register his meaning. When she did, she dropped the hand that was still brandishing the key to her side. "If it were, you'd have another hole in your head by now."

He stopped and rested one foot on the first step of the porch. "Guess I should be careful in the future not to get you keyed up." When her expression didn't change, he chuckled. "C'mon, Addie, where's your sense of humor? Admit I'm a wit."

"Only half." She firmed lips that wanted, badly, to smile. Leaning one hip against the railing, she observed, "You didn't track me down to crack bad jokes."

"No, I didn't. I tracked you down to give you this." He shifted the box he was carrying and held it out to her. "Consider it a peace offering."

She stared at it suspiciously, then at him. "Is it ticking?" The lone dimple beside his mouth deepened, a rakish dent that accentuated those well-formed lips. It would be easy, she imagined, for a more gullible woman to be charmed by it.

"I want to throw myself on the mercy of the court by making restitution." When she still didn't reach for the box, he shook it a little for emphasis. "I'm a little hazy on

my fairy tales. But I'm sure something terrible is supposed
to happen if you're still unshod by midnight.''

Her gaze bounced from the box back to his face. "You
bought me shoes?'' Her voice was incredulous.

"I'm almost certain there's a pumpkin in that story,
too.'' He considered for a moment, then shrugged off the
thought. She still hadn't taken the box, so he started up the
steps and pushed it into her free hand. "Let's go in and
see how I did on size.''

"I'm not letting you in to play shoe salesman at this
time of night.'' She held the box out to him. "I'm perfectly
capable of shopping for myself. And I don't need you buying me anything.''

"But I'm responsible for your mishap this afternoon.''

"No," she said, surprising him. "You're not. I can
blame cretinous designers, simple-minded purchasers, or, if
you're ungentlemanly enough to insist, my own lack of
grace. But it was hardly your fault.''

Her words caught him by surprise, although perhaps they
shouldn't have. She'd always had that core of honesty in
her, and had never hesitated to turn it on herself. It was
one of her most attractive qualities.

Because she seemed to expect a response he said,
"Okay. It was your own fault.'' And then enjoyed watching
her eyes heat and narrow. "But you're going to have to
take the shoes, anyway, because I refuse to go back into
that place to return them. I'm pretty sure the clerk thought
I was a cross dresser.''

This time she couldn't prevent her lips from curving. She
cocked her head consideringly. "You know, I think I can
see it. If you grew your hair out a little, wore it with more
height…you should stick to pastels, though. You're definitely a summer.''

Oddly satisfied that he'd made her smile, he reached out
and took the set of keys she still held. Ignoring her protest,

he moved past her and fit the house key into the lock. When the door gave, he pushed it open and gestured her inside.

She stepped into her house, if only to prevent him from doing so. "Enough, already, McKay. It's been a long day and I really...what are you doing?" He'd followed, crowding her in the darkened foyer.

"Making sure you get inside all right."

"I'm inside. The problem is, so are you."

Instead of the retort she'd expected, he pushed out an arm, shoved her behind him. "Stay back."

His whispered command drew her ire. "Listen, McKay, I'm not going to..."

He turned in the darkness, laid his fingers on her lips and walked her backward out the door by virtue of his superior strength. "Do you have a cell phone?" he asked, once they were on the porch.

She pushed his hand aside. "Yes. I keep it in case I meet idiots who won't let me into my home."

He ignored her words and reached for the door handle again. "Use it to call 911. There's someone in your house."

Chapter 3

It took a moment for Dare's words to register. When they did, A.J. made no move to obey them. She followed him back into the house, grabbed his shirt and gave it a yank. "Are you crazy? What are you doing?" she hissed.

With maddening ease, he moved forward despite her grip, felt along the wall for a light switch and flipped it on. "Get outside and make the call."

"Not unless you come, too."

Their whispered conversation came to a halt when the shadowy figure he'd seen earlier stood up, walked toward them. A.J. was plastered close enough to Dare to feel his muscles bunch.

"I didn't think you'd mind me making myself at home."

The familiar voice hit her with the strength of a blow. A peculiarly apt description, she thought, shoving aside the sudden swimming nausea. She could feel Dare shift, prepare to spring. Grabbing his shoulder, she said, "Don't. It's my brother."

His head snapped around to stare at her. She avoided his gaze by pushing by him to walk into the room, switching on a lamp. "Leo. This is a surprise." The understatement of her words was its own kind of mockery. "When did you get out?" As she waited for his answer, she took a rapid visual assessment. Her stomach dropped a bit further. On the surface at least, prison hadn't improved Leo Jacobs.

He had the lean, edgy look of a man too used to watching his back. His jaw was hollowed, and his mouth held its habitual twist of resentment. He'd worn it for as long as she could remember. A tumbler of scotch was held loosely in his hand. His drink of choice, apparently, was another thing that hadn't changed.

"A while ago," Leo said vaguely. His gaze was directed behind her. "Am I interrupting a date?" His smile was thin, bordering on insulting.

"How'd you get in here?"

A.J. sent a startled look Dare's way. Until he'd mentioned it, she'd been too shaken to even think about her brother's entry.

Leo flicked a challenging glance at him. "Better run along, pal. This is a family reunion. And you're not family."

Dare met the man's gaze, held it. "I think I'll stay," he said mildly. He moved to the wall and leaned a shoulder against it, crossing his arms.

Ignoring them both, A.J. went to the kitchen, turned on the light. And then cursed when she saw the broken glass on the floor. Striding back into the living room she inquired, "Ever heard of a phone call, Leo? Breaking and entering is a bad habit to take up so quickly after your release, isn't it?"

His eyes, the same color as her own, went sly. "I didn't know whether or not you'd want to see me. It's been a while since we've talked."

Moving further into the room, she set down her briefcase and the box she was still holding. "Who's your parole officer?"

"Coulson."

"He's good. Tough, but if you stay employed he won't give you any trouble." Because it gave her something to do with her hands, she picked up yesterday's newspaper, folded it into two neat halves. "Do you have a job yet? I might be able to find you something if you haven't."

Leo spread his arms along the back of the couch. "What? Sweeping up in some greasy diner?" He gave a harsh bark of laughter. "No, thanks. I've got something lined up."

She gave a brisk nod. "Good. Is there anything else you need?"

Her brother shoved his fingers in his wheat-colored hair. "In a hurry to get rid of me?"

The question arrowed a little too close to the truth. She denied it, anyway. "No. Just wondering if there was any way I could help."

"Well, that's a change. The way I remember it, when I needed help the most you were singing a different tune."

She gave a weary inner sigh at the bitter words. They were headed for familiar territory. The rerun wouldn't be pleasant. She cast a look at Dare. "You should go. My brother and I have a lot to discuss."

His level gaze saw more, far more than was comfortable. "I'll just clean up the mess." Pushing himself away from the wall, he disappeared into the kitchen.

Leo's gaze followed him. "So that's the type you go for. Way you always acted too good for my friends, we wondered if you were playing for the other team."

Her voice iced. "Your opinion is hardly surprising. You don't know me. You never did."

"Don't flatter yourself." The sneer in his voice was reflected on his face. "I had you figured out when you were seven. Still trying for the gold star on your forehead, aren't you, A.J.?''

It took effort, but she shoved aside the temper she could feel rising. "Let's not do this. Tell me what you need. I'll see what I can—"

He was off the couch and by her side in an instant, his hand gripping her arm. "You'll see what you can do for me? I asked you to do me a small favor once before, remember? But you couldn't sacrifice your sacred principles to help your own flesh and blood then, could you?"

Angry tendrils of pain radiated from his touch. "Take your hand off me or you'll be nursing a broken nose, bro. Promise.'' Their gazes clashed, warred.

He looked away first. His hand loosened its grasp, then fell to his side. There was a grudging note of approval in his tone. "Haven't lost that kick-ass attitude, have you?"

She resisted the urge to rub her throbbing arm. "I certainly had the role models for it.''

He turned, went back to pick up the drink he'd left on the table beside her couch. "Speaking of role models…how is dear old dad?''

"I wouldn't know.''

He sipped, watching her over the rim of the glass. "That's right, you cut him out of your life just like you did me, didn't you? You never did appreciate a damn thing he did for us.''

Memories stirred now, angry hornets with a still-painful sting. "What he did for us? What exactly would that be, Leo? You mean when he'd gamble all his paycheck so we went hungry for a week? Is that the part I'm supposed to admire? Or maybe I should be grateful for the way he'd come home drunk, and you'd try to convince him that I was the one who deserved beating instead of you.''

Leo's eyes went opaque. "Shut up.''

But the memories were raging now, wouldn't be quieted.

"I know Mom was grateful. There's nothing like a guy who puts you in the hospital half a dozen times a year." Her laugh was a little wild, emotions riding high. "And let's not forget the time he broke your arm because you wore his leather jacket. Yeah, Rich Jacobs is a real prince, all right."

"I said shut up!" The sound of glass shattering punctuated his shout. A.J. didn't turn to watch the scotch trickling down her living room wall. If she had, she would have seen Dare standing in the doorway, body tensed, fists curled.

"He wasn't that bad."

The choked-out words sounded like a plea somehow and defused A.J.'s fury as nothing else could. She fought for control, detesting the effort it took. "I don't know where he is. And if you have an ounce of self-preservation left, you won't try to find him."

He turned then, his shoulders slumping a little, and her heart twisted. Leo had always been the weaker of the two of them, despite his being older by two years. And Rich Jacobs was a man who'd preyed on weakness.

"Aren't you going to ask about Mama?" Her question hung in the air, suspended on gossamer threads.

He wheeled around, a cruel smile pasted on his face. "Yeah, how is the old lady? Still crazy as a loon?"

The oxygen seemed to clog in her lungs, before being released in a rush. "She's not crazy."

He shrugged, clearly unconvinced. "Couldn't prove it by me. She live here, too?"

"No." A.J. was filled with a sudden reluctance to share any more information. "She's at a place where she can get the help she needs."

"Maybe I should drop by, pay her a visit." He looked satisfied by her reaction. "Bet she'd be a lot more welcoming than you've been."

"I'm glad you stopped by," she said firmly. But there was no way she was going to tell him where their mother was placed. A.J. could fight her own battles, but her mother was defenseless; lost in a world where no one could follow. Her mental health was far too fragile to chance Leo's petty cruelties. "How are you fixed for money?" When he remained silent, she went to her purse and withdrew some bills. "I've only got a couple hundred, but if you get in a jam I can get you some more."

After a moment that stretched for an eternity, he reached to take it. "Conscience money?"

She met his gaze squarely. "I don't have a guilty conscience."

"Well, you should." His voice rose a fraction. "You had the contacts. You know judges. You could have pulled some strings, gotten those charges reduced. Or dropped altogether."

A wave of exhaustion hit her. It was familiar ground. It had been his topic of choice every visit she'd made to him in prison, until she'd spared them both and stopped going. "I don't have that kind of power. I wish you'd believe that."

He lowered his face to hers, and his voice was caustic. "Maybe not. But you wouldn't have done it even if it had been possible, would you?"

It cost far more than it should have to answer him honestly. "No." The flare in his eyes was a warning. She didn't back down, but met his temper head-on with her own. "You screwed up, Leo. You made the choices and you had to take responsibility for them. I believe in the system and I wouldn't have compromised that belief by trying to get special treatment for you, even if I could have."

He nodded, as if she was merely affirming what he already knew. But he didn't accept it, she realized with a sinking heart. He would never accept it. He brushed by her, headed for the door.

"Where are you going? Do you have a place to stay?"

"I've got a place." He turned far enough to look at her. "I might see you around later. Fact is, I just might pay the old lady a visit."

Her veins turned to ice. "I don't think that's a good idea right now."

"Well, sister dear, I never gave a damn what you thought. That hasn't changed." He opened the front door and was gone.

A.J.'s shoulders drooped a little at his exit. What was it about family, she wondered, that left her reeling like a boxer too long in the ring? She'd rather go through a lengthy cross-examination with Paquin than deal with her brother. They were like rats on a wheel, always circling and never getting anywhere. There was a time when she'd hoped for things to be different. She'd long ago accepted that they never would be.

She looked up then and saw Dare standing in the kitchen doorway, watching her with something dangerously close to sympathy in his eyes. She'd forgotten his presence. Defenses, long ago constructed, clicked into place.

"Well, that was a scene better played without an audience." Because she needed to move, she starting picking up the shards of glass from the tumbler Leo had broken, carefully placing the pieces on a newspaper. Without looking up, she said, "It's getting late. It would be best if you left." Better at least for her. It was always preferable to be alone until the inner storm had passed.

"Your brother's a charming guy."

"Leo?" Her smile was as brittle as her voice. "You'll have to forgive him. Some of his traits are genetically induced. They just flow through his blood like an oil spill."

"He hurt you."

Following the direction of his gaze to her arm, she ignored the undercurrent to his quietly spoken words and gave an embarrassed shrug. ''He lost the power to do that a long time ago.'' She shifted topics deliberately. ''All in all, it's been an…interesting day. You'll forgive me for wanting to see the end of it.''

''I can't go yet.''

''No? I don't see why not. It's getting late. You were uninvited.'' She didn't worry about being diplomatic, especially when a sudden thought struck her. ''How did you know where I lived, anyway?''

He cocked a brow at her, and she made a face. ''Of course, I forgot. Intrepid journalist that you are, no information is safe from you.''

''I was surprised to find that you'd moved.'' His gaze traveled around the room, as if comparing it to her former plush apartment.

She lifted a shoulder, wished him gone. ''I wanted something smaller. This suits me.''

As if recognizing the No Trespassing tone in her voice, he dropped the subject. But he still made no move to leave. ''What are you doing for the next couple days?'' At her blank look, his voice grew ironic. ''It's the weekend, Addie. What most people look forward to all week?''

She made a dismissive gesture with her hand. ''Probably work.''

''On the Delgado case?''

Her deliberate stare made words unnecessary.

''Sorry.'' He aimed a lopsided smile. ''Occupational hazard.''

Hazard was a word more appropriately applied to him, she thought. He should come equipped with flashing lights and warning signs. Caution. Big fall ahead. She'd skated closer than she'd like to admit to that particular edge two years ago. She had no intention of repeating the experience. "You were leaving, remember?"

"Can't leave before you try on the shoes I got for you," he reminded her. "I couldn't find anything to match that suit you have on. What do they call that hideous color, anyway?"

"Taupe." She bit the word off, damning herself for letting him get a rise out of her.

He went on easily, as if he didn't recognize the irritation in her eyes. "But I found something suitable." He gestured to the box.

Jerkily, she crossed to the table where she'd set it and lifted the lid, refusing to acknowledge the sliver of anticipation she felt. And then she stared, nonplussed. The sandals nestled among tissue paper were spike heeled, black, with criss-crossing slender straps that looked more decorative than practical. Dangling one of the sandals from her index finger by a strap, she asked, "What, pray tell, would you deem these suitable for?"

He was looking entirely too pleased with himself. "Well, naturally, I can't see you wearing them to work. Or jogging. But they'd look nice when you get dressed up for our date."

He was smooth. That last line was almost slipped in without notice. But A.J. was paid to be observant. "Uh-uh." She shoved the sandals back into the box. "No shoes. No date. No chance."

"I'll let you think about it," he decided. A man had to know when to make an exit, so he turned to go.

"I don't need to think about it." There was no use allowing him to believe that she was going to put up with his nonsense. Especially when she was certain where his real interest lay. "I won't let you jeopardize this case." If she felt a fraction of regret at the sudden blankness of his gaze, she made sure it didn't show. "Whatever is uncovered in the course of the investigation will not be made public, at least not unless Beardmore okays it. Hanging around me isn't going to win you any exclusives for your column.'' She braced herself, waiting for the explosion.

It never came. Though his eyes sent hot laser darts of blue fire, he gave her a curt nod. ''Fair warning. But you're going to have to get used to the fact that I'm going to know every blessed thing that happens in that investigation. My involvement doesn't have a thing to do with you. Delgado just happens to be another link in an investigation I've been working on since before we ever met. I'm not going to stop digging into it. I've got the time, and I've got resources at my disposal that even law enforcement doesn't.

''Because of my generous nature I'll give most of it to the cops, and through them, to you. You don't even have to thank me.'' His voice was as glacial as a polar ice cap. ''But, by God, you will stop treating me like I'm some second-rate hack who needs to seduce a woman to get inside info for a lousy article. You don't have to like me, Addie, but I've damn well never given you reason to disrespect me.''

The door closed behind him with a gentle snick, an understated emphasis to the quietly lethal tone he'd used. His departure left A.J. feeling small and petty and mean. She didn't care for the feelings. Maybe she'd misjudged McKay, now and two years ago. It was possible, she supposed, if he was as good as he seemed to think he was, that he'd come by that information he'd printed about her case entirely on his own. It was not even outside the realm of credibility that he'd been interested in her as a woman, rather than as an assistant state attorney. But regardless of his motivations, her decision wouldn't vary.

She went to the kitchen and got a rag, held it under hot water. Her reasons for shoving McKay out of her life two years ago were her own and had little to do with her job.

Allowing him to spend the weekend with her had been a mistake, and she'd moved quickly to rectify the unusual indulgence. Her mother was living proof of what happened when a woman allowed herself to get so wrapped up in a man that she'd risk her health, her independence, to keep him. A.J. would never repeat that mistake.

Reentering the living room, she began scrubbing the wall left sticky by Leo's tantrum. The vigorous movements were in tune with her determination. Spending her life alone was preferable to relying on a man for protection. In her experience, the only one she could rely on was herself. The knowledge didn't bother her.

She'd been taking care of herself all her life.

A.J. looked across the table in her office at Meghan Patterson and tried to keep the dismay from her voice. "Let me see if I've got this right. You're telling me that you didn't ever see Delgado in the alley when he was escaping with Connally's suspect."

The pretty blond woman returned her regard steadily. "That's right. I let Delgado believe I was the one who ID'd him. But it was my nephew, Danny, who actually saw the two men."

Her gaze sharp, she looked at Gabe Connally, who was sitting beside the woman. "You didn't tell me that."

"It gets...complicated." Meghan's voice was grim. "Danny was in the alley when D'Brusco and Delgado fled from D'Brusco's apartment after shooting at Gabe and his partner. We were at a toy store, where my nephew was choosing his birthday present. He was able to give a description of both men. And..." She gave Gabe a quick glance, and he took one of her hands in his. "...he was also able to pick up on what they were thinking."

Nonplussed, A.J. looked from Meghan to Gabe. "I'm not following you. You mean he saw their expressions and..."

"I mean he's psychic, Ms. Jacobs." Meghan's blunt pronouncement left A.J. speechless. "His mother, my sister, had the same telepathic abilities."

Carefully, scanning both of the faces before her, she discerned they were serious. Dead serious. So she tempered her disbelief with diplomacy. "That's an unusual claim."

Meghan inclined her head. She was obviously used to such reactions. "If you were to look up old media articles, you'd find my sister's ability has been well documented since her childhood." The evenness of her tone didn't disguise clashing emotions held in check.

"Wait a minute..." A.J. screwed up her brow, tried to summon hazy details. "There was something in the paper several months ago about a local psychic helping the police in a gang investigation...."

"Sandra Barton," Meghan said simply. "My sister. She was killed during the course of the investigation."

While A.J. tried to adjust to the information, Gabe interjected. "We found a videotape she made before she died. She'd been discovered by the two gang leaders, who forced her to use her ability to help them. There were connections between the case she was helping with and the one I was working on."

"And do any of those connections relate to my case against Delgado?" she asked.

"I think so." Meghan spoke again, and this time her eyes were haunted. "While Delgado was holding me he taunted me about Sandra's death. Her car had gone over the embankment on Pike's Hill Road. He said he wondered if I would scream the way she had when he ran her off that cliff."

Interest sharpened A.J.'s voice. "Delgado admitted to killing your sister?" At Meghan's nod, she looked at Gabe. "Was that before you got there?"

"Yeah." His hand squeezed his fiancée's, and the woman gave him a quick smile.

A.J. looked down, scribbled some notes on the pad before her. When she was finished, she tapped the pen rapidly against the paper, formulating her thoughts. "Okay, it sounds like there may be more to Delgado than the charges we've filed against him. But—" she raised a hand to stem the response Gabe would have made "—I can't use any of this without corroborating evidence. What about those two gang leaders Sandra was mixed up with? What's the likelihood of getting them to talk?"

Gabe was already shaking his head. "Both dead. Not coincidentally, their throats were slit by a blade the approximate weight and length of the one Delgado wounded Meghan with."

"I suppose it's too much to ask if there's any proof linking him to either of those deaths?" She read her answer in Connally's expression. Mentally crossing that lead off her list, A.J. tried another tack. "And the suspect Danny saw Delgado with? Dead?"

His smile grim, Gabe said, "He was found floating in the Hudson. Someone had opened his throat, too."

"Delgado was the last one seen with him." A.J. leaned back, considering. "His rap sheet includes charges stemming from assaults with a knife before, so it's clearly his weapon of choice. If I can find a way to get his criminal history introduced, that will help us prove deadly intent in Meghan's case, but other than that…"

"It's not enough." Meghan's voice was tight. "He needs to be held accountable for what he did to Sandra, as well."

Choosing her words carefully, A.J. said, "That's not the focus of this case. And I know it's hard to accept, but we don't have any proof of his involvement in it. It would be your word against his that he even said it, and possibly give his lawyer one more angle from which to attack your credibility as a witness.''

Eyes widening, the woman sputtered, ''*My* credibility?''

''She means because of our relationship,'' Gabe told her, his gaze never leaving A.J.'s. ''Paquin will try to establish doubt about your motives. Maybe try to say you're embellishing to help my case.''

''As if kidnapping and attempted murder needed any embellishment!''

The tart response had A.J. smiling. She was taking a liking to the woman. Some in Meghan's position would have been broken, or at least crippled, by fear. Instead the woman appeared determined to do whatever she could to nail the man responsible.

''You've got me interested in the ways Delgado seems entwined in your earlier case,'' A.J. told Gabe. ''I'm going to authorize a broader scope in the pretrial investigation. Of the most immediate interest, of course, are the instances of assault in the man's past…a history of threatening women, perhaps.'' She wouldn't be allowed to introduce Delgado's criminal record at the trial, but there was a chance she could introduce witnesses who would testify about his penchant for violence. And if she could actually find someone who had been threatened by him the way Meghan had, she'd clinch a conviction.

''About my nephew…I refuse to let any of this touch him.'' Gabe tried to interrupt his fiancée, but she went on despite his efforts. ''He won't testify, Ms. Jacobs. I won't allow it. And I want your word that what I told you about his abilities will never go further than this room.''

A.J. studied the couple silently. She was no judge of Meghan Patterson, having met her only today. But she knew Connally, at least by reputation. She couldn't imagine the cynical detective buying in to the idea of a child psychic. He seemed much too pragmatic.

"Unbelievable, huh?" The man accurately guessed her thoughts. "I thought so, too. But Danny was able to tell us where to find Meghan when Delgado had her. With his help, we knew right where to search. That was all the convincing I needed."

Recognizing the anxious look on Meghan's face, A.J. reassured her. "I can't think of a scenario where it would do our case any good to mention your nephew's…abilities. Just the opposite, in fact. And if a need arises for Danny to ID Delgado as the man he saw with Gabe's suspect, I'll arrange for him to videotape his testimony so he doesn't have to appear in court. You have nothing to worry about on that count. But I'd be lying if I told you that this doesn't complicate things."

The couple exchanged a look. "In what way?" Meghan asked.

"First off there's the relationship between the two of you." A.J. shrugged. "That was a twist I was prepared for, after meeting with Gabe last time. But I'm going to have to rethink my strategy now. I have to show Delgado's motivation for going after you…his criminal intent. Had you been the one who saw him with Connally's suspect, I could have contended he feared having you ID him as the last one seen with the guy before he wound up dead. Now if I decide to run that strategy, I have to contend he *incorrectly* thought you could ID him."

Meghan looked confused. "But that's exactly what happened. And I don't understand why there's a problem in the first place. He was caught red-handed when Gabe and Cal found me."

A.J. quirked a smile. Oh, to be that ignorant of the twists and turns of the justice system. "If you've spent any time at all around lawyers, you'd know that nothing is ever as simple as it seems." She thought it wise to ignore Gabe's sound of agreement. "Joel Paquin is an accomplished defense attorney. He's going to come up with so much smoke and mirrors, he'll have you questioning your own recollection of the facts.''

When she saw Meghan's expression go ashen, she almost regretted her candor. But it would be far better for the woman to be prepared. It would be A.J.'s job to counter whatever allusions the lawyer devised. She knew, especially in light of what she'd learned here today, that it would be the toughest assignment she'd ever undertaken.

Chapter 4

Dare spread the bills on the table, keeping a firm grip on them to avoid their being grasped away by greedy hands. The skinny red-faced man across from him glanced down and did a rapid count.

"That's not the amount we agreed on."

"I think you're forgetting our terms, Cooley. You get half for the tip, another half if it pans out."

"Where's your trust, McKay?" the man whined. "Geez, haven't my leads always been gold?"

"And haven't I always paid the other half when they are?" Dare countered. "So let's hear what you've got. Prove to me it's worth the price."

Cooley tried to feign disinterest, but the jittering of his foot under the table betrayed him. His ruddy complexion gave him the permanent appearance of embarrassment. Since Dare had failed to ever detect a hint of conscience in the man, the impression was peculiarly incongruous. "I've been thinking…this information is worth more than my usual fee. This is big. I got other markets for it."

Withdrawing the bills from the table, Dare replaced them in his pocket, watched the other man's gaze follow his action. "Stop trying to drive the price up. As soon as I walk out that door you'll be on the phone selling it to someone else, and we both know it."

Cooley didn't bother denying it. Although he objected to the term "professional snitch," preferring the more genteel "information broker," the fact remained that he made his living dealing facts for cash. With a philosophical shrug, he leaned forward and lowered his voice. "You're gonna love me for this, McKay."

"Given your hygiene habits, I sincerely doubt it. But if your tip's as good as you think it is, there'll be the usual bonus in it for you."

The promise seemed to satisfy Cooley. "You wanted information on Delgado? Well, I got you the best. I know the girlfriend he was shacked up with. Honey Stillwell."

"Old news. She skipped when Delgado was arrested. The police searched the apartment and came up with nothing." Dare felt a surge of frustration. This trip was going to turn out to be a waste of time, after all.

The smirk on Cooley's face said otherwise. "Well, I got the address she skipped to right here." He took a piece of paper from his shirt pocket, waved it in the air between them.

Dare reached for the paper, had to tug a bit to get the other man to release it. Reading it, he asked, "Is she there now?"

Cooley sat back and shrugged. "Don't know. I could find out for an additional fee."

Giving a short laugh, Dare pulled the bills out of his pocket and threw them on the table. "No, thanks. I'll check it out myself." He pushed his chair back and prepared to leave. Something caused him to pause. Cooley was already folding the money and shoving it into his pocket. "Who else have you sold this information to?"

The man's eyes went sly. "Can't divulge my customers, McKay. I got...whaddya call them things...scruples? Yeah, I got scruples."

"Well make sure your 'scruples' and your common sense take precedence over greed. Peddling this information could make you very unpopular in certain circles.

Dare turned and left the fast-food restaurant they'd chosen as their meeting place. A young woman brushed by, and he stepped back to let her pass. Her perfume assailed him, something deliberately suggestive and musky. For some reason it made him think of Addie, if only because of the contrast. Her scent was subtle, alluring and drifted through the senses like smoke. Memories rose, an emotional ambush. It was difficult to banish the intimate images of their two nights together. The curve of her jaw had fascinated him; so delicate to hide a will that strong. The sight of her sleeping, that inner guard momentarily lowered by unconsciousness. The softness sleep had lent to her face, and the drowsy surprise in her eyes when she'd opened them the next morning to discover him beside her.

Shoving his hands deep into his pockets, he set a brisk pace down the crowded sidewalk. But if he'd hoped to outrun the memories, he was doomed to disappointment. They trailed after him like wisps of fog. Endless pictures of Addie splayed across his mind like still camera shots— the stunned amazement on her face that had turned quickly to slumbrous desire when he'd slipped over her, into her. The feel of their bodies sliding against each other, friction causing heat to rise, temperatures to soar...

Turning into the parking lot where he'd left his car, Dare wondered ironically whether she was haunted in the same way by the mental images that refused to fade. He could attest that sheer force of will was no match for the stubborn memories of their time together. It suited him to blame Addie for that.

The night was pleasantly cool, with a capricious breeze that caressed the skin. Despite the weather, the figure in the shadows was perspiring. The car was late. It would be tempting to use its tardiness as an excuse to slip away, but fear was a powerful deterrent. Promises had been made. Money had changed hands. Actions had been taken that were irrevocable.

To avoid examining those actions too closely, the figure looked up and down the deserted docks one more time. During the day the place was a bustle of activity. At night, however, there was an eerie silence, broken only by the slap of the waves sending the wharf boards groaning.

The long black limo rolled soundlessly out of the darkness and pulled to a stop, lights doused. When the front passenger door opened, a familiar, large shadow got out.

The big man performed the customary body search with insulting familiarity. Then, stepping away, he gave an unseen signal and the back door of the limo opened. Familiar with the drill, the figure approached the door and stopped a couple of feet away.

Waiting in the darkness had been nerve-racking. Waiting for the voice to come from the interior of the darkened car was downright chilling.

"I trust you have something of value for me."

The figure nodded, pathetically eager, forgetting that the action was lost in the darkness. "I've seen all the information the state has so far against Delgado. There are no surprises."

The voice was distant, reproving. "Why don't you let me be the judge of that?"

Swallowing hard, the figure suppressed an urge to take a step back. "You said you knew about the police's evidence at the time of arrest. Jacobs doesn't have any more than that. She still hasn't interviewed the two witnesses from the school who saw him get into Patterson's car. She hasn't finalized her strategy for the preliminary examination.''

"In other words, you have nothing." The statement was uttered without expression, and invoked a terrifying desire to please.

"Well, there is one thing more. A man by the name of Dare McKay is hanging around her. He's a reporter."

"I know who he is." The words were laced with icy venom, and this time the figure did stumble back several inches. The man in the car, whoever he was, evoked money, power and evil. The silence that followed strained the already-tense air.

Finally the man spoke again. "I think we're going to adjust your assignment a bit. From now on, not only do I want to be apprised of each piece of information Jacobs has, I also want you to keep track of how much time she spends with McKay. Perhaps it wouldn't hurt to shake her up a bit, distract her from the case. I trust you can see to that."

"That wasn't the deal."

"I'm redefining our arrangement. Don't worry, you'll be suitably compensated. We'll meet again next week. I trust you'll have something of more value for me at that time."

The huge man loomed, shoved a packet into the figure's hand. Then he got back into the car, and the doors closed. The only sound in the darkness was labored breathing and the quiet whir of an electric window being lowered.

"This warning should be unnecessary, but you don't want to disappoint me. I have no tolerance for failures."

The limo left as silently as it had arrived, and the person left on the dock stumbled away. It wasn't until several blocks later that memory kicked in. In the dim glow of the

streetlight, the packet was opened to reveal a neat bundle
of hundred-dollar bills. Trembling fingers tucked away the
money to be counted in privacy.

Renewed strength was already flowing back into weak-
ened limbs. The assignment was taking an unexpected turn,
but it shouldn't pose much of a problem. Money could be
a powerful motivator.

The cab pulled to a stop beside a rusted Blazer that
looked as though it provided lodging for at least one family.
A.J. looked at the address on the paper she held, checked
it against the one on the dilapidated apartment building.
She gave silent thanks that she'd left her car at the office.
When Connally had called this morning to give her the new
information, he'd warned her that the neighborhood was
unsafe.

Leaning forward, she handed the driver his fee and a
substantial tip. "Keep the meter running and wait for me,"
she ordered. "I shouldn't be longer than twenty minutes or
so."

The driver shrugged, leaned forward and reset the meter.
She got out, walked toward the stoop, past hollow-eyed
children who were bouncing a ball back and forth, and
stepped around the derelict crumpled in a heap, still clutching his bottle. The steps swayed as she moved up them and
through the front door.

She found herself in a tiny foyer lined with mailboxes,
most of them damaged. There was nothing as modern as
an elevator in sight. She climbed three flights of stairs. Her
firm knock on the door of apartment 301 was met with
silence. She tried again. "Ms. Stillwell?" She punctuated
her words with renewed pounding. "It's Addison Jacobs,
assistant state attorney for Cook County. I'd like to speak
to you."

"Now that's a surefire way to get her to open up the

door. There's not a person alive who wouldn't want to talk to the law.''

Whirling around, A.J. saw Dare leaning against the wall behind her. ''What are you doing here?'' she demanded. A sudden thought struck, and her eyes narrowed suspiciously. ''Did you follow me?''

''As enticing a prospect as that would be,'' he replied, only a hint of irony in his voice, ''it so happens that I was in the neighborhood.'' When her eyebrows rose skeptically, he went on. ''I've just left from checking here myself. Already found out that she's left for work.''

Although she was loath to request any information from him, she found herself asking, ''Do you know when she'll be back?''

He studied her, not answering. Today she was wearing a beige suit, as ugly as the other ones he'd seen her in recently, and, his gaze dropped, matching shoes. Her blouse was white, her hair combed to a perfect gloss. With the briefcase in her hand, she presented a no-nonsense air that screamed authority. He could only imagine Stillwell's reaction when faced with her.

''She'll be back late,'' he said, belatedly responding to her question. ''If she comes back at all.''

She frowned. ''Why would you say that?''

''If you're here, that means the police have already contacted her, interviewed her.''

He was right, although she wouldn't give him the satisfaction of saying so. Connally had called her office to report the conversation shortly after he'd left her. When the detective had expressed a concern about the woman taking off again, A.J. had lost no time coming over to make sure she had a chance to speak to her.

Gathering up her briefcase, she started down the hallway. ''I can come back later.''

''You do that.''

It was the innocence in his tone that gave him away. She turned on him. Since he'd been following her so closely, her action placed them only inches apart. Determined not to let their proximity disconcert her, A.J. gave him a challenging look. "Do you know something that I don't?"

He pretended to give her question solemn consideration before answering. "Nope." He moved by her and headed for the stairs. Now it was her following him, a situation she didn't particularly care for. "You're not going to be hanging around here all day staking the place out in hopes of catching her, are you?"

"Nope." He took the stairs rapidly, and it was an effort to keep up, wearing heels.

"So you must be pretty sure that she'll be coming back tonight."

"Nope."

They moved through the foyer and outside, down the steps. She reached for his sleeve, pulled him around. "Dammit, McKay, quit being so cryptic. What are you up to?"

"I'm not up to anything. You go ahead and check back later. Try after midnight."

"And what are you going to be doing?"

He deliberately misunderstood her. "After midnight? That's kind of a personal question, Addie. I thought those parts of our lives were off-limits."

She managed, barely, to avoid grinding her teeth. He usually had that effect on her. "Where are you going right now?"

"Me?" He turned, started to amble away. "I'm going to go talk to Honey Stillwell."

A.J. looked at her cab and back at McKay. It was hard to tell if he was jerking her around or if he could really lead her to the woman.

"So you know where she is?" She had to call the words

after him, because she refused to scuttle in his wake like a friendly puppy.

"I might."

This time her jaw did clench. "Yes or no, McKay. And turn around. I refuse to have this conversation with your back."

With exaggerated care he did as she requested. "I might know where she is. I won't know if she's there until I check, will I? And if she's not in that spot, I've got a couple others to try."

Giving up, she walked toward him. "So tell me."

He pursed his lips, shook his head. "I don't think so."

She restrained an urge to land a fast right jab to his gut. "You could get yourself in trouble if you're withholding information from an officer of the court."

This time he did laugh. "You're cute when you get all legal and uptight, you know that? But I don't have any hard facts, just some leads I picked up from her neighbors. If you wanted to, you could canvas the neighborhood, too."

Intending to do just that, she turned to go. His next words stopped her. "Of course, I can't imagine any of them talking to you. You've got law stamped all over you, and that's bound to make folks around here a little leery."

She tapped the sidewalk rapidly with the toe of one shoe. "I'll take my chances."

"Good luck."

She sent a quick glance around the area, dismay filling her. He was right, damn him. It'd be difficult to get any of the people in this area to even open the door, much less talk to her. There had to be an easier way. But it wasn't simple to turn back to him and say, "Wait. I'm coming with you." And it certainly wasn't simple to watch him shake his head.

"I don't think so."

There was a limit to her patience. "Listen, McKay, if

you've got a lead on where Stillwell might be, I'm coming
along. I don't want to take the chance that she might take
off before I can talk to her myself.''

He shoved his hands in his pockets, enjoying himself.
Addie in a temper was a sight to behold. Her face was
flushed and her eyes were shooting sparks. He tore his gaze
away from the quick rise and fall of her chest and countered, ''Connally has already spoken to her.''

''I always speak to all potential witnesses myself, as a
follow-up. Don't you move an inch.'' She stalked back to
the cab, took out a bill and handed it to the driver. Then
she approached McKay again, who was obediently staying
put. If he made one crack about her wanting to tag along
with him, so help her, she'd deck him.

He was wiser than that. He merely waited for her, then
strolled along beside her. Silence stretched, long enough to
be awkward. After a few minutes he observed, ''Nice day.''

''It *was*.''

''My car is a couple blocks up the street. Do you want
me to carry your briefcase for you?''

''No.''

He shrugged. ''Care to make a friendly little wager?''
Her glance slid to his. ''I bet I find Stillwell in the first
place I look.''

She quickened her pace. ''So?''

''So if I'm right, then you'll wear a real dress on our
date together.''

''And if you're wrong, you'll wear one,'' she shot back.

A broad smile crossed his face. She hadn't told him there
was no possibility of a date ever happening. It was pathetic,
he reflected, how such a little thing could give him hope.

''Okay, lose the jacket.''

Her look, her voice, was deadly. ''I beg your pardon.''

''C'mon, Addie, look at this place. No one in there is

going to talk to us with you looking—'' he gestured with
his hand ''—the way you do.''

Realizing the truth in his words didn't make her any
more eager to comply. She unbuttoned the suit jacket and
slipped out of it, her movements jerky.

''Okay, now the blouse.'' Her gaze whipped to his and
he raised a hand placatingly. ''I mean, just loosen it a bit.
Unfasten the top couple of buttons.'' When she didn't move
to obey, he went to help her and nearly lost his fingers in
the attempt.

''I can manage my own clothing,'' she snapped. ''I've
been dressing myself for some time now.''

''From what I've seen of your wardrobe, that comes as
no surprise.'' He surveyed her critically. There was still a
starched quality to her that clothes couldn't counter. He
reached out a hand, raked it through her hair, tousling the
careful styling. He was barely quick enough to pull away
before being raked by her long fingernails.

''Do you enjoy living dangerously, McKay?''

He ignored the quietly lethal tone. ''That's probably as
good as we can do. C'mon.'' He opened his car door.
''We'll put your briefcase in the trunk.''

She got out and rounded the car. ''I'm taking it in with
me.''

''No, you're not.'' He unlocked the trunk and it swung
open.

It was difficult to say which she found more annoying—
the calm certainty in his tone or the look of exaggerated
patience on his face. ''I need to take notes if she talks.''

''You can write your notes when we get back outside.''
He unwrapped her fingers from the handle of her briefcase,
tossed it in the trunk and closed it. The lid on her temper
lifted.

''Listen, McKay, I'm getting sick of your high-handed
ways.'' She poked an index finger at his chest for emphasis. ''Quit giving me orders. And while we're at it, quit

putting your hands on me, or you'll find yourself facedown on the sidewalk, kissing concrete.''

It was tempting to remind her that there had been a time, albeit a brief one, when she'd liked his hands on her. A time when he'd been kissing her. But neither of them needed the distraction of those particular memories at the moment. He grabbed the hand that threatened to maim him and held it firmly. ''Now you listen. You're out of your element here. Will you admit, at least, that I have a certain expertise in tracking people down and then getting them to open up?''

Their gazes clashed. ''I've been conducting interviews for years.''

''Yeah, on your own turf. In your office. In courtrooms. The last thing we need is for you to start your cross-examination routine. If Stillwell is in there, she has to be handled delicately. She's probably still raw from being questioned by Connally earlier today. Given her relationship with Delgado, it's doubtful whether she has a real high regard for the law. You could screw everything up the first time you open your mouth and start spouting legalese.''

It was maddening to admit that his argument made sense. It was even more maddening to realize that his hold on her hand had loosened, that his thumb was caressing her skin. She yanked away, all too aware of the heat left in the wake of his touch. ''There's nothing to stop me from going in there and talking to her by myself.''

Unsurprised by her show of stubbornness, he made a sweeping motion toward the door. ''Go right ahead. I'm sure she'll tell you everything she told Connally. Care to place another little wager—on which of us gets more information?''

She glared futilely at him. His electric-blue eyes were somber; not a hint of amusement showed on his face. He was, she realized, as serious about his job as she was about hers. If she did as she'd threatened and questioned Stillwell separately, she'd never know what, if anything, the woman had told McKay. And she didn't trust him to tell her, either.

Without another word she started toward the door. He reached it first and held it open. She sailed by him, only to stop short several feet inside the dark interior. "McKay," she hissed. "This is a strip joint."

"Can't get anything by you."

Her elbow caught his ribs in a not-quite-accidental jab. It was almost worth it. Rubbing the spot where she'd caught him, he said, "One guy I talked to from Stillwell's building claims Honey works here. Says he's watched her show." He led her to a table in the partially filled room, well back from the stage and runway. He doubted Addie would appreciate a closer vantage point.

She was slow to seat herself in the chair he pulled out for her, so he reached over, tugged helpfully at her skirt. A scantily clad waitress was shuffling in their direction. Before Addie could open her mouth, Dare sent a winning smile to the other woman.

"What can I get for you."

"Coffee for me. Addie?"

"I don't want anything."

Dare looked back at the waitress. "She'll have a soda."

"Ten dollars."

Dare reached into his pocket, withdrew his wallet. Taking out a ten and a five, he handed both to the woman, saying casually, "We're hoping to catch Honey's act. She on today?"

The ten went in the pocket of the waitress's apron. The five disappeared beneath it, to be tucked in the woman's garter. She took an inordinate amount of time slipping the bill in securely, all the while exposing her shapely leg. "She's next. If you stick around, though, I'll be on in a couple hours.'' It was clear the invitation was issued for Dare's benefit. ''It'd be worth your time.''

''I'm sure it would be.'' He gave her an easy smile which she returned before moving away.

''Ten dollars? You must have some expense account, McKay.'' There was no way A.J. was going to give him the satisfaction of commenting on the waitress's blatant interest.

''It's just a thinly disguised cover charge. Don't tell me you've never heard of juice bars? These places have to be licensed, but they skirt some scrutiny by not applying for liquor licenses.''

The music started, and a woman entered the stage with an obvious bump and grind. Whatever reply A.J. would have made was forgotten as the dancer began shedding the little apparel she was wearing. When the stripper assumed an almost impossible position, all the time swaying to the music, A.J. winced. That had to be uncomfortable.

Dare noted the pained look on her face and nearly chuckled. He couldn't imagine an environment where she would be more plainly out of her element. The action on the stage held no interest for him. The woman beside him did. Strippers had lost any allure they'd once held when he was seventeen and had discovered there was far greater satisfaction to be had in being the one to remove a woman's clothes. He doubted Addie would appreciate the sentiment.

A bored-sounding announcer introduced the next dancer, and a new woman pranced on stage. ''The waitress will deliver a message to Honey that we want to speak to her. Let me do the talking at first.'' Dare raised a hand to forestall the protest he sensed on her lips. ''Believe me, in a place like this, the woman is going to be a lot more willing to talk to a man than to another female.''

Because she couldn't refute his words, she acquiesced gracelessly. ''All right, but I'm going to have questions of my own before we're through.'' She watched as the woman from the stage approached them, wariness in her expression. And then she watched Dare spring into action, rising and showing the woman to a seat.

He was good, she was forced to admit, as Honey Stillwell visibly relaxed beneath his charm. The woman dealt with A.J. by ignoring her, which was fine for the moment. She was content to listen for a while.

After Dare had spent what A.J. considered to be an inordinate amount of time complimenting Honey on her show and ordered her something to drink, the dancer appeared to be completely won over. Her interest didn't waver when he introduced himself, nor when he stated his occupation. It wasn't until the first mention of Delgado that she showed the first sign of visible unease.

''Now whaddya wanna talk about Paulie for? He's old news.'' Honey scooted her chair a bit closer to Dare's and leaned toward him so that her skimpy robe gaped at the neckline. ''You and me could make some news of our own.''

His smile was pure sympathy. ''Bet you're tired of that topic, right?''

''You said it,'' she crooned, smoothing one shapely hand up and down his arm. ''I left our apartment as soon as I heard he was in trouble. I said to myself, I said, 'Honey, you don't need none of that trouble coming your way.''' Her red-lined lips pouted as she added, ''Don't know how they tracked me down to my new place.''

It apparently didn't occur to her to ask Dare the same question, and A.J. was fairly certain she knew why. The woman was giving a good impression of being smitten, and Dare, the fool, appeared to be enjoying every minute of it.

He leaned in closer to the woman with a conspiratorial air.

''Wasted your time, didn't they? If you'd had any information the police could use, you'd have already called them, am I right?''

''That's just what I told them detectives,'' Honey said, giving Dare's arm an approving pat for his understanding. ''I haven't seen Paulie since he got himself arrested, and I ain't gonna. Not that I'm not a loyal kind of gal, but I didn't really even know him that well, ya know?''

Questions churned inside of A.J., questions that, for the moment, went unuttered. She sat with barely concealed impatience as Dare skillfully extricated bits and pieces from the dancer without seeming to interrogate her. Honey had lived with Delgado for about four weeks, in her apartment. They'd met, she admitted artlessly, when he'd come to the club and seen her dance. He'd been good to her at first, spending lots of money on her and taking her to fancy restaurants.

''How about toward the end?'' Dare asked. ''Did he change at all?''

For the first time Honey's gaze met A.J.'s, then slid away. She lifted a shoulder, sending the flimsy robe in a precarious slide. ''He wasn't that bad. Had a temper, I can tell ya that.'' Delgado had, they learned, with Dare's careful prompting, been prone to vicious bouts of violence. But although Honey admitted to suffering a few black eyes at his hands, she denied ever being threatened with a knife. And there had never been any visitors to their apartment, so she had no idea who he'd associated with.

''How about phone calls?'' A.J. finally put in, growing frustrated. ''Did he have a cell phone?'' She knew from the report that there had been no regular phone service in the apartment.

''None I ever saw. Don't think he ever talked to anyone, least not when he was with me. Never saw him make a phone call or get any letters.'' She stopped, as if struck by a thought. "He mailed one once, though. Least, he had me do it for him. Said it was to his sister."

A.J. and Dare exchanged a glance, an invisible band of energy tightening and humming between them. "Do you remember where she lived?" she asked, scarcely daring to breathe.

Honey appeared to reflect, then shrugged. "Can't remember. Iowa? Ohio?" She shrugged, as if the mental exercise had exhausted her. "I know her name, though. Nancy." She began to giggle. "Nancy Clancy. Isn't that a hoot? I remember it because it rhymes."

Chapter 5

"Pretty productive day for your first time at a strip joint," Dare observed as they left the table.

"I've got to call Connally. If Honey had told him the name of Delgado's sister, he would have mentioned it to me." Addie sent him a pointed look. "It seems pretty convenient that she just happened to bring it up with you.

"It's understandable." They reached the exit, and Dare pushed the door open. As they stepped outside, he blinked rapidly. The sunlight was blinding after the dim interior of the club. "People naturally offer more information when they're comfortable. It goes without saying that their comfort level when talking to police isn't particularly high. Especially if they live their lives on the fringes of legal."

He kept up with her easily, although she was covering the distance to his car with the longest strides she could manage. He crooked a grin at her. "You gotta admit, we made quite a team in there. If you ask me real nice, I might even let you tag along once I track down Delgado's sister."

Upon reaching his car, she paused and waited for him to unlock it. "I'm sure Connally will manage fine. Your services won't be needed."

Had she been looking at him she would have seen the shimmer of anger in his eyes. He leaned in front of her and slipped the key into the lock. "That doesn't sound very grateful, Addie. Remember, if it weren't for me you'd still be pounding on closed doors begging for info."

Her fingers clasping the door handle, she faced him squarely. "I'm not denying that you managed to pick up what could be a valuable lead. But these matters are best left to the police to investigate. Your involvement only complicates the case." She began to pull the door open.

He pushed it shut again. And to make sure it stayed closed, he kept his palm firmly planted on it. "You know, that sounded suspiciously like a kiss-off." His even tone did little to disguise the dangerous emotions seething beneath the surface. "But I shouldn't be surprised. You have a nasty little habit of kicking people aside when you're done with them."

If the barb stung, she made sure it didn't show. He could almost see her defenses surge, click into place. Angling her jaw, she said, "Let's drop the references to ancient history, shall we? It's unfortunate that you have difficulty dealing with rejection, but it's not my problem."

The casual dismissal in her voice nudged his temper upward. It was so easy to be reminded of another time when she'd dismissed him just as effortlessly. Just as emotionlessly. He shifted his weight, crowded her against the side of the vehicle, and his voice went soft and low. "Are you sure you don't have any problems with ancient history?"

A.J. brought her hands up to push against his chest, but he rendered the matter useless simply by moving closer. "No images to haunt?" The words were whispered against her jaw. He was so close his lips brushed her skin as he spoke, and an involuntary shiver chased down her spine. His head dipped and he found the pulse below her ear. "No memories to rise?"

A shudder worked through her as his mouth made its way along her jawline. The act took an eternity. Plenty of time for her to react, either physically or verbally. To break free and return their relationship to what it should be—that of adversaries.

So it was telling that during the interminable moments while his sculpted mouth hovered above her own, she remained motionless. It was shock, she told herself. Sheer surprise at his audacity. But even as she had the thought, it felt like a lie. The flavor of anticipation threading through her was too unmistakable, the pull of temptation too strong. When she finally gathered her wits to form a reaction, it was already too late.

His mouth covered hers. The pressure was firm—a little bit angry and a whole lot hungry. She tasted the demand on his lips and fought against it. In a delayed sense of self-preservation she tensed, began a self-defense move that women were born knowing. But as if sensing her intention he crowded her against the car, his long legs pressed against hers, every inch touching. It was too close, and she felt a sliver of panic, realizing that the moment she'd sworn never to repeat was playing out again.

Dare didn't lessen the pressure. Pleasure with Addie was fleeting, and before he was done she'd remember that pleasure, every last minute of it. She'd be branded by the same images that had seared themselves into his mind, his memory.

He cupped her nape, brought her face closer, and immediately was sidetracked by the soft skin beneath his hand. It reminded him of other places on her body he'd once discovered, exquisitely feminine places. Just as soft. Just as sensitive. His lips unconsciously softened as they twisted against hers. Dim alarms sounded in his head. If he'd stopped to listen to them he might have realized that his attempt to awaken the memories for her was bound to send his own rioting. But he didn't stop and he didn't listen. Her scent, her taste, wiped his mind clean.

A.J. fought to keep from going boneless. Thought was getting increasingly foggy. She'd never denied the man was potent; that was a large part of his danger. Her hands clutched his shoulders. He was tracing the seam of her lips with the tip of his tongue, and she recalled just how wicked that tongue could be. The press of his body kept her nearly motionless, and she remembered when she had twisted beneath him, the feel of his weight, his heat. The erotic images, once so securely dammed, rushed forward, one streaming into the other.

Steeped in the scent of her, the taste, it was all too easy for Dare to lose track of his original intent. In his attempt to summon her memories, he was being swamped by his own. The silken texture of her mouth was familiar. Intoxicating. And he knew in that instant that he'd been caught in his own trap. For if Addie was recalling how it had been between them, so was he. If she was remembering each moment of their time together, he was, too. And the hell of it was, at this instant he couldn't bring himself to care.

Cupping her face in his hands, he slanted his mouth over hers. Her fingers closed around his wrists, but she didn't push him away. Her tongue touched his in what might have been an accident, then lingered. He encouraged it with his own, and their tongues tangled, wove, their tastes melding.

Glass shattered nearby, and raucous laughter drifted through the air. The blast of noise took longer than it should have, to register. His eyes opened, and the sight of Addie filled his vision. She gazed at him, her eyes slumberous and a little confused, vulnerable for a moment in a way she rarely allowed herself to be. "Ancient history, Addie?" he murmured. "Are you sure it's really dead and buried?"

She blinked, and he noted the instant that comprehension returned. The fingers on his wrists tightened, and she violently shoved him away. Because he knew it was wisest, he allowed himself to be moved.

"Is there no level too low for you to stoop, McKay?" She sidestepped away from him, uncertain whether the distance was for his benefit or for her own. "I don't know what you were trying to prove, but try it again and your social life will be impaired for a week. God gave me a knee and I know how to use it."

If he hadn't heard the tremor in her voice, he might have reminded her that she'd had plenty of opportunity to stop him and had failed to do so. Conscience rose, and it was damned inconvenient. With savage movements he yanked her door open. "Get in."

Her tone was incredulous. "After that display? Not a chance in hell."

His teeth snapped together. "I still have your briefcase in the trunk. If you want it, get in the car. Now."

They stood there glaring at each other, gazes battling, neither prepared to give. Then she glanced at the trunk, pressed her lips together and complied, slamming the door shut after her. Grimly he rounded the vehicle and got in the other side, started it. Stirring up complications was something he did on a daily basis in his professional life, but in his personal life he liked to keep things simple. And there was nothing in the least bit simple about Addison Jacobs.

A.J. gave an inordinate amount of attention to the acts of buttoning her blouse, slipping into her suit jacket. She attempted to stem the constant replay in her mind, trying to stoke her resentment for McKay. But her recriminations were all for herself.

What was it about this one man that could continually shatter her control? How did he so effortlessly shred years of caution and restraint? The questions taunted, and she could no longer dodge the answers. There was history between them, yes. History she was eager and determined to forget. But it wasn't buried. Not when the memories were still so clear and could be beckoned so easily.

She'd thought once that she could give in to her physical response to him and still keep her emotions separate. She'd been wrong. In the short weekend they'd spent together, he'd managed to charm her, captivate her, devastate her control.

The man was still charming. He was still devastating. And he was still able to break through her defenses with an ease that terrified her.

When Dare double-parked outside A.J.'s office building, she was out of the car before he had it in gear. Since she knew he had a trunk release in his car, there was absolutely no need for him to get out of the vehicle at a leisurely pace and round the car to unlock the lid. Unless, of course, he was intent on torturing her, dragging the humiliating moments out as long as he could.

When he handed her briefcase to her and met her gaze, she made sure her voice was steady. "I'll call Connally and update him on the lead with Delgado's sister. If you come up with something else in the meantime, I suggest you keep him informed." She took the case, turned away.

"I always do." He reached out and took her arm when she would have taken advantage of a break in traffic to dart across the street. "Dammit, Addie, wait a minute." When she glanced at him, the sight of her bland demeanor trapped the words in his throat. She was too good at that—donning an icy mask that gave no hint of her thoughts, her emotions. It was easy, when faced with that expressionless persona, to believe that was all there was of the woman—an icy exterior, cool calm logic and a will of steel. Although he'd caught glimpses of something else inside her—humor, softness and an unlikely vulnerability—they were never more than that. Mere glimpses. A man could be forgiven for believing he'd imagined them.

Except…the taste of her still lingered on his tongue, her scent still trailed through his senses. He rued the moment he'd ever believed he'd seen more in Addison Jacobs than she showed to the world. And he most sincerely regretted trying to prove its existence to her a moment ago.

Apologies were bitter, and best gotten out as quickly as possible. He muttered an expletive and dropped her arm, jamming his fingers through his hair. "I'm sorry, okay? I've got no excuse. You just drive me crazy sometimes."

Her brows arched. "A short trip, it would seem."

Ignoring the gibe, he plunged on. "It appears that you've been right all along. It'd be best if we spent as little time in each other's company as possible."

There was a flash of something in her eyes, there and gone too quickly to be identified. "We agree on something at last." She turned then, posture regal, and started across the street. Dare slumped against the car and watched her go.

There was, he decided, reason to consider his sanity. False modesty aside, he could have any number of women just by picking up a phone. Women who were sweet, funny, smart and a whole helluva lot more interested in having him around. Women he could spend time with and not have to battle through a coat of armor to discover what made them tick. Women, in short, who were the opposite of Addison Jacobs in almost every way.

He had just enough self-preservation left to realize that he needed to find one of those women, and take his mind off the one he couldn't have. The one he didn't want, anyway, he assured himself, as he slipped back into his car. He and Addie were like two hot wires: touch them together and sparks flew. The analogy was a little too close for comfort.

The sound of screeching tires wasn't unusual enough to snag his attention, but when it was accompanied by the blaring of horns, he did look up. And then froze in the act of slipping the key in the ignition. A car was bearing down insanely fast, without regard for other vehicles or pedestrians.

His eyes widened, and his head snapped around. Throwing his door open, he shouted, "Addie!" She was halfway across the street when she looked up, then froze. Giving the speeding vehicle one wild look, she broke into a run. But she was wearing heels, and her strides were hampered by her skirt. "Dive!" he urged, running toward her, unmindful of the sound of brakes screeching, people shouting. "Dive and roll!"

The scene slowed down, took on movie-like slow motion. Her fingers released her grip on her briefcase...she threw her body forward...out of the path of the car...until it swerved at the last instant, its bumper catching her in the hip.

Dare sped across the street, dodging the cars that had parted for the runaway vehicle, his gaze fixed on the figure crumpled on the pavement. The impact of the car had sent her rolling almost to the curb. She lay crumpled in the gutter, amid the day's debris. A siren sounded in the distance. He skidded to a halt beside her, dropping to his knees. "Addie!" His voice was urgent, a vise squeezing his chest. "Look at me, baby. Open your eyes."

As if in response to his frantic command, her eyelids fluttered, then rose, but her gaze was unfocused. A river of relief ran through him, and reaction set in. "Don't move.

We'll get an ambulance and take you to the hospital, get you checked out.''

As he spoke his hands were running gently, expertly over her body, checking for broken bones, watching her face carefully for a wince of pain.

''No...hospital. Help me...get up.''

''Not a chance.'' He picked up her wrist, held it lover-like in his hand while he took her pulse. His brows drew together as he noted her dirty, bloody palms. There was no way he was going to move her. She could have a concussion, a back injury. He wasn't taking any chances. He took a handkerchief from his pocket and wrapped it around her hand that had taken the brunt of her fall.

A voice sounded near his ear. ''I called the cops as soon as I saw that guy driving like a lunatic. They ought to be here pretty quick.'' As if to validate the words, the sound of the siren drew even closer.

Dare became aware for the first time of the crowd that had grown around them.

''Damn fool...idiot could have killed somebody...came out of nowhere and...'' The disembodied voices ebbed and fell around them.

''Is this hers?''

Dare turned and took the briefcase that bore scuff marks from its contact with the pavement. Addie took advantage of his distraction and rose to a sitting position. ''What the hell are you doing?'' he demanded when he turned around and saw what she'd done. ''You might have a head injury...a broken bone. You need to be checked out by a doctor.''

The pallor in her cheeks was belied by the strength in her voice. ''What I need is to get out of the street. I'm fine. Really.'' She put a hand on his shoulder and struggled to her feet. He had to support her or risk having her crumple again. ''The car just grazed me, that's all.'' Under his disapproving frown she stood, swayed a bit, then tried to shake free of his hands.

"Yeah, you look fine, sweetheart. You surely do." The savage tone in his voice had her glancing at him warily. "But even given your superpowers, bullets bouncing off your chest and all that, you're still getting examined by a doctor."

The protest she would have made was interrupted when a police car wheeled around the corner and pulled to a stop beside them. Dare could see Addie draw herself up, shoulders straightening, hand smoothing her hair. It was amazing, really, the metamorphosis the woman could pull off in a matter of moments. And perhaps even more amazing when she was able to converse with the two patrolmen, stating the events in succinct terms, as if she wasn't even now standing there bleeding.

Bleeding. His stomach lurched viciously. Not only were her palms scraped, but her knees and shins had been injured from her fall. She should have them tended to, and then she needed to have her hip and wrists examined. She'd taken the brunt of the impact on her hip, and broken her fall by extending her hands.

The second patrolman approached Dare for his statement but he'd been too concerned about seeing Addie in danger to note many details. All he could relate with any certainty was the color of the car and its make. From the resigned expression on the cop's face, it was apparent the other bystanders had been of little more assistance.

He shifted away from the crowd that had collected around them and addressed the cop interviewing Addie. "I think you guys have gotten all you're going to. Ms. Jacobs needs to get to a hospital." He ignored the baleful gaze Addie threw his way and focused on the patrolman, who was nodding his head in agreement.

The officer addressed Addie. "You can call us tomorrow

for an update. We've got what we need for now. The guy's right. You should see a doc.''

"I'm fine. I was shaken up, but that's all.''

Dare recognized the authoritative tone of her voice and prepared to do battle. "You could have internal injuries.''

With a simple lift of her brows she managed to convey her skepticism at the suggestion. He moved closer, lowered his voice. "Quit being so bullheaded and see reason, would you? You should have some X-rays.''

She concentrated on unwrapping the handkerchief from one palm and rewrapping it around the other. "I'm all right. Really.'' Her eyes met his then and held. "I imagine I'll have a chorus of aches and pains making themselves heard tomorrow, but there's nothing broken.''

"You can't be sure.''

"No doctors. No hospitals.''

Her words were edged with a hint of something that Dare would swear was panic if he didn't know her so well. But he was too familiar with her stubbornness to give the possibility more than fleeting consideration. He folded his arms across his chest and surveyed her. "Just what are you planning to do? Waltz in to your office this way?'' He saw by the shift of her gaze that she hadn't planned that far. He pressed his advantage. "Or maybe you've decided to find a drugstore that's running a special on pantyhose and Band-Aids. You could always clean up in the restroom of a fast-food restaurant.''

She reached for her briefcase, and he saw her wince as the handle connected with her raw flesh. "I'll go home to change, of course.''

He clenched his jaw to stem his arguments. There was no point in noting that clasping a steering wheel would be torture when she couldn't even hold her briefcase without pain. The whole thing really wasn't his concern, anyway. Hadn't they just agreed that their best strategy was to steer clear of each other? So it was completely self-destructive to say resignedly, "C'mon. I'll drive you."

The look she shot him was justifiably wary. "How do I know you won't take me to a hospital instead?"

Because the thought had occurred, he kept his expression innocent. "No hospitals." He clapped one palm to his chest and held up three fingers on the other. "Promise."

If possible, her gaze became even more speculative. "Wrong hand, McKay."

He shrugged easily and switched hands.

"Something tells me you were never a Boy Scout."

"Not for long, anyway." He took the case from her hand and began guiding her across the street to his car. "I got tripped up on parts of the Scout law—particularly the reverent bit."

A.J. walked beside him, limping only slightly. "Why am I not surprised?"

"Probably because you have a totally misguided distrust of me." He opened the car door, handed her gently inside. "You'll be happy to know, though, I still believe in the Scout motto. I'm always prepared."

"I'm not sure this is a good idea." Warily, A.J. looked around the hallway as Dare opened the front door to his apartment. "It would have made a lot more sense if you'd just driven me to my place."

Dare unlocked the door, swung it open and ushered her inside. "It would have taken twice as long. I assumed you wanted to get back to the office as soon as possible."

Because he was right, she kept further protests to herself. But that didn't mean they weren't bouncing and colliding inside her. She preceded him into the apartment and stopped in the foyer, glancing around. Her first impression was one of neatness. The large living area before her looked comfortable and lived in, but there was little clutter. A pair of battered running shoes had been discarded in front of the couch, as if their owner had shed them to prop his feet on the coffee table. She looked at the kitchen to her side and felt a little better when she saw a few dishes stacked next to the sink. It looked homey and, more dangerously, a little intimate.

Dare appeared to be completely unaffected by the cozy atmosphere. He waved her to the couch. "You may as well get rid of those pantyhose. They're ruined, and we have to treat your legs." He disappeared into another room, but she could hear him nearby rummaging through drawers.

His suggestion was easier stated than carried out. Once A.J. slipped out of her shoes, she reached under her skirt and began to shimmy out of the nylons. When she got them to her knees however, they were stuck to the scraped skin, and freeing them was agony. Deciding that quick pain was preferable over slow torture, she yanked them the rest of the way down, biting hard on her lip to stifle her gasp of pain.

When Dare returned with an armful of first-aid supplies and a small bowl of water, she'd seated herself gingerly on the edge of the couch, the wadded up nylons clutched in her hand. He frowned when he saw her legs. "Guess we should have cut them off."

She eyed the small mountain of items he'd piled on the table. "Are you always equipped to do major surgery?"

His mouth quirked. "I guess so, courtesy of my dad. It's kind of an old joke between us." He cupped the back of her calf in one hand and pressed a warm washcloth to her knee. Her breath hissed out before she could prevent it.

He glanced up. "Hurts, huh? Cleaning the wounds is always the worst part." He continued to work with a quick efficiency that was at the same time curiously gentle. "Every birthday, Dad sends a first-aid package to remind me of all the patching up I used to require."

Recognizing the distraction for what it was, A.J. seized it gratefully. "You were prone to accidents?"

"More prone to brawling. My dad was a disc jockey, and we did a lot of moving around. In a new neighborhood there's always a few who like to try out the new guy."

She was, in a horrified sort of way, fascinated. "You beat them up?"

"Got my ass whipped on a regular basis."

The breezy admission unexpectedly made her laugh. "I know about tough neighborhoods." Their homes had always reflected her father's fortunes at any given moment. When he brought his paycheck home with some regularity, they'd lived in small houses that were fairly presentable. However, when booze and cards took their toll, their homes were more often apartment buildings much like Stillwell's. The memory alone was enough to make her stomach clench. It was infinitely preferable to listen to Dare's banter than to linger on memories better kept tucked away.

"I know it's difficult to imagine, but I wasn't always this studly male specimen you see before you. I was small for my age until I was about twelve."

"Unfortunately," A.J. noted dryly, "your modesty didn't improve with age." She barely noticed when he finished cleaning one leg and started on the other.

He didn't disagree with her observation. "What can I say? I was the youngest of four, with three sisters. I was doted on throughout my entire childhood."

Over his head she rolled her eyes. Somehow the acknowledgment didn't surprise her. "Really? One would never guess it."

His fingers squeezed the back of her calf in a quick warning. "Sarcasm is highly inadvisable when I hold your welfare in my hands. Literally." He shifted back to the original subject. "It wasn't as great as it sounds. There were definitely downfalls to having four females in the house. I can't tell you how many times I had to play Barbies.''

She smiled imagining it. ''Ever consider that might have been the reason you got beat up?''

''If so, it was worth it. I don't know if you've no- ticed—'' he looked up, flashed a grin ''—but Barbie's stacked.''

She resisted the urge to kick him with her free foot. ''Something tells me you were a depraved child. Appar- ently some things can't be outgrown.''

He chuckled, set aside the cloth. Applying generous amounts of ointment to the scraped areas, he reached for the bandages. ''A few things have changed. I prefer my dolls to be talking and breathing, although—'' he gave her a wicked look ''—I still enjoy undressing them. There.'' He rocked back on his heels, surveyed his handiwork. ''Damn, I'm good. Is that a professional job or what?''

A.J. considered the leg he'd swathed. ''Very nice. Why don't you complete the job, and I could go to work dressed as a mummy?''

''Everyone's a critic,'' he muttered, already applying bandages to her other leg. In short order he had that one done and reached for her hands to repeat the process.

''I don't mean to sound ungrateful.'' She was thankful for his help, as uncomfortable as it made her to accept it. ''I'm just not used to letting people do things for me.''

One corner of his mouth kicked up, but he didn't raise his gaze. ''Now there's a surprise. Is that why you don't like hospitals?''

''No.'' She knew her answer was curt, but she was un- willing to expound on it. There were entirely too many memories associated with nameless hospitals, faceless nurses, somber social workers. The memories, like so many others from her childhood, were best avoided.

He didn't say anything for several minutes, and, studying

his bent head, she realized she'd offended him with her abruptness. She felt oddly ashamed, especially in light of all he'd done for her this afternoon.

The silence stretched, became awkward. She gazed around the room, her eyes lighting on the bookcases lined with books and pictures. And one award plaque that she could identify even from where she sat. "That's your Pulitzer on the shelves there, isn't it? Dennis mentioned you'd received two."

He applied bandages to one of her palms, then switched to the other. "That's the second one." His voice was as short as hers had been earlier.

"Where's the first?" He was silent so long she thought he wouldn't answer. Although she detected a rigid set to his shoulders, his touch remained gentle.

"I gave the first to my father."

His brusque tone was as clear as a No Trespassing sign. It shouldn't have felt like an affront. Not when she was so adept at posting those warnings herself.

It was with an unusual doggedness that she continued the conversation. "He must be very proud of you."

His fingers stilled for a moment, before he finished applying the last bandage. "There." He turned to pile up the supplies again. "You're not exactly as good as new, but it's an improvement." He glanced at her bare legs a moment later and frowned. "I can't say that I've got any spare pantyhose lying around for you."

Earlier she would have seized the opening as an opportunity to fire a caustic remark. Then he would have laughed off her words and responded with an easy, immodest reply. But something had changed in the last several minutes, and she wasn't certain how to counter it. "I can slip these shoes on without nylons. I just need to get rid of the worst of this dirt."

He eyed her skirt as she indicated the stains and, giving

a nod, he rose. "You can scrub it off in the bathroom. Washcloths are in the cupboard, and there's a blow dryer in the top drawer." He stopped, grimaced. "What am I saying? You can't clean it without getting your bandages wet. C'mon."

As she trailed after him, A.J. was distinctly aware that his reluctance mirrored her own. "I'm sure I can manage…" Her voice tapered off as he gestured for her to seat herself on the edge of the tub. Feeling at a distinct disadvantage, she did so. Glumly she realized that the bandages were going to attract a lot of attention that she would rather avoid, as well as hamper her work significantly. Not for the first time since the mishap, she silently cursed the fool who had caused this whole situation.

Without a word Dare knelt before her with a warm washcloth and began scrubbing at the worst of the dirt. She tried to hold the skirt material taut, but he finally had to grasp the hem with one hand to keep it from bunching up.

She shifted uncomfortably. His knuckles brushed against her knee as he worked, branding her with each light touch. She was acutely aware that the only thing that separated his hand from the flesh on her thigh was two layers of fabric. Somehow the act seemed more intimate than his earlier ministrations.

Unbidden, images floated across her mind, teasing wisps from their lone weekend together. They'd showered together, in what had started out as a languorous interlude. But the steadily rising temperature had had nothing to do with the water. A.J. swallowed hard, willing the memories back to the pocket in her mind where she usually kept them. But it was too late. She could almost feel again the slide of wet skin against wet skin. Hands skating for purchase, fingers clutching at damp, heated flesh. The pounding of the water over them, echoed in the movement of their bodies moving together, riding passion to its explosive crest.

"You know, I think that's good enough." She jumped up from her perch, stepped by him carefully. "I can manage the blow dryer. Maybe you could call me a cab. I hate to think of having to drag you downtown again."

If he was surprised by her barrage of words, his expression didn't show it. He rose, as well, tucked the wet cloth on the towel rack to dry. "I'll go make the call."

When she reentered the living room, his back was to her, as he gazed out the window to the street below. He turned at her approach.

"Good timing. The cab should be here any minute."

They looked at each other for an emotion-charged moment. "I appreciate all you've done." A.J. gestured awkwardly at the supplies still piled on the table. "I'm sure you didn't expect to have to play doctor this afternoon." As soon as the words left her mouth she wanted to call them back. They were an open invitation for one of Dare's famous double entendres.

The expected witticism didn't come. He merely nodded. "It was the least I could do. If you hadn't been so furious with me maybe you would have reacted more quickly when that car appeared."

Whatever she'd been expecting from him, that wasn't it. Her shrug was self-conscious. "I think we've covered my lack of grace previously. Let's lay the blame where it belongs, on the idiot driver." He didn't respond, just shoved his hands in the pockets of his jeans, drawing her attention to the way his action drew the material tauter across his hips. She cleared her throat. "I'd better go down to the street to wait for the cab." She retrieved her briefcase and then turned for the door.

"I meant what I said earlier."

She turned her head quizzically. Dare hadn't moved a muscle. "What?"

"About steering clear of each other. You were right. That's best for both of us. I'll do my part."

"I...thank you." Her reply sounded inane, even to her own ears. She let herself out of his apartment with indecent haste. And as she pulled the door shut after her, she was acutely aware of an absurd sense of loss.

Chapter 6

A.J. had always found work to be a great diversion from troubling thoughts. And if her job wasn't proving to be as complete a distraction as she could wish for, her experience in court that morning provided, at least, a measure of satisfaction.

When she entered the reception area outside her office, Song took one look at her and said, "You look pleased. Good day in court?"

"I nailed that scumbag to the wall." The memory of the armed robbery case still had the power to warm. "Tripped him up on the cross-exam. He contradicted himself so many times his public defender will never be able to undo the damage in closing arguments."

She paused by the woman's desk to take the messages she held out. "Any other calls?" Song shook her head, and A.J. suppressed an emotion she refused to identify as disappointment. She hadn't heard from Dare since she'd left his apartment two days ago. It would be comfortable to believe that she was relieved he was keeping his vow to maintain his distance. Comfortable, but not totally truthful.

Song lowered her voice. "I hate to tell you this, but Mr. Stanley is waiting in your office."

Her good mood abruptly evaporated.

Shrugging helplessly, the woman said, "He claims the two of you have a meeting and decided to wait. I told him I could just contact him when you came in, but…"

But Mark had insisted, and the woman hadn't wanted an unpleasant altercation with a superior. Imagining the scene, A.J. gave her a grim smile. "Don't worry, Song. I'll take care of it."

She opened the door, stepped into her office. Mark Stanley turned from the window to face her. Shutting the door with a little more force than necessary, she said, "You're a little early, aren't you? I thought our appointment wasn't for another hour."

He flashed his trademark smile. "I had some extra time, and I heard Gaffney was ahead of schedule. I figured you'd be getting done early. Since I have another commitment later this afternoon, I was hoping we could move our meeting up."

Silently, she walked to her desk, deposited her briefcase on it.

His look was quizzical. "You're not mad that I'm in here, are you?"

Deep breathing took the edge off her voice, if not her temper. "I'd prefer that you do me the courtesy of respecting my privacy."

He gave a helpless shrug. "Sorry, I had no idea you were so touchy about your space." The silence stretched, until he fidgeted slightly under her steady regard. "Are we going to have a problem?"

They had, A.J. thought, a much bigger problem then the man would ever admit. But she wasn't about to give him the opportunity to run to Beardmore and accuse her of not playing nice. "Not as long as this doesn't happen again."

"Fine." The word was imbued with the soothing civility of a man dealing with a hysterical female. A.J. found the tone every bit as irritating as his behavior.

"You said you wanted to finalize strategy for the prelim," he reminded her. "I wouldn't lose sleep over it, if I were you. I figure the only reason Paquin's going through with it is for the opportunity to grandstand to the press."

Opening her briefcase, she withdrew a legal pad and crossed to a nearby table. She'd spent quite a bit of time considering Paquin's motives, and hadn't liked any of the conclusions she'd drawn. Most felonies arrived in court after the defendant had waived the preliminary examination. The state didn't have to show reasonable doubt at this stage, and it seemed apparent that Delgado would definitely be held over for a trial. But it was never wise to dwell on the obvious when dealing with the wily defense attorney.

Seating herself at the table, A.J. gestured for Mark to do the same. "My first impression was the same as yours." She dearly wished she could continue to believe it. "But Paquin's more devious than that. He's got a reason for proceeding with the prelim, all right. I'm guessing he's going to try to get the charges dismissed or reduced to a misdemeanor for trial in district court."

Mark stared at her for a moment before giving a disbelieving hoot. "C'mon. You're giving the man too much credit. He's playing to the media, pure and simple. Sure, he may go in there and blow some smoke, but there's no way he can convince a judge to reduce the charges."

She tapped her pen against the pad before her. "I'm counting on that. But he's not going to go in there empty-handed, either. I know this guy, Mark. He's counting on the reduction, and he'll have something to back his plea up."

Folding his arms across his chest, Stanley leaned back in his chair, clearly unconvinced. "Like what?"

"I'm still drawing a blank on that," she admitted. "I expect him to concoct some fairy tale explaining away a connection between Delgado and Patterson. But Paquin will have to have proof if he wants to show reasonable doubt doesn't exist." She reflected for a minute, then shook her head. "I've given it a lot of thought, but I can't figure what he might be planning."

"I think you're wasting your energy. We'd be further ahead if we spent our time…"

Song stuck her head in the door, interrupting the other lawyer. "You've got a phone call, A.J. Someone from St. Anne's Hospital?"

A greasy wave of apprehension rose swiftly, was ruthlessly suppressed. "Thanks." She stood on trembling legs to cross to her desk, snatch the phone up. Later she wouldn't be able to remember the entire conversation— only a few phrases registered.

"Can't calm her down…agitated…"

Voice controlled, she said tightly, "I'll be right there." She replaced the phone, reached for her purse. "We'll have to postpone this, Mark."

His expression was disapproving. "But we really need to…"

She was already out the door, striding past her assistant's desk. "I need to take some comp time, Song. I won't be long."

She hoped, with a strength born of fear, that she spoke the truth.

A.J. had the cab drop her off three blocks from the hospital, because she could walk the distance faster than the driver could maneuver through the snarled traffic. She didn't halt by the front desk, and the nurse on duty was forced to follow in her wake down the hallway. "I didn't even know you had a brother, Ms. Jacobs." Her tone was reproving. "Normally we like to be apprised of any family members who might come to visit."

"Is he still here?"

"Yes, he's in with her now."

Violence was a mainstay of her childhood, and she had nothing but loathing for those who reverted to it. But right now it was boiling in her veins, throbbing for release.

Halting in her mother's doorway, she took in the tableau before her. Leo sat in a chair facing their mother's, his back to A.J. But it was Mandy's expression that held A.J. spellbound. How long had it been since she'd seen that kind of animation in her face? It had been twenty-three days since her mother's regression to a near catatonic state. It had been much, much longer since she'd been heard to laugh. The sound of it now had A.J.'s throat knotting.

"I see you have a guest, Mama." Her voice as normal as possible, she strolled into the room. When Leo turned to look at her, their gazes met, warred. Then she focused on her mother again, still marveling at the change in the woman. She'd deal with her brother later, she vowed grimly. But not here. Not in front of their mother.

She crossed to the older woman and bent to kiss her cheek, breathed in the smell of her shampoo. Scents evoked the most powerful of memories, and A.J. could never smell peaches without thinking of her mother. She kept her supplied with the familiar shampoo, in a futile hope that the scent would help ground the woman to reality in a way that medications and therapy often failed to do. Lately, the times were all too frequent when the aroma was the only familiar thing about the woman.

For a moment Mandy's eyes clouded with confusion, before the mental haze lifted. "A.J.!" Her gaze shifted back to Leo. "A.J. is here. She never forgets."

"And who could forget a beauty like you?" He clasped both the woman's hands in his own, while she beamed. "I told you I'd come back, didn't I?"

It was doubtful he'd told her anything of the kind. A.J. couldn't remember the last time Leo had visited their mother, but it was long before he'd gone to prison. She'd told herself that their mother was better off for the slight. Leo had a way of causing friction wherever he happened to be. But it was difficult to deny the pleasure his presence was bringing her now.

Strolling to her mother's side, A.J. put a hand on her frail shoulder in a gesture that was unmistakable. Taking in her protective stance, Leo's lips twisted. He gave Mandy's hands a squeeze and rose. "I have to go now, but I'll come back soon. I promise." He bent to kiss his mother's cheek, and her fingers clutched at his shirt.

"Don't leave again, Richie. Please don't go."

The words sent daggers of ice stabbing deep into A.J.'s heart. Her throat clogged. "Not Richie, Mama. It's Leo, your son."

The older woman didn't seem to have heard her. Leo was attempting to unclasp her grip from his shirt, but she held fast. "It'll be different this time, Richie, you'll see. We can be happy. I'll make you happy."

Her voice had become shrill. Experience had taught A.J. that without intervention, hysteria would be the next stage. She slipped from the room and summoned a nurse. "My mother's becoming upset again. You may need to sedate her."

She didn't wait for the nurse to hurry down the hallway for reinforcements. She reentered the room to find Leo bent over their mother, her hand clasped in his, speaking soothingly.

"Next time I come you'll put on your best dress and we'll go out to do the town right. Just like we used to.

Remember?'' The memory seemed to calm her, because her grip loosened and then fell away.

"Next time," she repeated dreamily. "Next time, Richie."

Leo rose and turned to go. A.J. followed him out the door, and when they were several yards away she grabbed his elbow, pulled him around. "What the *hell* did you think you were doing in there?"

Pulling away, he made a show of smoothing out his sleeve. "What do you mean?"

It was far more difficult than it should have been to resist the urge to pound comprehension into her brother. And it would give him far too much satisfaction were she to try. Hands fisted at her sides, she struggled for a composure that continued to elude her. "Do you have any idea what you just did back there? The damage you might have caused?"

Chin at an arrogant tilt, he said, "What I did was get the old lady's attention. For the first time in about a month, from what the nurses told me."

A deep breath filled deprived lungs, but did nothing to lessen A.J.'s fury. "You have her believing you're Dad, for God's sakes! She's no closer to reality now than she was when she wasn't speaking at all!"

"Then she's no further *from* reality, either. Matter of fact, it's hard to imagine her further gone. The old gal's a complete fruitcake, isn't she?"

Oddly enough his callous remark brought calm, layering over the anger. His attitude, after all, was so very familiar. "Sympathetic as always, Leo. Your sense of family loyalty is overwhelming."

His mouth thinned. "Something we have in common."

Pushing aside the welter of emotions caused by the earlier scene, she reached for logic. "I'm sure you couldn't have known what your appearance would do to her. That's why it would be better if you call first before coming back. I need to talk to the doctor, get his opinion…''

"Do what you want. His opinion won't matter a damn to me, and neither will yours. If I feel like coming back, I will." A crafty smile formed on his lips. "I promised her, as a matter of fact."

"I pay the bills. I can control Mama's visitors, especially if the doctor says it's in her best interests. If you continue to upset her, I'll do it."

She barely flinched when her brother's fist slapped against the wall next to her. His face was a tight mask of anger when he shoved it close to hers. "It's no wonder the old lady didn't recognize me. You always did try to keep us apart."

Age-old weariness rose in her. Leo had a convenient way of twisting things around so responsibility rested with everyone but himself. Arguing with him was futile, so she distracted him with a question. "How did you find out where she was staying, anyway?"

He shifted away, mentally as well as physically. "You're not the only one with contacts, you know. Matter of fact, I just might talk to a few other people I know." His smile was taunting. "I wonder what kind of case I'd have if I hired a lawyer to force my dragon sister to let me see dear old mom?" He cocked his head for a moment, as if contemplation of the idea gave him great pleasure. "If I were you, I wouldn't push, A.J. Because you never know when I'll push back." With that he turned and walked jauntily down the hall, as if he hadn't just stabbed a knife deep in her heart and given it a savage twist.

She had just enough self-control to wait until her brother was out of sight before sagging against the wall, her head drooping. Is this what family was? This violent emotion, these depths of despair? She couldn't understand people who gave their love so freely, so carelessly, without consideration for the consequences of letting someone close. Far better to chance loneliness, she thought, than to hand someone an invitation to shred her feelings whenever the mood struck.

"Ms. Jacobs?"

It was habit that had her straightening immediately, her features smoothing. "Doctor Gannon. Have you had time to evaluate the change in my mother?"

The doctor's seamed face was set in serious lines. "The truth is, I'm just not sure what it means yet. It's hard to tell whether the new medication took effect, if the alteration was caused by the unexpected arrival of your brother, or if it was a combination of the two. At any rate, Mandy still appears quite confused. She didn't recognize her son. As a matter of fact, his presence at first really seemed to upset her. How long has it been since she's seen him?"

"Seven or eight years, I think."

Gannon nodded. "No surprise then. But mistaking him for her ex-husband...does your brother resemble your father?"

Not in looks. The thought was swift, and better left unspoken. "No."

"Well, despite her confusion, this change may well be encouraging." He gave her a bolstering smile. "She recognized you today, I'm told. Given time, she may remember your brother, as well. We'll know more after we've had additional time to observe her." He gave her arm a reassuring squeeze and walked away. A.J. focused on his journey down the hallway without really seeing the doctor at all.

Psychiatry, she'd been told, time and again, was an inexact science. Who could really understand the workings of another's mind, or understand what precipitated the gradual slide from reality? Logic told her she'd never be certain. Instinct told her differently. Her mother had loved Rich

Jacobs, if their relationship could be dignified by the word. She'd tolerated beatings, infidelity, emotional and psychological abuse. And when she'd finally faced the fact that their life together would never change, she developed a psychological haven where just the opposite was true. Mandy Jacobs had handed her heart to the man she loved, and he'd used the very strength of her love to destroy her. Of that A.J. was certain.

The certainty never failed to terrify her.

When she came face-to-face with Dare in the courtroom, the intervening days since the scene in his apartment abruptly vanished.

"Hello, Addie." His face was sober, his voice expressionless. Sending a quick glance over her form, he asked, "Looks like you're healing okay."

"I...yes. I'm fine." She gripped her briefcase handle more tightly with fingers that had gone damp. The scrapes that still marred her shins were disguised, at least somewhat, by the dark nylons she wore. As more people entered the room, they shifted to the side, still facing each other.

Awkwardly she said, "I want to thank you again. For a few days ago, I mean." She tried for a smile. "With your skills you could moonlight as a medic."

"Given your distaste for hospitals, I suppose it wouldn't hurt for you to have your own private physician on call."

She would never know whether he'd intended to volunteer himself for the position. At that moment Mark looked back from the prosecution's table and frowned. She took a step backward. "I need to get settled before the judge enters."

He nodded, his face carefully blank. "Good luck."

But as she headed to the front of the courtroom, it felt more like she was hurrying away from, rather than toward something.

*   *   *

A.J. lost her customary calm and gaped across the courtroom at Paquin. "You've got to be kidding!" She ignored the nudge Mark Stanley gave her, and suffered a glare from the judge.

The defense attorney gave her a smug look before addressing the judge again. "From Ms. Jacobs's reaction, it's apparent she hasn't been apprised of all the facts. But I'm prepared to prove that this wasn't a kidnapping attempt at all, but a consensual meeting between two people involved in a romantic relationship. Detective Connally was insanely jealous at Patterson's interest in my client, and broke in on them when they were engaged in one of their—" he coughed discreetly "—tête-à-têtes." His lowered tone perfectly conveyed a man embarrassed to be betraying another's peccadilloes. "What we have here, Your Honor, is a love triangle, and a contrived story by the police to discredit the other suitor for Miss Patterson's affections."

"Your Honor." A.J. shot from her chair. "The contrivance exists solely in Mr. Paquin's imagination. In his eagerness to see his client freed, he's manufactured this…" She gave an incredulous laugh. Paquin wasn't the only one who could showboat. "…this fairy tale. We have witnesses who will testify that Meghan Patterson was being held against her will."

"And I can produce witnesses who will attest that my client and Miss Patterson had been engaged in an ongoing sexual affair."

A.J. heard the strangled gasp behind her, knew it'd come from Meghan. She kept her attention firmly on the judge. "This is a pathetic attempt to manipulate this court, Your Honor, into dropping felony charges against a known criminal."

Judge Holley gave her a reproving glance from over the top of her bifocals. "I'll be the one to decide if this court is being manipulated, Ms. Jacobs." She turned to Paquin again. "You say you have witnesses to support your claim?"

Joel folded his hands before him urbanely. "Yes, Your Honor. I have three of them here with me today."

Swiveling in her chair, A.J. noted that the courtroom was sparsely populated. Prelims didn't normally garner a lot of attention. Out of the corner of her eye she observed Dare seated in the back, typing on a laptop. It wasn't difficult to pick out the three witnesses Paquin was referring to, as they were the only people seated directly behind the defense counsel's table.

"Well, let's hear from your witnesses, Mr. Paquin."

At the judge's words, she sank in her seat. A.J. slid her legal pad closer and prepared to take notes. But sitting quietly throughout the witness's testimony proved excruciating. When given the opportunity, she grimly cross-examined each of the three. The lone woman of the group professed to work as a maid at a motel she claimed was frequented by Delgado and Meghan. One man was a bartender who insisted the two of them had often been seen at the bar where he worked. And the third was a gas jockey at a station on the outskirts of the city. His testimony was perhaps the most damaging. He stated that he'd seen the couple on several occasions, often engaged in a heated argument as he filled the tank on Meghan's car. Which he proceeded to describe, down to the make and license number.

A.J. fired question after question at each of the three, attempting to pin them down to specific dates and times. Each was able to recall the specifics she asked for, which was in itself suspect. Few had memories that sharp. She was unable to lead any of them into a contradiction. But of course, she was working at a disadvantage. She hadn't had the luxury of checking their stories out for herself.

In the end she had to rely on the strength of the testimony

of the detectives and Meghan to convince the judge. Detective Madison presented an articulate picture of the abandoned restaurant Meghan had been held in, describing her gagged-and-bound state when he'd entered the room behind Connally.

A.J. was somewhat concerned about Gabe maintaining his calm, but she needn't have been. He stated the facts in clear, concise terms and remained stoic during Paquin's attempts to discredit him. Her respect for the detective grew. His words were uttered without heat; not even an inflection gave him away. But his eyes... She wondered how Paquin could stand before him and not be seared by the threat emanating from the man.

Meghan wasn't quite as composed, although she was struggling admirably to maintain control. She'd had a nasty shock when Paquin had spun his tale, and there were a couple of occasions when her voice shook while answering. But she, too, exhibited a surprising strength when faced with the defense attorney's questions. The delicately built blond met Paquin's gaze head-on and flatly denied his spin on the events.

In the end, of course, it came down to Holley. A.J. waited with an outward calm she didn't feel, for the judge to render her decision. It was telling that she wouldn't have had any doubt about the outcome even a few hours ago.

The woman on the bench frowned as she re-read her notes. With the streaks of gray mingled in her brown hair and her world-weary eyes, she looked every day of the fifty-nine years she was credited with. But she had a conservative reputation, and A.J. was banking on that to work in the prosecution's favor.

The judge looked up, removed her glasses. "I am naturally troubled by these two diametrically opposing views. It is difficult to overlook the testimony of the defense's witnesses."

Behind her, A.J. could hear a barely audible groan emanating from Connally.

"But I can think of no more credible witnesses than two highly respected Chicago police detectives. Their testimony leads me to my decision to uphold the charges the state has brought against Mr. Delgado. The trial will proceed as planned."

Even as she released a breath from oxygen-starved lungs, Paquin was on his feet. "A trial may take months to schedule. I'm requesting bail be set so my client can be free to assist in his own defense."

Rising, she said smoothly, "The state objects to bail being set, Your Honor. Mr. Delgado has been charged with a very serious crime. He has a history of priors, and no permanent address. Without a job or family in the state, he's a decided flight risk."

The judge pursed her lips. "Again, I have to agree with the state. But I will do all I can to ensure a speedy trial for your client, Mr. Paquin. You and Ms. Jacobs get together and provide me with a list of dates to begin, shall we say…three months from now?" She stood, signaling that the proceedings were at an end.

Exchanging a grim glance with Mark, A.J. reached for her calendar and rose, as well. The deputies began to escort Delgado from the room, and she headed for Paquin's table. As the prisoner shuffled down the center aisle, she heard a scuffle and jerked around to see Madison step in front of Connally, who looked on the verge of lunging for the defendant. Her gaze stabbed at Delgado and caught his offensive grin. In spite of herself, she felt revulsion snake down her spine. She'd prosecuted some reprehensible characters, but this one was in a class by himself. With his deepset eyes, prominent bones and bald head, his skeletal face never failed to give her a chill.

She waited until she saw the rigidity seep from Connally's limbs before she turned back toward Paquin. The smile the defense attorney gave her was avuncular, his tone smug. "A.J. You've come to discuss a plea bargain, I assume."

Rather than give him the reaction he was clearly expecting, she merely raised her brows. "Hardly. I am, however, going to be ready to press charges for perjury." She smiled blandly. "If the situation calls for it."

Paquin's gaze frosted. "I don't like your insinuations."

"I can't say I care for the recent implications in this case, either," she responded, deliberately misunderstanding him. "But if you think this fairy tale you've spun for the judge's benefit is going to convince the state to reduce the charges, you're deranged."

He threw his head back and chortled. His aides swept their belongings from the table and piled them in briefcases before moving away. When he looked at her again, there was real mirth in his eyes. "I can always count on you to entertain me, A.J. Just don't let that fighting spirit of yours blind you to the inevitable."

She cocked her head. "Inevitable? I look forward to dismantling your witnesses in court. If I were you, I'd worry about how it's going to reflect on you, once I prove their testimony was manufactured."

Any vestiges of humor had long since fled his face. "I welcome you to try. Don't be surprised, though, when I find even more people willing to come forward and attest to the same thing." He bared his teeth. "I'm afraid my client and Ms. Patterson really weren't very discreet."

She shook her head slowly. "I've seen you take some pretty huge risks in the courtroom, Joel, but I've never known you to commit professional suicide. You must have a lot hanging on this one. More than I imagined."

He flipped the lid of his briefcase closed, snapped it shut. The small click sounded louder than normal in the almost empty courtroom. "If you knew me even half as well as you think you do, you'd know that I always play to win. Be very careful, A.J. After I destroy you in court, Beardmore is going to kick your career down to the basement. I look forward to that day." He picked up his briefcase, prepared to leave. "The day you come crawling to my firm."

He walked away, and she let him go. Song could always call his office and set up the dates the judge mentioned. She'd already spent as much time as she could stomach in Paquin's company. Dealing with the man invariably left her with a strong desire to wash her hands.

Crossing to her table, she gathered up her briefcase and notes. The room had cleared, save for Mark, the detectives, Meghan and, of course, Dare McKay. It was easier somehow to avoid looking at him. To avoid thinking about him. So she turned her gaze to Meghan and gave her an apologetic smile. "This whole afternoon has been trying for you, I'm sure."

The other woman couldn't quite hide a shudder. "I'm not certain what I was expecting, but it wasn't the sordid scenario Paquin came up with." Her hand didn't move from Connally's arm, as if with her touch alone she could keep them both composed.

"We knew he had something up his sleeve when he insisted on going through with the prelim," Mark said. "A.J. just wasn't able to predict what direction he'd take."

"He wants the charges reduced so his client can skate," she said flatly. "That isn't going to happen." She looked at Connally and his partner. "Now that we've got dates and times from these so-called defense witnesses, we'll proceed by shooting holes in their stories. Start with Stillwell. See if she's able to contradict Delgado's absence on any of those..." She broke off, seeing the look shared between Dare and the detectives. "What?"

"I just told the detectives..." Dare's somber gaze met

hers. "I can't find a trace of Honey Stillwell. Her apartment's empty and she hasn't shown up for work for two days."

"She skipped town?"

"Hopefully." Dare's flat tone gave none of his thoughts away.

She gave a mental shrug. "If we decide we need her, she can be found again."

"Maybe." Gabe didn't sound hopeful.

Turning toward him, she said, "Maybe?"

"The man we obtained the information from last time…" Gabe's eyes cut to the reporter. "The same guy who then sold the information to McKay, isn't going to be of any more help in this case."

"He won't be helping anyone," Dare put in, his eyes flinty. "He was found in a Dumpster this morning with three bullets in him. If Honey Stillwell is very lucky, she left town before suffering the same fate."

"You're sure you can counter this story of Paquin's?"

It was the third time Beardmore had asked that particular question, and A.J.'s answer was no less emphatic for being repeated. "I'm certain of it." She leaned back in her chair and resisted the urge to slip off her shoes, rub her arches.

"This development took us by complete surprise," Mark put in, with just the right amount of concern in his voice. "A.J. thought Paquin might be up to something, but wasn't able to predict exactly what he'd pull. There's no telling how many more of these phony witnesses he'll line up. We're going to be kept running in circles trying to chase down the validity of all those stories. In the meantime Paquin is taking the next three months to get prepared."

A.J. considered the clock surreptitiously. It was long past dinnertime, and she hadn't eaten since she'd devoured a day-old doughnut at her desk that morning. She wanted to get to St. Anne's before it got much later, but Beardmore was exhibiting a strange need for reassurance.

"Connally and Madison will be looking into the backgrounds of the three he had in court today," she said. "I'm sure they'll turn up something. And I'm not wasting my time trying to discredit an endless list of so-called witnesses he throws at us. I'm going to discredit his entire argument. I've instructed Meghan to make a schedule of her activities for the last couple of months. Paquin claimed she left her nephew at home in the apartment late at night to go out and meet Delgado. Meghan is certain we can find people in her building who will help us prove otherwise."

"I hope it will be as simple as A.J. is making it out to be." There was just a shade of doubt in Mark's tone.

She turned her head, sent him a little smile. "Why don't you concentrate on interviewing those witnesses from her building, Mark?" The suggestion effectively quieted him.

Dennis smoothed a well-manicured hand over his hair. "Well, I have faith in the two of you. Couldn't be more confident." He gave them his polished smile. "But I don't think I have to remind you how important this case is to this office and, I don't mind saying, to me.

"I've had some very influential people in the city question me about my political aspirations. Very wealthy people." Somehow he managed to look pleased and modest at the same time, a credit to his acting abilities. "In complete confidence, I'll tell you that I'm seriously considering a run for Cook County state attorney."

"Congratulations, sir." A.J. and Mark responded in unison, although A.J.'s voice was noticeably less enthusiastic. Rumors of the man's plans had circulated through the offices for weeks. And since the current state attorney had been a desk commando and had never tried a felony case, a big win on this case would provide credibility to Beardmore's candidacy.

Beardmore paced her office like an orator. "I don't need to tell you what a case of this magnitude could do for this office, A.J." He stopped, gave her troubled look from beneath his beetled brows. "Or, what my political opponent could do with a defeat."

His meaning was as clear as if he'd etched it in glass. "Believe me, sir, I'm going to do everything in my power to make sure we win a conviction."

He stared at her a moment longer, then nodded. "I want you to pull out all the stops, because we know that Paquin will. We'll have to be prepared to step outside our normal parameters, fight fire with fire." Then, having apparently used up his quota of clichés, Beardmore left her office, trailed closely by Mark.

She took a deep breath, rubbed her forehead. Paquin, the snake, had called it correctly. Her career hinged on the outcome of this case. A loss might not only spell the end of Beardmore's political ambitions, but relegate her to pleading second-rate cases any first-year law student could handle.

Sitting in the office, staring blinding at the wall, she thought about Beardmore's words. He'd been right about one thing. She was going to have to fight fire with fire. Her stomach jangled with nerves as she contemplated her choices. She just hoped she didn't scorch herself in the process.

Chapter 7

Since she'd mentally rehearsed the scene in the car on the way over, A.J. was able to suppress all but a sliver of unease as she knocked at Dare's door. But when it swung open to reveal a broad, naked chest, tapering down to a flat stomach left bare above unbuttoned jeans, all her persuasive words and polished speeches slid abruptly down her throat.

Dare leaned his shoulder against the doorjamb. "Wrong time of year to be selling Girl Scout cookies."

She was aware she was staring dumbly, but found it difficult to switch mental gears. "I…ah…if I'm interrupting something I could come back. Or call." Once the idea was formed, it began to seem extremely sensible. She took a few steps back. "I'll call. Or you can. When you're not busy. Later."

He raised a brow. "You're here. Might as well say your piece."

The tidy little speech she'd planned seemed suddenly ridiculous. "If you have company, it would be best to talk tomorrow." During the course of the statement she inched away, shortening the distance to the elevator.

A natural curiosity came in handy in Dare's line of work. But at times like now, it was the bane of his existence. He cocked his head, considered her. He couldn't imagine what would have Addison Jacobs voluntarily seeking him out, and after hours, to boot. And he damned himself for wondering. Given their last few run-ins, any guy with an ounce of sense would be making tracks in the opposite direction. He liked to believe he had more than his share of intelligence.

Which didn't explain why he stepped aside, opened the door wider. "C'mon in."

He noted her hesitation before she complied, the way she made sure to keep a safe distance between them, and he shut the door behind her with more force than necessary. She'd stepped no further inside than his foyer, and was looking everywhere but at him.

"Oh, you were working?"

He didn't follow her gaze to the glow of the computer screen on the desk in the kitchen. "Yeah. I was getting a column ready to turn in." He folded his arms across his chest, intrigued despite himself. There was something else on Addie's mind, and it was becoming increasingly apparent that whatever it was, she wasn't at all comfortable with it.

She looked at him finally and drew a breath. "Since you heard Paquin today, I think you have a pretty good understanding of what I'm up against. He's going to keep throwing these phony witnesses at us to keep us busy checking them out, and prevent the investigation from focusing solely on Delgado."

Cautiously he said, "I think that's a given."

"Makes you wonder what he's afraid we'd find in the man's past, doesn't it?" Speaking of the case seemed to relax her as nothing else could. He could almost see the tension seep from her limbs in tiny increments.

"Connally checked his past. But then, you know that." He couldn't resist the veiled jab. He wasn't sure where she was heading with the conversation, but he wasn't in the mood to make it easier for her.

"We know he hasn't been arrested for ten years. But when it comes to what he's been up to…"

"Can't find any employment records. No property in his name. No permanent address. Hasn't paid Social Security or filed a tax form. He hasn't even applied for a driver's license."

She inclined her head, granting him that one. She had no doubt that he'd exhausted those leads himself. "So whatever Delgado's been doing for the past decade, he's made a point of doing it quietly. Why would anyone bother to go to such lengths to leave no records if he were living a model life? I've been thinking that maybe I should give Connally's original hunch more credence." The next few words seemed to pain her. "And yours."

He clutched his heart, feigned shock. "Are you, in an unusually roundabout fashion, telling me that I was actually right about something?"

His sarcasm had her relaxing a fraction, if only to show irritation. "Don't get cocky, McKay. I'm not ready to buy any theories on how he's spent the last ten years without some evidence to back it up. But I am beginning to think it would help my case to do a little more digging into his past."

He dropped his hands, hooked his thumbs in his pockets. "And you're telling me this, because…"

Her mouth flattened. "I'm telling you that I've reconsidered." He could only imagine what the next few words cost her. "I may have been too hasty when I asked you to steer clear of the investigation."

His shock was real now, but he did a better job this time of hiding it. "*May* have been?"

He thought, he was almost sure, he could hear her teeth snapping together. But to her credit she didn't lose her cool but looked him straight in the eye. "Beardmore wants a win pretty badly on this one. So far I've got two detectives who have their caseloads to juggle along with the investigation aspect of the case, one assistant state attorney for whom the same can be said, and myself. It occurred to me that I'd be a fool to discourage you from digging up any details you can that might help put that scumbag away."

A cynical smile twisted his lips. As if she could have stopped him in the first place. "And what led you to this abrupt change of heart?"

"It's partly due to a chat I had with Dennis about an hour ago. And partially from the look on Meghan Patterson's face after the prelim."

The words had him dropping his gaze. "That had to be tough on her."

"It will continue to be tough on her," A.J. predicted grimly. "Because Paquin is going to drag her reputation through the gutter with this defense route he's taking. She's well-known in this city. She comes from one of Chicago's oldest families. When the trial starts, the media coverage will be brutal."

If she expected him to object to her words because he was part of that media, she'd be disappointed. Dare well knew how reputations could be tarnished, lives ruined, just by the breath of scandal surrounding a person. And somehow, even when the suggestions proved false, it was the scandal, not the exoneration, that the public remembered.

"Do you think Paquin believes that line of defense will convince Meghan to drop the charges? Any chance of that happening?"

A.J. lifted a shoulder. "I'm sure the devious jerk had all

kinds of reasons for doing what he did. She and Connally are pretty adamant about holding Delgado accountable for his actions. She's also convinced he was instrumental in her sister's death.'' She stopped then, frowned. ''But if there's a chance that the publicity surrounding the case could have an adverse effect on her nephew, well…I'm not sure what she'll decide.''

He nodded, remembering quite well how protective Meghan was of the six-year-old boy. ''So now you're figuring that the facts as they stand might not be enough.''

''I want more.'' The uneasy woman who had entered his apartment had vanished. He was much more familiar with the one facing him now, wearing a mask of determination. He found he preferred her like this. Addison Jacobs. Righter of wrongs. Protector of the downtrodden.

The flash of admiration he felt wasn't totally comfortable. It would be much easier to believe that she'd made the decision to use him again because he could be of help. And if he wasn't so convinced of her genuine concern for the victims in this case, he'd choose to believe just that. ''So why are you here, Addie?''

She never backed down from an unpleasant task, he'd grant her that. ''I'm here to tell you I'm interested in hearing whatever you uncover.'' He began to nod, unsurprised, but she wasn't finished. ''And that I want to be involved in every step.''

That snared his attention as nothing else could have. ''You mean you want me to report to you.''

''No, I want to go with you when you follow your leads. Have you traced Delgado's sister yet?''

He could see where this was headed, and it was time to take a detour. ''I don't know for sure where to find her.'' Under her silent stare he felt like a perjured witness. He had the woman's date of birth and social security number, and had actually found record of some traffic tickets in her name in Ohio. But he wasn't lying when he said, "I'm still digging. I was going to go to Ohio tomorrow and see what I can turn up, but it's going to be hit-and-miss." He was talking faster now, as if speed would sway her where logic wouldn't. "You'd be better off waiting to see if I have any luck. Then you could accompany Connally when he questions her. He and Madison may even find her first." Humility had never been his strong point, but a desperate man was a well of creativity.

"The potential witnesses in this case have a way of disappearing," she noted flatly. "I do plan to accompany Connally and Madison when they question people. I also plan to accompany you."

He couldn't remember when he'd heard a worse idea. Hadn't they already been through this? Hadn't he recently, in a fit of blinding stupidity, suggested the very thing? But that was before he'd been reminded of all the reasons the two of them should stay far, far apart. Before he'd touched the satiny skin on her thigh and been reminded that the silkiness was repeated on every square inch of her flesh. And before he'd spent interminable minutes kissing her, recalling things that would be much better left forgotten.

He'd since regained his senses as well as his cognitive functioning. "I don't think so."

Her expression took on a superior cast that was more than a little provocative. "Just what is it you're afraid of, McKay?"

Brows skimming upward, he folded his arms across his chest and contemplated her. "*Afraid?* Me?"

Her fingers clenched against her leg in an uncustomary show of nerves. "I think we're both mature enough to put our personal feelings aside, don't you? This case is important. I want Delgado convicted. I'm willing to do what it takes to accomplish that. You convinced Connally of your theory on the man's past. Let's get some proof."

The unusual sight of Addie flustered, even a bit, was a diversion he didn't need. ''You'll get your proof, along with a prediction. When we start digging into Delgado's past, we're going to find ourselves tripping over Mannen, too.''

It wasn't until he caught her smile that he recognized the pronoun he'd used. *We.* Cursing himself for being all kinds of a fool, he gave in with little grace. ''Be ready to leave at seven tomorrow morning.''

Puddle jumpers weren't high on A.J.'s list of favorite things, but the takeoff at O'Hare went without incident. It would, Dare had asserted, save time to fly to Ohio and rent a car. The plan made too much sense to argue with. It didn't appear wise to argue with Dare right now, at any rate.

Her gaze slid to the man next to her. He'd been remarkably quiet since they'd met at the airport. There had been no teasing comment about her simple black pants and jacket, no arch remark about her willingness to spend time with him. No, there had been very little conversation at all. And she suspected that she knew what was weighing on his mind.

''I heard from the officer who investigated that driver that nearly hit me. The car had been stolen, then abandoned. Probably some kid out for a joy ride.''

''That's possible, I guess.''

''I also heard from Connally last night. He had more information on the homicide of the snitch…Cooley?''

Dare's jaw tightened. ''Yeah, I talked to Connally, too.''

From his reaction, it appeared she'd accurately guessed the reason for his preoccupation. ''You aren't to blame for his death.''

Voice expressionless, he countered, ''Aren't I?''

''No.'' Her voice was firm. ''Your number may have been found in his pocket, but Connally said the man made his living selling information to the highest bidder. He'd dealt with him several times himself. It was a high-risk business.'' She paused a beat for emphasis. ''One filled with dangers.''

He finally looked at her then, and his eyes had gone flat and steely. ''What are you suggesting, Addie? That it wasn't his connection to me that got him killed?''

''I'm suggesting that you have no idea how many people he'd dealt with recently, nor all the information he was selling. There's no reason to believe his death was linked to you.''

His mouth twisted. Her words failed to shake his certainty of just that. Cooley wouldn't be the first innocent victim to get caught up in the deadly struggle between Mannen and him. A scene from the past burned a path across his mind, and he almost flinched. It was always the sounds from that day that seemed most prominent. The roar of the explosion, the screams, the wail of sirens…

It was tempting to give up when he just looked away without comment, but A.J. tried one more time. She, of all people, knew about regret, the suffocating weight of it, that could paralyze and haunt by turns. ''Haven't we all made enough mistakes that we have to live with? Do you really need to accept guilt about something you had no control over?''

His tone was challenging. ''You sound like the voice of experience. Do you take your own advice?''

Her gaze went past him, to focus on the cotton-batting clouds. ''I'm trying,'' she murmured finally. ''I am trying.''

She didn't consider how much she'd exposed about herself with those few words. It had just occurred to her that a reporter who felt responsible for the welfare of a street snitch was far more admirable than she'd like to believe. It was doubtful that such a man would stoop to rifling her notes for details to support a story.

Shifting in her seat uncomfortably, she acknowledged that the thought wasn't a new one. The facts stated in his article two years ago had closely reflected details she'd had documented in her briefcase, and she'd seized on the coincidence to support a decision she'd already made. He'd gotten too close to her, too fast, and that had scared the hell out of her. That had been the truth two years ago.

And despite the passage of time, it was just as true today.

"So where do we begin?"

"With Clancy's last-known address."

"How do you know she's still there?"

His tone was patient as he checked for traffic before merging onto the freeway. "She may not be, but it's a starting point. If she moved on, chances are she left traces. Mail has to be forwarded, employers notified, licenses renewed. You wouldn't believe the information available on people in the county courthouses."

Actually, she had no trouble believing it, having haunted the courthouse herself digging for facts relating to her cases. They were, indeed, a gold mine of information. Drivers' licenses, property purchases, mortgage applications, liens, criminal judgments, pet licenses... If Nancy Clancy still lived in the county, she had no doubt they could find her.

However, when they went to the address Dare had acquired, the current occupant was an unshaven man dressed in stained sleeveless T-shirt and khakis, who appeared to be nursing a hangover. He'd been living there for three months, he told them, and had never met the former occupant. So in the end, Dare and A.J. ended up in the local courthouse, just as he'd predicted.

Seated at a table beside him, A.J. stared at the computer screen until her eyes threatened to cross. Pulling up Clancy's driver's license had yielded the same address they'd visited. Although they found one drunken driving conviction from three years previously, there was no sign of the woman's name in any of the other sets of records they accessed.

She slid a glance at Dare. He was slouched over the table in a boneless position that would have her spine screaming after only a few minutes. From the looks of him, he could go on like this for hours. She imagined that there had been occasions when he'd had to.

Giving an inner sigh, she went back to her work and began to access the county property records. After several minutes she paused, almost unwilling to believe what she'd found. She grabbed the briefcase she'd set on the floor beside her chair and laid it on the table, snapped the locks open.

Dare looked up questioningly. "Did you pack a lunch in there or something? Because I could go for a hot ham and cheese on rye right about now."

She was rifling through her notes. "I don't suppose you remember Paul Delgado's middle initial."

"T for Thomas."

"And his birthdate is…" She checked the sheet she'd been looking for, then compared it to the name on the screen. "January 11."

"A Capricorn," he agreed, coming over to look. "What are you getting at? Did you find Delgado's name on there?"

She leaned to one side to allow him to see. "No, but I found a Paul T. Belgado with a birthdate and social security number that matches our guy." She couldn't prevent the hint of smugness from tingeing her voice. "Looks like he bought some property down here about four months ago."

Clancy's house was several rungs above her former dwelling. "A spelling error," Dare muttered for the fifth time. "If I told you how many times I've run into dead ends because some idiot types the wrong letter or number..."

"Don't pout." She reached over and patted his cheek. "It's not attractive."

He captured her hand and shot her a pointed look. "Neither is gloating."

"I'm not gloating," she corrected, discreetly tugging to free her hand. "Just stating a fact."

That familiar grin of his made an appearance, and something jittered in her chest. His amusement was infinitely preferable to the grimness he'd exhibited on the plane. So suffering through that megawatt smile was preferable, wasn't it? That was the sole reason she let her hand rest in his a moment longer than necessary. Why it took yet another moment to gather scattered senses.

"Am I expected to stand idly by while you charm Clancy like you did Stillwell?" The question was posed to distract them both.

He lifted a shoulder, opened the car door. "Can't say I know what to expect this time, so I'll have to play it by ear."

It took a moment for her to understand his meaning. She hurried up the walk after him. "Don't you think it'd be wiser to have a plan?"

"Not if I'd have to shuck it in the first ten seconds." He climbed up the steps and lifted his hand to knock at the front door. It was opened almost immediately by a preteen girl who surveyed them sullenly. "If you're selling something, they'll never buy it. They never buy nothing."

She was pushed aside by a thin-faced woman who looked them over sharply. "You cops?"

Even as A.J. opened her mouth to answer, Dare let loose a laugh. "God, no. Do I look like a cop?"

A fraction of the suspicion in the woman's eyes faded,

but she remained visibly wary. "You can't always tell. Whaddya want?"

"I'm trying to locate Paul Delgado. I was told he lived here."

"He don't." The woman made as if to close the door.

Puzzlement was plain on Dare's face. "But I understood he owned this property."

"He does, but he don't live here. I'm his sister. He bought the house for me."

Dare exchanged a meaningful look with A.J. The trouble was, she had no idea what the look meant. Neither, apparently, did Clancy. "Is there a problem?" the other woman asked.

"There might be, ma'am." Dare turned from her to address A.J. "Would you go back out to the car and call the home office? Tell them we're running into a bit of a snag here, and that we'll be longer than expected."

She was savvy enough to play along, but she knew when she was being ditched. "Oh, I think that can wait, can't it? We're not that late."

He acted as though he hadn't heard her. "Tell them there might be a problem with section 512 article 6, will you? They'll understand how sticky that can be."

Her glare had no effect on him. He turned his bland smile back on Clancy, and A.J. was left to grit her teeth and walk back to the car.

She sat fuming in the vehicle for a full minute before she remembered that she was supposed to be acting as though she were making a phone call. Whether that was really a necessary part of this ruse, or whether it had just been a handy excuse to get rid of her, she had no idea. She suspected the latter, but just to be sure, she opened her briefcase with movements made jerky by irritation. Pulling out her cell phone, she pretended to place a call.

From the corner of her eye she watched the front porch.

After several more minutes the screen door was opened wider and Dare was stepping inside. They disappeared in the house, but the child they'd spoken to earlier came out again.

For lack of something better to do, A.J. watched her. Her lethargic movements and heavy sighs screamed boredom, an emotion A.J. could empathize with at the moment.

Rolling down her window, she smiled at the girl, getting only a blank look in return. "Can't find anything to do today?"

It was apparent by the girl's long pause that she was debating whether she was bored enough to talk to A.J. Tedium eventually won out, because she sauntered closer to the car. "There's never nothing to do in this town. 'Cept go to the public pool, and she—" her head jerked toward the house "—never buys me a season's ticket."

A.J. thought there was more than the usual childish discontent sounding in her voice. "Maybe your mom is having a hard time making ends meet," she suggested.

"She's not my mom!" The correction was swift and fierce. "And the only reason she never has money is because she spends it all on her clothes and her hair. That and running around with whatever jerk she's dating at the moment."

The girl flopped down on the grass beside the car. "My dad had to buy this place, because she always wasted the money he sent her." She rolled her eyes, the gesture far older than her years. "They think I don't know he sends her money to take care of me."

A thought occurred, so preposterous that A.J. could scarcely credit it. "Who's your dad?"

The girl sent her an impatient glance. "You should know, you came here looking for him. It's Paul Delgado."

"An hour and a half." A.J. grated the words out between clenched teeth. "You must be losing your touch, McKay.

It usually only takes minutes before women start pouring their hearts out to you.''

She could have sworn she saw him wince as he steered the car away from the curb. ''Now, A.J., don't be like that. I just didn't want you to be placed in a tough position, professionally. Ms. Clancy was a tough sell. I couldn't rely on my natural wit and charm. I had to get creative.''

A vivid imagination could be a blessing or a curse. She made no attempt to keep the suspicion from her voice. ''Do I want to know just how creative you got?''

He hesitated, thinking of the tale he'd spun about his fictitious banking employer and a mix-up in Delgado's accounts. Sometimes details were better glossed over. ''Don't you think you'd be happier not knowing?''

She opened her mouth, shut it again. The fact that he was right didn't mean she was any happier about being relegated to the back seat in today's affairs.

''Clancy wasn't going to talk to us, especially if we told her who we were. You saw how uncooperative she was. The situation called for some innovation.'' He gave her a self-satisfied smile. ''And it certainly paid off. Because guess where Delgado keeps many of his personal effects?''

''Here, of course. He visits about once a month.'' Enjoying his startled look, it was her turn to smile. ''You're not the only one who came up with some information. Bet you can't guess who the girl at the house belongs to.''

His eyes widened satisfyingly. ''No way.''

She nodded. ''Exactly my reaction. That poor kid has Delgado for a father.''

Dare turned on to the freeway back toward the airport. ''What a life she's got ahead of her. Especially when he spends the rest of his years in prison.''

A.J. felt a flicker of pity. She could well imagine the child's hopelessness, her despair, once she really got old enough to understand just what kind of man her father was. She was already far older than A.J. had been before a similar realization had dawned on her. Her own father had been a monster, and she'd often felt like she was the only thing standing between him and her mother's fragile grip on reality.

As a barrier, she'd proved remarkably ineffective.

"Aren't you even interested in what I found in there?"

She welcomed the diversion his question presented. "You're telling me you actually got the woman to let you dig around in his stuff?"

"Not as much as I would have liked. She was watching me pretty closely. But I was able to come up with this."

He reached in his pocket, pulled out a small black notebook and tossed it to her.

Aghast, A.J. stared at it. Her voice was strangled. "You removed something from the house? McKay, do I have to remind you of the laws surrounding the chain of evidence?"

Pretending to consider, he finally said, "No, I don't think so. I had permission to be in the house, and Clancy actually told me I could take this with me." He may have persuaded her that the book merely listed dates of bank transactions, but he saw no reason to burden A.J. with extra details. "Since I'm turning the information directly over to an officer of the court, I'd have to guess that you would have a 75 percent chance of getting it admitted as evidence, if necessary. That's assuming it's tied to a crime in the first place."

She glared at him. "In your case I'd say a little knowledge really is a dangerous thing."

"And a little knowledge just might break this case wide open," he said imperturbably. "Take a look at it and tell me what you think."

Reluctantly A.J. opened it. On the first few pages there

were numbered notations. "Okay, I'll bite. What are these supposed to mean?"

"Look at the combination of numbers. They could stand for dates, couldn't they?"

She flipped through the pages, saw he was right. "If so, the oldest one dates to almost ten years ago." Even as the words left her mouth, she realized their significance. "Almost as long as Delgado's been out of prison."

Dare gave her an approving look. "Exactly. Maybe we've got some information there that's going to link Delgado to Paulie the Knife."

A.J. was already shaking her head. "Let's not leap to conclusions."

"Somehow I thought you'd say that. Look at the date that's fifth from the bottom." A.J. did. It was less than four months ago. "Do you remember Meghan telling you Delgado bragged to her about killing her sister? I'll have to check to be absolutely certain, but I think we'll find that the date will correspond with the day she died."

Chapter 8

A.J. and Dare met Connally at district headquarters and waited as he fed the dates and Delgado's MO into the national Criminal Apprehension database. Several of the dates matched those on which homicides had taken place, the oldest having occurred almost a decade ago.

The discovery of Clancy's house, and its owner, was enough to convince a judge that Delgado's permanent address had been discovered. A search warrant was issued and his personal belongings in Ohio were seized. Hours blurred for the next few days as a mountain of new information accumulated. At the end of each day, all A.J. could do when she went home was fall into exhausted slumber.

But the lack of sleep was a small price to pay for the sudden rapidity with which the case was beginning to gel. Connally and Madison were combing through the evidence from Clancy's house, and Mark Stanley had already uncovered some very unsavory information about two of Paquin's supposed witnesses.

And A.J. found herself, strangely enough, in Dare McKay's company for more hours than she cared to count.

Their time together was going without incident. If nothing else, their forced alliance had shown her that they could spend time in close proximity without personal memories distracting them.

At least, they didn't appear to be distracting Dare. He was acting, finally, more like a casual acquaintance than a one-time lover. He was polite and charming, while holding his wicked sense of humor in check.

Which explained why she was fairly comfortable sitting in his apartment that evening, at a computer near his, digging into archives from newspapers across the country. The kitchen counter was strewn with fast-food wrappers and her third diet soda was within reach. After Connally had found homicides that might match the dates in Delgado's book, she and Dare had split the cases. During the day she made calls to the detectives who'd worked the investigations, acquiring more facts about each. She became more and more confident that they were on the right track. The tiniest bit of information they stumbled over just might be the key to tying Delgado's identity to that of Paulie the Knife.

She took a break for a moment, rubbed her eyes. Glancing over at Dare, she saw he was still concentrating fiercely on the article he was reading, a pair of gold wire-rim glasses perched on his nose.

There was an odd kick in her stomach at the sight. How was it possible for a man to look studious and sexy at the same time? And why was she even thinking of how the man looked when it had been she who'd insisted on a strictly business relationship between them? Embarrassed, she switched her focus to her screen, but not before he caught her staring.

"What's wrong?"

"Nothing." She could feel a mortified flush crawl up her

cheeks. She hadn't blushed since Mrs. Goetz caught her peeking in the boy's bathroom in third grade. "I've never seen you in glasses before, that's all." A knowing smile started to play at his lips. To wipe it off, she added, "They make you look halfway intelligent."

A lone dimple flashed. "Addie, you've really got to stop fawning over me. Your lavish compliments are getting downright embarrassing."

Deliberately she changed the subject. "Some of the dates in Delgado's book haven't been linked to one of these homicides. Does that mean he turned a job down? That he failed at a hit?"

Dare reached up, unfastened a button on his shirt. Her gaze immediately arrowed to the bared triangle of golden skin, before bouncing guiltily away. "I suppose either is possible. But since one of those dates corresponds to the date of Meghan's sister's death, there may be a more likely explanation." As he spoke, he unbuttoned his cuffs and folded his sleeves back. "What if it means he didn't use his preferred method of murder? That for whatever reason, circumstances forced him to deviate from his knife?"

"You mean like when he ran Meghan's sister off the road."

He linked his hands, stretched his arms out in front of him. "Maybe some jobs have to look like accidents. If so, we'd have a devil of a time ever linking him to them."

The explanation made as much sense as any. It was still difficult for A.J. to be dealing with so many suppositions. She was far more comfortable with facts. But she was willing to accept the change in her methods, if it meant that she could defeat Paquin and get Delgado put away. With renewed purpose she turned back to her machine.

Dare was slower to follow suit. Her armor had grown increasingly less noticeable, aided, perhaps, by his manner toward her. He'd been as circumspect as a priest. Well, almost. Surely priests didn't indulge in the kind of erotic thoughts that occasionally played across his mind. But working so closely with Addie had convinced him that he was firmly in control of his emotions. A relief for a man unaccustomed to being led around by them.

Night fell unusually early that evening, and he rose to switch on some lights. Clouds were bumping and colliding against the darkening sky, signaling a storm blowing in from the lake. Dare opened the sliding door leading to the small terrace and enjoyed the cool air's promise of rain.

"Hmm. You should come look at this."

At her voice he turned and padded back to the kitchen, knelt by her chair. She pointed at a name on the screen. "This article in the *Indiana Star* details the trial of a Frank Benson six years ago. He was quite a busy guy, apparently. Into drugs, prostitution, lone-sharking..." She broke off, scrolled down further into the story. "He was acquitted of most of the charges, probably because the witnesses who were going to testify against him kept disappearing. But they did manage to convict him of the murder of a rival drug lord." Her gaze raised to his. "Guess how the guy died?"

His fingers crowded hers on the keyboard as he tried to scroll down the story. "He had his throat cut?"

"Right." She batted his hand away, closed out of that article and opened another. "He's been screaming his innocence to high heaven, and now his case is awaiting appeal." She leaned forward, skimming the article until finding the part she wanted to show him. She pressed the command to highlight the block of text. "He claims it was another drug lord who ordered the hit and then framed him to get two rivals out of the way at once."

"So you're thinking this Benson might be innocent?"

"I'm sure he belongs in prison, if not for this crime, then for a multitude of others. But if I were to speculate..." She looked at him, plainly in unfamiliar territory without empirical evidence at hand.

"What if he's telling the truth?" Dare finished for her. "Warring drug lords sound like the sort of people Delgado would be involved with."

She lifted a brow. "Long shot?"

"Probably," he affirmed, and watched her face fall before he added, "but definitely worth checking out."

"I think so, too." She smiled, a delighted flash of teeth that tightened his chest and thickened his blood. He didn't look away. He couldn't.

It was moments like these that were so hard to forget—when defenses lowered and glimpses of the Addie she hid from the world were revealed. The contrast aroused primitive emotions far better left unidentified.

Seeing the expression on his face, her smile faltered, faded. There was something naked in the way he gazed at her, something suggesting hot sin, seductive danger. She wished she wasn't intimately acquainted with that look. She wished she could deny her response to it.

Desire thudded in her veins. If only she didn't have an exquisite memory of being over him, under him, seeing those eyes blaze just that way, until they reflected nothing but her. If only she could deny the power there was in being wanted, with just that kind of intensity.

A breath shuddered out of her. She was helpless to stem the memories that picked that moment to swarm. Her gaze fell to his sculpted lips, remembered their taste. It wasn't that she no longer had the will to resist the man. She just failed to recall the need to.

Their mouths met, soft, oddly tentative. And then came that slow, gradual sink into pleasure that tilted her world in a way that always alarmed later. Much later. Now there was only the pleasure of it, the increasing pressure, and awareness receding to be replaced with demand.

Dare cupped her face in both his hands and leaned into the kiss. Hunger rocketed through his system. He traced the seam of her lips with his tongue, coaxed them open. And when they did, need rose up, edgy and fierce.

He reached for her fingers, tugged, and she obeyed his urging. Slipping out of her chair, she sank to the floor, until they were knee to knee. All the while their mouths mated, teeth clashed, breath mingled. She touched his chest where it was bared, and the feel of his warm flesh spiked her own temperature. As if they had a will of their own, her fingers went to the buttons on his shirt, unfastened them one by one. And then went on a sensual discovery, skating over sinew, bone and muscle. Exploring angles and intriguing hollows, gorging her senses on the journey.

He shoved a hand in her hair, pulled her closer. He wanted everything she had to give, more than she'd ever given before. And he wanted, quite desperately, for her to offer it freely. Without reservation.

He dragged his mouth from hers and strew hard, desperate kisses along the delicate line of her jaw, to the pulse at the base of her throat. His need to touch her was fueled by the wake of heat her hands left on his skin. Sparks flickered just below the surface of his flesh. He unfastened the first button on her blouse, skimmed his hand over sensitized flesh.

Her world rocked on its axis, and her hands rose, fisted in his hair. That first contact had spurred unchecked desire, a restless craving. With one gentle finger he traced the swell of her breasts above her bra, before dipping between them. She gasped, the sound caught by his lips.

The evidence of her passion sent a hot ball of lust hurtling through him. His hands went to her waist and he pressed her to him, unable to bring her close enough. Need surged from a primal place, desperate and demanding.

"Don't deny this, Addie," he rasped, his mouth skating

over her collarbone. "Don't deny us." It was a measure of his desire that it took several moments to realize that her body had gone stiff at his words, her lips unresponsive. And when he raised his head to look at her, he already knew what he'd read on her face.

Fear. Pure and unadulterated, it smashed his longing with a brutal fist. He didn't know if the emotion was directed at him or at herself. The distinction really didn't matter. The end result was the same.

The bleak realization knifed through him, leaving a sense of desolation that was staggering. He rose, wanting to haul her in his arms again, knowing that he couldn't. She was that fragile. That vulnerable. To keep from reaching for her, he shoved his hands in his pockets, watched her stumble to her feet and fasten her blouse with shaking fingers.

She turned to go, head bent, then hesitated. He willed her to leave without a word. There was nothing to say. No reason to say it. An instant later he got his wish, and she walked out of his apartment, closing the door quietly behind her.

Dare backed up slowly, leaned heavily against the couch. He didn't know what Addie was so afraid of, but he knew it was powerful. Whatever it was had kept her running from him for over two years now.

There was a glow of distant lightning in the sky, heralding a storm's approach. A.J. didn't heed it. It was the storm within that absorbed all her attention. She found a parking place close to St. Anne's, carefully positioned her car and turned the key off in the ignition.

Then she rested her forehead against the wheel, as the emotions twisting inside knotted her stomach and pounded at her temples.

Drawing deep breaths, she fought for control. A control that had been noticeably absent while she'd been in Dare's arms. A control that, if she was truthful with herself, had been receding fractionally for some time.

Only an hour ago she'd been congratulating herself on her ability to work side by side with McKay without any personal complications rising between them. *Complications.* A wild laugh welled up in her throat. What a word to describe what had just happened. Again. She'd fooled herself once that she could give in to that kind of desire. That she could warm herself with that wealth of heat he transmitted, without ever risking more. Without ever giving more.

And now it appeared as though she'd deceived herself yet again. Because it was becoming glaringly apparent that she couldn't be near Dare McKay for any length of time without her defenses crumbling, one tiny bit at a time. A man who could so easily dismantle her careful guard, thread his way past her resistance, was more dangerous than any criminal she'd ever prosecuted. More dangerous, at least, to her.

Wearily she raised her head. Thunder rumbled ominously. The lone woman passing by on the sidewalk sent a wary glance skyward and increased her pace. With conscious effort, A.J. pushed aside the emotions that troubled and taunted, and reached for that cool logic that served her so well. The memory of how McKay could shatter it so easily was a troubling thought better saved for another time.

Movements jerky, she got out of the car and approached the hospital. She needed to have herself firmly under control when she saw her mother. When she was alert, Mandy could be incredibly attuned to, and affected by, the emotions of others.

Nodding at the nurse on duty, she walked by without pausing to visit. When she got to the doorway of the room, her mother looked up, and the recognition on her face sent waves of relief crashing through A.J. It had been like this for too long. A constant roller coaster between hope and despair. Even once she'd convinced her mother to leave Rich Jacobs, especially then, she'd never been completely certain what she would find when she went home. A sad, broken woman huddled in a corner of a room, weeping for the man who'd beaten her, nearly killed her. Or one calmer, but gradually slipping farther from reality.

"I painted today," Mandy told her. "Sister Jean wanted me to paint the fruit, but I painted a picture of her instead. Do you want to see?"

A.J. admired the painting, and some of the tension seeped from her limbs. At times like these, she could almost let herself believe they were a normal family. A daughter stopping by after work to visit her mother, while both shared their days. It was a normalcy she'd longed for desperately all her life, one she'd never achieved.

But it was a milestone of sorts that her mother was speaking again, responding to those around her. And as the minutes stretched into an hour, A.J. focused on the change in Mandy's condition. And if more troublesome thoughts of Dare McKay and her inexplicable attraction to him were merely held at bay for the moment, she could at least enjoy the reprieve while it lasted.

It lasted exactly seventy-five minutes. The discreet bell sounded, signaling that visiting hours had ended. A.J. replaced the brush she'd been using on her mother's hair and bent to kiss her goodbye.

When she straightened she saw the man standing in the doorway. Protectiveness rose to war with apprehension. "Leo."

"Called your office and your house. Figured you'd be here." He sauntered into the room, his gaze landing on his mother for a moment before shifting away. "I need to talk to you."

Of course. A surge of old bitterness rose. He normally

surfaced when he needed something. She hadn't heard from him since the last time they'd met here, and from what the nurses told her, he hadn't been back to visit their mother since then, either.

"Rich?" Mandy's words were a thread of sound, a note of wonder in them. A.J. almost felt guilty for being compelled to shatter it.

"No, Mama, it's Leo. Remember? He came to see you before."

"Not Rich." The woman in the chair smiled tremulously, clung to A.J.'s hand. "Of course. It's Leo. Leo's here."

Leo moved forward, bent, dropped a kiss on their mother's cheek. "Ma. How ya doing?" Almost immediately, he looked back at his sister. "I need to talk to you now."

"Leo was such a good tree climber. Remember?"

Startled, A.J. took her eyes off her brother to look back at the older woman. "Remember what, Mama?"

Her mother's gaze was faraway. "You both climbed such tall trees. Your dad would get angry. He didn't like you in the trees, but you climbed them, anyway. He couldn't keep you out of them."

A.J.'s gaze flicked to her brother, saw understanding, and an all too familiar resentment in his eyes. One small house they'd lived in had had a postage stamp yard, containing two huge trees. Only one had had branches low enough for nimble children to scramble up. They'd sought refuge there when their father, in drunken fits of rage, had chased them from the house. It had been terror that had them scrambling up the trees, rather than any sense of childish adventure.

"You fell out once, A.J. Remember? You weren't as good a climber as Leo."

Bitterness twisting her lips, she answered, "Yes. I remember." She recalled the time Leo had shoved her from the tree, as her father had stood at its foot and screamed up at them. Remembered the ground rising up to meet her, the air crashing from her lungs.

But most of all she remembered the whistle of her father's belt as it sang through the air, lashing her again and again until exhaustion or intoxication had slowed his movements, sent him stumbling back in the house. She recalled every moment of pain. Every second of furious resentment that had tasted too much like hatred for an eight-year-old child.

Suddenly driven to move, she patted her mother's shoulder and reached for her purse. "The nurse will be coming soon to put you to bed, Mama. I'll come back tomorrow."

"You'll come back tomorrow," her mother repeated. Her hands twisted tightly together on her lap. "And Leo will come back tomorrow. And Rich will come back tomorrow, won't he." She turned her face up to her daughter's pleadingly. "Tomorrow we'll be a family again. Won't that be nice?"

Nausea snaking through her stomach, A.J. squeezed her mother's hand, tried for a smile. "Good night, Mama." The oxygen in the room seemed to vanish. She almost ran for the hall, where she collapsed against the wall and fought air into her strangled lungs.

Old memories could rise at any time and still throb like an open wound. She swallowed hard. It was so much easier not to feel at all. So much easier to shield oneself from all the pain and misery that vulnerability could bring. She hadn't been vulnerable since she was a child. She'd sworn that she never would be again.

"Can't see that she's getting any better." Leo strolled out, pointed his index finger toward his head, made a circling motion. "Hope you aren't paying these doctors too much. All you're getting here is a fancy nuthouse."

Gritting her teeth, A.J. counted to ten. "She's progress-

ing.'' The doctor had told her that, and she clung to the
assurance with a kind of desperation. She knew too well
that for every month of progress, there could be two of
deterioration. That the barriers could come up, and Mandy
could be back in her own world at any time. It was easier
to focus on the hope offered by the doctor's prediction
rather than to dwell on her mother's past history.

Leo lifted a shoulder. "Whatever. I hear you talked to
Coulson. What'd you tell him?"

It took a moment to search her memory. She'd almost
forgotten the brief conversation she'd had with her
brother's parole officer. He'd called a couple days ago to
inquire about Leo's whereabouts. She'd had little to tell
him.

"What should I have told him? That I had no idea where
my brother was? That he must have acquired a taste for
prison because he sure seems bent on landing back there
again?"

"I missed one lousy meeting." His voice was sullen.
"And he's acting like I went on a crime spree. Making
threats about revoking my parole."

She sighed, considered banging her head against the
wall. "What do you expect, Leo? The meetings with Coulson are a condition of your release. If you screw up, you
go back to prison and finish out your term. Is that what
you want?"

"That'll never happen." His eyes, his voice, were flat.
"I was doing a little traveling for my job and didn't get
back in time."

"Well, here's a bit of advice. Next time you need to
reschedule, call him first. Save yourself some headaches."
She pushed away from the wall and began walking away.

"Wait a minute. I wanna know what you told him when
he called you." Menace was stamped on his face. "You

didn't screw me over, did you? Because if you badmouthed me to him..."

She whirled around, frustration mounting. "I didn't tell him anything, Leo. How could I? I don't know where you live. Where you work. I don't know anything about your life, so how could I even begin to guess where you might be when he couldn't reach you? I just promised to tell you he was looking for you if I saw you."

A little of the suspicion left his expression. "That's all?"

She folded her hands together, afraid reaction from the day's events would cause them to tremble. "Like I said, I don't know anything I could tell him. What traveling did you have to do, anyway? What kind of job do you have?"

His gaze skated away from hers. "I'm a salesman. Gotta meet clients at some odd hours, sometimes."

She blew out a breath. "Fine. Just don't mess this up for yourself." She continued out of the hospital, him trailing after her.

"You know, this is some place." He seemed inclined to chat. "Does it cost extra for her private room?"

"It's included in the package," A.J. said shortly, her steps brisk. An expensive package it was, too, but she was determined to keep the best possible care for her mother.

"She knew me today, huh?"

Slowing, she glanced at him. "Yes, she seemed to. She...it comes and goes, but I think she's becoming more lucid all the time."

He snorted, stuck his hands in his pockets. "Lucid. Hell of a word for someone still waiting for the husband who threw her out to come back to her."

She shouldn't have reacted. She knew it at the time, but he was too intimately entwined in her childhood and knew just what bruises still throbbed. "He didn't throw her out, we left, remember? I finally convinced her to get out before he killed her. Killed all of us."

"Yeah, that was a real cushy life you took us to, wasn't it?" he drawled, face twisting. "A stinking women's shelter with not enough food and people crying all night."

"The only difference between it and home was that we were safe there," she shot back. "And you didn't wait around for a better place to come up, did you?" He'd gone back to live with their father within days, and in the ensuing years she'd seen him only intermittently. Usually when he wanted something.

"I was old enough to take care of myself." At seventeen, she supposed he had been. And she'd been old enough to take care of her mother, to find them a room above a diner and arrange for jobs for both of them. Old enough to understand that her mother's grasp on reality slipped a little more every year, and that the doctors at the free clinic had been able to do little to help her.

They'd reached the double front glass doors, and she saw that the promised storm still hadn't transpired. "Ever see yourself in a place like this, A.J.?

His words stopped her, even as her hands were on the door. She turned her head, regarded him impatiently. "What do you mean? I *am* here."

He shook his head. "No, I mean *in* here. Or a place like it." He watched her with a careless little smile on his face, but his eyes were as cruel as his words. "Ever wonder if craziness is inherited? If you'll find yourself losing your grip, a little at a time, until someone takes pity and locks you up so you can sit and rock like that old lady in here?"

She wanted, quite badly, to hit him. To force him to retract the words, the thoughts, the ugly possibility. It was shocking to feel that level of violence, causing her vision to haze and her limbs to tremble. "Shut up, Leo."

"C'mon." He threw a companionable arm around her shoulders. "You can't say it hasn't occurred to you? It has to have. You've seen how she is. Probably started slipping at about your age, ever think of that?'' He laughed, as if the idea amused him. He leaned closer, lowered his voice. ''Ever ask yourself if crazy can be inherited like blond hair and brown eyes? Ever wonder who would take care of you like you take care of the old lady?''

She shoved away from him savagely, taking him by surprise, so he fell back a couple of steps. ''You are a sick sadistic bastard, you know that?''

He eyed her then, bared his teeth. ''Yeah, well, that's inherited too, right? With our parents, we've got both to pick from. Which would you choose? Sadistic or crazy? Think about that one for a while.'' He turned, pushed open the door and exited.

She didn't follow him. She couldn't. Not while his words, those careless mocking words, still echoed in her head.

Ever wonder if crazy can be inherited, A.J.? Ever wonder if you'll end up in a place like this someday?

Icy fingers trailed down her spine, chilling the skin. Because of course he was right. Late at night, when sleep refused to come and she had only memories for company, she frequently wondered those very things.

Thunder crashed around the city, swords of lightning scoring the sky. Icy splinters of rain drenched the skin, chilled the bone. Frothy whitecaps dashed wildly against the moorings as the wind whipped across the lake. But through it all, it wasn't nature's threat that paralyzed limbs and struck terror to the heart. It was the threat emanating from the man in the limo.

The storm faded to insignificance as the figure on the dock faced judgment.

''I warned you about disappointing me.''

Later it might occur that the voice had been audible despite nature tantruming around them. Danger had a way of honing the senses. "I've been providing you with the information I promised. Didn't I tell you that Jacobs acquired some notes Delgado kept that she's tracing to old homicides?"

"You did. But her continued zeal for this case leads me to believe you've failed to adequately distract her."

A familiar large shadow loomed closer, and the figure shifted uneasily. "I arranged a distraction. But she's not the type to scare easily. She'd die before failing her job."

The voice was smooth, the flat side of a blade. "An excellent suggestion."

A wild gasp of breath was drawn into strangled lungs. "Not a chance. I didn't sign on for murder." The huge man stepped closer, raised his gun silently.

The voice from the car sounded again. "No? Then you'd best find a way to keep your commitment to me, hadn't you?" The distinctive sound of a safety being released punctuated the words. "My patience is running out. The next time you fail me, you won't walk away from our meeting."

The cold gun barrel pressed into flesh, exerting vicious pressure. Pride forgotten, the figure cringed. "It wouldn't be quick." The gunman's voice was low, rough. "It wouldn't be easy. I'd kneecap you first. A person can live a long time with both knees shot out. Before it was over you'd beg me to finish it. And I would."

He pressed the barrel harder, then lifted it away, stepped back. "With pleasure."

"I'll…I'll think of something." Never had a promise been made so rashly, fear motivated by self-preservation. "You can count on me."

"For your sake, I hope so." The meeting was over. The message had been delivered, the figure dismissed.

As the limo rolled through driving sheets of rain, the

large man spoke. "If we're not getting the results you want, maybe it's time to look elsewhere."

"Nonsense, Peter." Long graceful fingers reached out, adjusted the back-seat stereo until strains of a favorite concerto filled the interior of the car. "You're too quick to resort to violence. I believe we provided adequate motivation to convince our associate to follow through."

Unused to explaining himself, the man in the luxurious back seat fell silent. It would be most efficient to get rid of Jacobs for good, but discretion must be exercised. He could ill afford the scrutiny a homicide would generate right now. He'd have to be satisfied with diverting the attorney from the case to shake her concentration, and distract McKay, as well.

The music melted into a solo piece, and he closed his eyes to better appreciate the weeping of the harp. All would go according to plan, he assured himself, despite the fact that he seemed surrounded by incompetents. Delgado, the bungler, had deviated from his instructions by not killing Patterson immediately, and then compounded his error by allowing himself to be caught. At least Paquin could be depended upon to follow orders to the letter.

He was an inordinately patient man, and firmly believed in the satisfaction brought by revenge served cold. He smiled slightly, eyes still closed, his hand rising in an imaginary conduction of the exquisite music. There would come a time, when this was over, when they would all pay. Each who had cost him time, money, resources. The anticipation was sweet. Connally, who'd proved to be a conspicuous thorn in his side, would certainly be taken care of. As would Patterson, who'd caused this unpleasantness, and even the esteemed assistant state attorney if she continued to prove meddlesome.

But it was the thought of McKay's demise that gave the most pleasure. His death would necessitate a bit more finesse. It would include profound suffering. Crafting his end would be almost as entertaining as the act itself.

The music faded, and he drew in a breath, savoring the final strains. Taking a handkerchief from his breast pocket, he dabbed a tear from his eye. The concerto never failed to move him.

It was such a lovely piece.

Chapter 9

Dare awoke in a sweat-soaked tangle of sheets. A restless night filled with dreams of an unattainable woman had left him aroused and frustrated. An ice-cold shower relieved the first condition but not the second. With an uncertain temper and no one to take it out on, he had to content himself with his thoughts. They made for unpleasant companions.

He couldn't imagine what had made him think that last night with Addie would be any different from the times before. That she wouldn't turn tail and run. That she'd let herself want, to need, without that incomprehensible fear taking over. He was, he figured, ten kinds of fool. Why else would he let himself continually get ambushed by this pointless bolt of lust?

If there was a part inside that slyly reminded him that unrequited lust had never packed quite this kind of wallop, he was in the mood to ignore it. The way he would ignore Addison Jacobs until he was positive he could look at the woman without wanting to shake her for hiding from the truth.

Except…except that there wasn't a dishonest bone in her body. She was painfully truthful with everyone, with the exception, perhaps, of herself. He wished he knew what brought that sheen of panic to her eyes, just when he thought that he'd reached her on some level. He wished she trusted him enough to tell him.

He gave a humorless laugh. While he was harboring futile hopes, he might as well wish she'd show up at his door this morning wearing nothing but whipped cream. One possibility was as unlikely as the other.

He strode over to his computer and stood looking over the notes the two of them had taken last night. They'd made some progress, and the lead that intrigued him the most was Frank Benson. Someone had committed the murder that the man had been convicted of. If by chance Benson was telling the truth, it'd be interesting to see if he had any ideas on the identity of the killer.

Moving quickly, he gathered up some of his materials and headed for the office. He'd get answers more rapidly using his resources there. And the *Register* held a distinct advantage over his own home. There the rooms wouldn't hold images of Addie nor be filled by her scent. He was uncomfortably aware that the mental pictures he carried of her wouldn't be as easily evaded.

Two hours later he strode into Reetz's office and slapped a folder down on the man's desk. "You're a brilliant man, Creighton, you know that?"

"Uh-huh." Reetz twirled around in his chair and kept wary eyes on the reporter. McKay in this good a mood generally boded trouble.

"You knew what I needed before I did. A vacation, you said, remember?"

The editor searched his memory. "Yeah. I guess."

"So I decided to take your advice. I'm going on vacation."

Brows shooting upward, Reetz said, "You can't do that now. You've got columns due, assignments to cover…"

Dare tapped the folder he'd dropped on the man's desk. "There's a week's worth, but I might not need that long. I'll let you know." Already he was striding from the office.

"You gonna try Cancun?"

"Nope." Stopping at the door, Dare tossed him a grin. "I've got a flight to Indiana in two hours."

The taxi let A.J. out a block from the Fidaldo Café. When Song had given her a message from Paquin requesting a dinner meeting, her first instinct had been to decline. She wasn't eager to sit down with the man on a good day, and today certainly wouldn't qualify as such. She'd gotten little sleep the night before.

She ducked that memory and focused on the matter at hand. Professional curiosity had eventually gotten the best of her. She couldn't imagine what the other attorney had to say, but she wasn't going to pass up the opportunity to hear it. Not when it offered a possibility of gleaning his trial strategy.

The restaurant was located in an area that developers hoped to turn into a trendy piece of real estate. The neighborhood had been left to deteriorate for years, with boarded-up buildings lining the sidewalk and crack vials piled in the gutters. A few brave souls, believing in the developer's plans, had opened businesses in the area. So, newly renovated buildings stood among the shabby ones, dotting the area like dazzling jewels landscaping a slum.

The street in front of the restaurant was closed for repair, and as she made her way to the restaurant she stepped carefully over the broken concrete on the sidewalk. Although her appetite was uncertain, she wasn't averse to the idea of keeping busy. Especially since the alternative would have her going home and spending the evening alone.

It was amazing how quickly she'd gotten used to Dare's company after work. It had only been a couple of days, after all. But like every other aspect of her life, he'd wound his way into her subconscious, so that too many minutes of the day were spent thinking of him. And remembering the fool she'd made of herself last night.

That wasn't the sort of thought to guarantee a return of her appetite, so she deliberately shifted her attention. A man stumbled from an alley just ahead of her, and she slowed, looked around at the near-deserted streets warily. There was a couple window shopping across the street, so she relaxed a bit when the man came in her direction.

"Is it six o'clock yet?" he asked, when he'd reached her.

Keeping her distance, she checked her watch. "Half past."

"Damn. She stood me up again." He stalked past her muttering something about knowing better, and she felt a wave of understanding. She'd known better to than to let her guard down around Dare McKay, but that hadn't stopped her from relaxing it, had it?

The window shoppers entered one of the buildings and A.J. examined the canopy of her destination up ahead. The Fidaldo was supposed to serve a very decent French meal, and she felt a stir of interest. If the meeting with Paquin was productive, she might find herself hungry, after all.

And then all thought fled as an arm shot out of the alley she was passing and yanked her inside.

Shock warred with disbelief, but it didn't keep her immobile for long. She jabbed her elbow out and wielded her briefcase like a club. But another body joined the first, this one crowding her from behind. And while she wrestled to free herself from the first shadowy figure, the other wrapped an arm around her throat, clamped a foul-smelling rag over her nose. Shapes, colors danced before her eyes before her knees crumpled beneath her and everything went black.

Indiana's maximum security prison was rimmed with massive concrete walls, which were topped with electric fencing. Rifled guards stood watch in towers dotting its perimeter.

The sound of his footsteps rang in the nearly deserted corridor as Dare followed the guard to the visiting area. Frank Benson's lawyer had been understandably eager to have his client meet with an investigative journalist. Of course, he'd probably assumed Dare's interest in the case was due to the upcoming appeal, and Dare didn't try to disabuse him of the idea. He *was* extremely interested in Benson's appeal, especially in the information the other man thought would free him.

He seated himself at a long wooden table in the room the guard showed him to, and waited impatiently for the inmate to be brought in. There were already several other people seated nearby.

A door clanged open and Dare raised his head, watched a guard escort another prisoner into the room. He recognized the man immediately from the grainy photos that had appeared in the newspaper articles. Short and stocky, with dark hair and a swarthy complexion, Frank Benson was dressed in the regulation prison-issued blue jumpsuit.

The guard waved the man to a chair across from Dare's and directed a look that encompassed them both. "Keep your hands where they can be seen at all times. No touching, no passing anything across the table." He shuffled away, and Dare looked at the man he'd come to meet.

"I'm Dare McKay, Mr. Benson."

"The reporter. Right." The man settled as comfortably as possible in the chair and regarded him from narrowed dark eyes. "My lawyer says you might be interested in my story."

"Only if you have specifics to support your claim."

"Oh, I got specifics, all right. I didn't do the murder, I can tell ya that right up front." The man had a smoker's voice, low and raspy. He drummed the table with blunt, short-nailed fingers.

"I read the newspaper reports from the trial, but I'd like to hear your side of the story." Dare took a notebook and pen out of his pocket.

"Well, if you read the papers, you know I was supposed to have iced Andrew Dorsey. Andyman, they called him. He was running a trade in Gary, west side. I had a legitimate business, a dry cleaners there."

"I assume the government thought you were running a similar 'trade' from your dry cleaners," Dare guessed wryly.

The man wagged his finger. "They thought it. They didn't prove it, though. I was found innocent of those bogus charges."

"Go on."

"Well, there's another guy on the east side, Paddy Mulcahy, and he's into everything. He's got the bookies, the sharks, drugs..." Benson spread his hands. "Greedy bastard, too, tries to horn in on everybody else's interests."

Dare dropped his pen, sat back. "I'm still waiting for specifics."

"I'm getting to 'em." Benson looked around, leaned forward, and lowered his voice. "Well somehow this Mulcahy gets the same idea the police got, that I was trading from my legitimate business. But he was wrong, like the cops was wrong." He waited until Dare nodded his understanding. "So Paddy gets himself the idea that he can get rid of Dorsey and me at once by killing one and framing the other. That's how one of my cards gets left in Dorsey's pocket, like maybe he'd had some dealings with me. And then the cops come and talk to me, and I tell 'em I don't know nuthin', which I didn't. But they get a warrant to search my place, and damned if they don't come up with a knife and Dorsey's blood on one of my shirts.'' He pushed away from the table, slouching in his seat, as if disgusted by the retelling. "Like I'd be dumb enough to ice Dorsey and then keep the evidence.''

"That'd be stupid, all right.'' Dare almost smiled. The man's outrage seemed as much for the insult to his intelligence as to the supposedly wrongful conviction. "But you must have something more if you've been granted an appeal.''

"Sure I got more.'' He reached up, scratched a jaw already stubbled with shadow. "It just so happens that I know a hit man was in town at the time. Goes by the name of Paulie the Knife.''

An itch worked its way up Dare's spine and under his skin. "How'd you know he was in town?''

Benson gave him an impatient glance. "'Cause I saw him, okay? Came into my place a couple times. Recognized him right off, 'cause him and me, we did some time at Leavenworth back in the eighties.''

He'd have to check his notes to be sure of the date, but Dare did recall reading that Delgado had served one sentence at the Kansas prison.

"Go on.''

"So he says he was in town, came by to look me up. I never thought nuthin' about it. He knew I was moving back to take over the family business when I got out. So we talked some, mostly about guys we both knew in the joint.''

"Did he have that nickname in Leavenworth?''

"Earned it there. Had a real bad temper, Paulie did, and there was a guy in the dining hall who'd come by his table a couple times a week, and he'd like—'' the man folded his arm, made a jabbing motion with his elbow ''—nudge him, ya know? Make him spill something. So Paulie, he said how he ain't gonna take that.''

A minor offense, Dare considered, for which to contemplate violence. ''What'd he do?''

''One day he causes a diversion, palms another guy's spoon. And he takes it back to his cell and works on it every night after lights are out, till he's got a pretty decent shiv. Then he waits till he catches the guy in the shower. The next thing ya know, the guy's in a body bag, and he sure as hell ain't gonna be nudging Paulie at lunch no more.''

''And you saw him do the killing.''

''Sure I saw it. Me and a couple other guys. But we all left before the guards came round.''

''Did you ever tell anyone this story?'' At the man's blank expression, Dare continued, ''I assume there was an investigation.''

Benson lifted a heavy shoulder. ''Yeah, sure, but none of us said nuthin'. The guy shouldn't have been nudging no one like that, anyway. No one's gonna take that.''

Drawing in a breath, Dare wrote furiously for a few minutes using a shorthand that made sense only to him. When he was finished, he set the pen down, studied the man. ''So you knew Paulie was in Gary. How do you get from that to him killing Dorsey?''

''It took me some time,'' the man admitted. ''But I got an associate in here, just showed up couple of months ago. Used to do some work for me, and he disappeared before my arrest, with some of my…'' The man stopped, frowned and seemed to struggle for the right wording.

''With some of your dry cleaning?'' Dare asked dryly.

''Yeah.'' Benson smiled, showing nicotine-stained teeth. ''Yeah, he used to deliver some of my dry cleaning and then he disappeared with a delivery. So when I see him in here, I says to him, you owe me something. And he says he don't got no money.''

"So you threatened him."

"I made him some promises," the man corrected. "So then he says he's got something better to give me, he can give me some information. I says I gotta hear it first and then we'd see if it's worth saving his—'' He stopped himself, reworded. "We'd see what it's worth. So he tells me how Paulie gave him five grand to take him one of my shirts and then later to hide a package in my place at the dry cleaners. On account of he was in and out of there all the time.''

Dare regarded the man for a moment. "And he can identify Paulie?"

"Sure he can."

"And do you know what Paulie's real name is?"

Benson looked at him as if he was crazy. "Of course, I was in the joint with him, wasn't I? It's Delgado. Paul Delgado.''

It was dark. So dark. A.J. attempted to drag her eyelids open, but they seemed weighted. Consciousness was returning in an ebb and flow. Sickness swirled and rose in her stomach; her head pounded. She could hear voices—their pitch but not the words. Were the words important? She wished she could think.

She tried to wet her lips, which felt parched and dry, and found she couldn't. Panic rose swiftly, battling with the fuzziness in her mind. Jerking her head, she tried again. Again she failed.

"She's waking up." The voices abruptly stopped, and footsteps approached her. When words were spoken again they came from right in front of her. "Hey. You awake?" An ungentle hand slapped her cheek a couple of times. "Nighty-night's over.''

There was a high-pitched giggle, quickly muffled. "Maybe she thinks it's still night 'cuz of the blindfold," the giggler suggested.

Comprehension returned sluggishly. Her eyes were covered. And she must have tape over her mouth. Flexing her limbs, she discovered she was seated. Her arms were tied in back of the chair, her legs bound together.

"I'm gonna take this tape off, but if you try to scream, it goes back on, right after I clip you on the jaw. Got it?"

She would have agreed to almost anything at that point. She started to nod vigorously, stopped when the hammering in her head increased.

There were fingers on her face, then the tape was ripped off in one painful motion. A.J. filled her lungs, then something wet splashed her face. "Here, drink this." A metallic-tasting cup was pressed against her lips, and she sipped. Water.

"What the hell am I doin' this for. Get over here." It took her a moment to realize he was talking to the other man. "It ain't my job to play nursemaid."

The cup was removed before her thirst was quenched, which was probably best. Just the taste she'd had was already stirring uneasily in her stomach.

"Okay, whadda we do now?"

The one who seemed to be the boss sounded impatient. "How many times do you gotta be told this? We wait. We wait until we hear something."

Although her faculties had returned, she couldn't make sense of their words. She remembered...Fidaldo's. She was going to meet Paquin at the restaurant he'd suggested. A man had spoken to her, then passed by. Was he the one who had grabbed her? But no, there had been someone in the alley. The second man? And what did they want with her? Her mind whirled with questions. But there was only one answer she was certain of.

She'd never been in so much danger.

* * *

Dare slept in the next morning until nine, a luxury for him. He'd taken a red-eye flight out of Gary and arrived home after midnight. He'd still been keyed up and had toyed with the idea of calling Connally then and telling him what he'd discovered. He'd figured the detective wouldn't thank him for it. But this morning when he tried to contact the man, neither he nor Madison were at their desks. Dare left a message for the detectives to call him and dropped the phone in disgust.

It was hell having some hot news and having no one to share it with, no one with whom to hash over the possibilities. He thought of Addie and then immediately discarded the idea. The memory of her reaction the other night was still too raw, too painful. And he was in no hurry to reopen that particular wound. It would be easier from now on to work directly through Connally and let him feed her the information she needed. A bit laborious, perhaps, but a man's ego was a fragile thing. It could only take so much battering.

He wanted, desperately, to believe that ego was all that was involved.

He showered, shaved and fixed breakfast. Over eggs and waffles he reflected that he could really get used to this vacationing thing. As he was clearing the dishes to the counter, the phone rang and he answered it cheerfully. "You've got McKay."

"Mr. McKay, I hope you don't mind me calling you at home."

His brows drew together as he tried to place the voice. Automatically he walked over to check the caller ID box. Chicago Courthouse. His tone was decidedly more cautious when he said, "May I help you?"

"It's Song Wynn. Addison Jacobs's assistant." The inflection at the end of her statement made it seem a question.

Just the mention of Addie's name had his muscles bunching. "Sure, Ms. Wynn. What's up?"

"I'm wondering…well, this may seem strange, but… have you seen Ms. Jacobs?"

Something in her voice tipped him off—a thin veneer of calm, over ragged nerves. "Not since the night before last. Why?"

"I'm sure it's nothing to be worried about. She just hasn't come in yet this morning, and there's no answer at her home. It isn't like her to be late, especially when she had a meeting scheduled this morning with Mr. Beardmore." The woman lowered her voice. "He's already asked for her twice. I know there has to be a good reason for her tardiness, but it's unlike her not to phone in. I tried the hospital where her mother is, but the nurses haven't seen her since the night before last, either. And I don't know anyone else to call."

Wait a minute. His mind stalled a sentence back. Her mother was in the hospital? Had he even known she had a mother around here? No. And that was probably only one in a multitude of things that Addie hadn't shared with him.

Then the rest of the woman's words registered. And when they did, Dare felt the first inkling of unease. "Wouldn't she call if she had gotten delayed?"

"I think so, yes. She's always very dependable about things like that." Worry had crept into the woman's voice. "Nothing like this has ever happened before."

Something in his gut clenched. He pulled out the chair from the kitchen desk and sat. "You'd better tell me everything."

A.J. had lost track of time. There was no way to tell if it was day or night, for the blindfold hadn't been removed, not even when she was released from the chair to use the bathroom. The tape was taken away from her mouth only to give her water, and once to feed her a greasy hamburger.

The first man, the one who seemed to be in charge, had gone out several times, once bringing back food. From the rustling noises of the wrappers, she'd thought it must have come from a fast-food place. Right now he was gone again, and she was wishing that he'd return. He seemed to be a calming influence on his companion, who was getting bolder all the time.

Her captor's fingers threaded through her hair, and her skin crawled with revulsion.

"Kinda boring, ain't it? You and me could find a way to pass the time. No one would ever have to know." She could feel his breath bounce off her face, knew he'd squatted down in front of her. Turning away, she swallowed hard against the surge of nausea. "Randy wouldn't never find out. You sure can't tell him, can you?" He seemed vastly amused by his witticism, giggling madly.

Logic warred with repugnance. *Randy.* That must be the name of the first man. She hoped she'd have a chance to use that knowledge. Then that thought fled when a hand touched her throat, slid down the front of her blouse.

A.J. exploded with a violence that shocked them both. Throwing her weight to the side, the chair tottered, fell over. The resulting crash mingled with the man's curses and the shouts of another.

"What the hell is going on?"

The man called Randy had returned. She shuddered with a combination of reaction and relief. It was ridiculous to feel safer with the man who appeared to be the mastermind of her kidnapping. Ridiculous while she still had no clue to his motives.

There was a distinctive sound, fist meeting flesh. "I said, what's going on? I told you to watch her."

"I was! I did." The second man's voice was farther away now, sullen. "She just keeps doin' that, knocking the chair over like that. Thinks she's gonna make a racket someone will hear, probably."

There were footsteps approaching, then a fist grabbed her hair. She could feel the kiss of cold steel against her face. "You're wasting your time, lady." The voice was as smooth and lethal as the blade. "There's no one around to hear. No one who knows where you are. There's just you. And there's us." The blade was removed, and the tip pressed beneath her chin. "But if you want to make trouble, there'll just be us. Got it?"

He exerted enough pressure to break skin, and she drew in air sharply through her nose. Then after an interminable moment, the blade was removed. "Leave her like that. She got herself into that position, let her stay that way."

She lay there, her face pressed against cool cement, the grit on the floor ground into her face. Concentrating fiercely, she tried to figure a way out of her predicament. She was used to taking care of herself. But for the life of her, she couldn't think of a single way out of this mess. If she could convince them to take the tape off her mouth, she could at least try to reason with them. Bribe them. Threaten them. Whatever worked. But lying on the floor, trussed up like a Christmas package, she had little hope of coming up with a workable plan.

It was getting increasingly difficult to stem the tide of desolation. She couldn't come up with one reasonable plan for getting herself out of this.

And she couldn't think of a single person who would come looking for her.

Dare tried Addie's house first, but got no answer to his knock. After considering his options, he entered the same way Leo had gained entry the last time Dare had been there.

He hated to consider what she would have to say about another broken pane.

If there had been a measure of uneasiness at violating her privacy, it dissipated upon searching her home. She hadn't been there last night. Her bed didn't appear to have been slept in, and the tub held no hint of moisture.

The discoveries had the first hint of panic sprinting up his spine. If it were anyone else, he would assume she'd spent the night with a friend. A lover. Though the thought burned, he forced himself to consider it as he drove back downtown. And then rejected it with a vehemence that was only partly personal. He'd be willing to bet that Addie wasn't involved with anyone else. She'd made it painfully clear how she felt about relationships.

Perhaps the most bizarre part of this whole story, Dare reflected, was the phone call Song had related to him. The woman had explained that she'd received a phone call from Joel Paquin and relayed the message to Addie that the other attorney wanted a meeting. But when Dare had called Paquin's office, the man denied having made any such call.

Heading in the direction of the restaurant, he reached for his cell phone. He was getting a real bad feeling about this whole thing. It was time to find Connally.

''You comin' back pretty soon?''

The words sent glaciers bumping through A.J.'s veins. She didn't want to be left alone with the second man again. Even Randy's cruelty was preferable.

''I'll be back when I'm back.''

''Yeah, well bring me some comics or something. This is boring work, ya know.''

She didn't hear the other man's answer. But her ears did pick up the sound of a door closing. The small sound seemed prophetic.

She waited, her breathing choppy. After several moments

footsteps shuffled toward her. Then she experienced a sense of disorientation, as her captor righted her chair.

"You got dirt on your face." A rough thumb smudged it away. "You oughta be grateful. Randy woulda left you like that. You're grateful, right?"

It seemed politic to nod.

"You sure musta pissed someone off," her captor continued conversationally. His hand rested on her shoulder, and she tried to shrug it away. His fingers tightened, squeezing. "You oughta be nicer, ya know? Way I see it, I might be the only one makes sure you get out of here alive."

She fairly shook with the effort it took to remain motionless. A moment later she was certain the effort had paid off. His grip loosened, fell away."

"That's better. Whaddya say you and me play a game?"

She could hear him moving, wished desperately to see. Not knowing what was going on around her made her helplessness that much more terrifying. She felt the tip of a knife pricking her collarbone. Anger and fear made a huge hard ball in her throat, impossible to swallow around.

"You like games?"

She shook her head violently and the knife shifted, popped the top button off her blouse. The sound of it hitting the floor, rolling, seemed abnormally loud in the stillness.

"Wrong answer, doll face. Let's try again. You wanna play with me, right?"

She remained still. Her lack of response, however, didn't seem to please him any more than her last one had. The tip of the knife traced down an inch, removed another button.

"This is gettin' fun." The glee in her captor's voice couldn't quite disguise the growing thickness in his tone. His breathing quickened, and she swallowed hard against a surge of sickness that threatened to swamp her. "You and me are gonna have a lotta fun, doll face.'' Another button was popped away from her blouse, the tiny sound of it hitting the floor punctuating his words. "We've gots lots of time before Randy gets back."

By the time Connally and Madison had arrived, Dare had already searched four nearby buildings and found nothing. After conferring for a few moments, the men split the surrounding area and fanned out.

"Remember, if you find something, call me on the cell phone.''

Anxious to restart the search, Dare merely nodded, started away.

"I mean it, McKay." Gabe's voice followed him. "Don't do anything stupid."

That gem of advice, Dare reflected grimly, as he peered into windows of nearby abandoned buildings, came a bit too late. He could have used it before he slept with Addie two years ago. Before this case had drawn them together again. Or even before he damn near made love to her a couple of nights ago. *Stupid* didn't even begin to describe a man who got so wrapped up in a woman that the thought of her in danger tied his insides in knots. Especially when that woman had made her disinterest so clear.

Not content just to look into some of the buildings, he went around the back to investigate. The detectives would probably prefer not to know how he was getting into them. It helped that most had fallen into such disrepair that many windows were shattered. All it took was a little more help and they broke completely out, allowing him entry.

Although there were plenty of signs that some of the buildings had been occupied recently, it appeared most likely that the occupants had been vagrants or teenagers looking for a place to score.

Moving on to another building, however, he heard a

sound and stopped to listen. It sounded like someone was in the old warehouse before him. Given the sound of the laugh he heard, Dare figured it was a teen. He rubbed at one grimy pane, attempting to see inside. When he was unable to make anything out, he moved around the corner. He pulled some old barrels over, stacked them precariously and climb atop them to peer into the window. The scene he witnessed stopped his heart.

A man wielding a knife stood before a figure tied to a chair. Wildly, Dare craned his head, attempting to see around the man's shoulders. Recognition was difficult, as the captive's face was nearly covered by a blindfold and tape. But he'd seen that gray suit before.

Later he would be amazed at how quickly reason could be swamped by emotion. There was nothing civilized about the red haze that swam across his vision, the violent primal emotions that engulfed him. He was overwhelmed with a raw fierce rage, the kind that burned through the veins and fired the blood. The kind that spelled certain death for the man inside.

Nimbly, he jumped down from his perch and rounded the corner to the street side of the building, rang Connally. "Yeah, I've found her." He read off the building's address.

"Okay, wait for us to arrive. Do you hear me, McKay?" The detective's voice was adamant. "Don't even think about going in there before we—"

The command was cut off when Dare broke the connection, replaced the phone in his pocket. Waiting wasn't an option. Addie was inside, alone, defenseless. She wasn't going to be alone much longer.

The air inside the dark building was cool, but it was revulsion rather than the temperature that was responsible for the iciness of A.J.'s skin. She could feel her blouse gaping open, felt the flat edge of the knife smooth across her chest. "I'm gonna untie you from the chair now. You gonna behave?" She could feel the ropes loosen, although her wrists were still tied securely together. She wasted no time. Launching herself forward, she tried to use her head to ram into where she thought the man's chest would be.

She wound up face first on the concrete, struggling for a breath. Dimly, she was aware of the man laughing, before she was roughly grabbed and turned over.

"Eager, aren't you? Well, good. That's the way I like 'em."

Her arms came up, and her bound wrists caught him in the jaw.

"Bitch!" Stars exploded behind her eyes, and her face rocked back with the force of his blow. "You're gonna be—"

She was aware of his stillness first. It took another moment to realize the cause. Then the sound came again, a pounding from somewhere outside. Her captor's weight was off her, and she could hear him moving away. She lost no time raising her secured hands to her face, trying to pull off the tape. But her fingers were numb, clumsy from lack of circulation, and she cursed futilely as she fumbled with the task. The noise had stopped as quickly as it had begun. Her moment of opportunity was rapidly fading.

She managed to loosen a portion of the tape, filled her lungs and tried to yell. "Help." The word was more a croak than a shout, and she swallowed, tried again. "Help me."

Swift footsteps approached, and the tape was refastened. "You're costing me some energy, doll face. You better be worth it."

Although she fought wildly, she was restrained again. "Now where were we?"

A crash sounded, and her captor rose. She heard curses, the sounds of a struggle. Wildly she attempted to loosen her blindfold. Not knowing what was going on around her was as frightening as the situation itself. Then there was a final thwack and a groan, the sound of a body crumpling.

Hearing footsteps, she rolled to her knees and raised her bound hands in an unmistakably combative stance.

She heard a low chuckle, one filled with relief, and something else not easily identified. "A fighter to the bitter end, aren't you? It's all right, baby," the voice soothed, "it's over."

Disbelieving, she stilled as gentle hands went to her blindfold, pulled it way. It took several moments for her eyes to adjust, but she didn't need to depend on vision to identify that touch, that voice.

And when Dare McKay wrapped his arms around her, A.J. sagged against him and wished with all her might that she could hug him back.

Chapter 10

Dare removed the tape and bonds. Without her conscious permission, her arms twined around his neck, clung tight. "Those childhood brawls of yours came in kind of handy. Not everyone would have the experience to come in and kick ass." Her words were muffled against his chest.

His voice sounded strangled. "Well my motto has always been to walk softly and carry a helluva big board."

A laugh shuddered out of her, and his arms tightened. "Did he hurt you?"

She shook her head, not wanting to consider what her captor had had in mind. "I'm all right. A few scratches."

He crooked a finger beneath her chin, raised it so her gaze met hers. "Did he *hurt* you?"

Belatedly, his meaning registered, but it was a moment before she could answer. She was too entranced by the thread of lethal danger underlying the words. "No." Tension seeped from his muscles, an infinitesimal bit at a time. "You have impeccable timing."

Then he gathered her back to his chest, held her close. "Hardly." His mouth brushed her hair as he spoke. "You must have been here for close to twenty-four hours already." Just the thought had the power to send alarm sprinting anew. He could hear the detectives approaching through the back door. He'd rung Connally to update him, cut the detective's rebukes short.

He didn't want to think about what could have happened during Addie's captivity. Didn't want to consider what he would have done to the man who was still out cold on the floor if he'd found her injured. The savage rage had receded, but he was left with a confusing jumble of feelings. He didn't have the first clue how to identify any of them.

It was a guilty pleasure to stay like this, holding Addie close. And far, far too tempting. But he forced himself to gently untangle himself from her arms. With one swift movement he pulled his jacket off and handed it to her. Then he stepped between her and the detectives to offer her a modicum of privacy while she switched the garment for her ruined blouse.

"Is she all right?" Connally's voice was terse, and beneath the words was a hidden meaning Dare understood all too well.

"She's fine."

Madison had gone to examine the figure on the floor who was just beginning to stir. "Bet he's gonna have a helluva headache," he observed, deftly slipping cuffs on the man's wrists.

"He's lucky to be waking up at all." Dare's flat tone had both detectives eyeing him carefully.

"Who said there's never a cop around when you need one?" A.J. was determined to keep the shakiness from her knees, to keep a smile pasted to her face. The weakness in her limbs must have spread to her mind. That could be the only explanation for the way she'd clung to Dare a moment ago, unwilling to let go. That same weakness had her longing to be back in his arms again.

"Do you have any idea who this man is, Ms. Jacobs?"

She turned at Madison's voice to look at her former captor. "I'd never seen him before. There's another one who seemed to be the mastermind of this whole mess. This one," she nodded toward the man Cal was pulling to his feet, "called him Randy."

"I think the lady's had enough for one day, don't you, detectives?"

Although Gabe opened his mouth to answer, one look at Dare's face seemed to change his mind. "Of course. A.J. can come by tomorrow, and we'll take her statement then."

"Don't be ridiculous." She rubbed her hands together to rid them of some of the grime, hoping the friction would lend some warmth to her chilled blood. Because she could feel the disapproval radiating from Dare in waves, she meticulously avoided looking at him. "There's no reason we can't get this taken care of right now."

Dare caught Gabe's sideways glance, as if the man expected him to object. He turned away, silent. Experience had taught him the futility of trying to look out for Addie. It was a lesson he'd been clubbed with often enough. She didn't need him to protect her. She didn't need anyone.

Dare stood with his shoulder propped against a file cabinet, just a little apart from the detectives and Addie. She was a model of courage under stress. Under different circumstances he might have admired her fortitude. Right now he could only curse it. It was probably just his imagination that her voice wavered from time to time before she could control it again. That her limbs occasionally quaked in a shudder that had nothing to do with the air-conditioning and everything to do with reaction.

"We'll check with Paquin again, of course." Gabe

tapped his pen against his palm. "But Dare says when he called him he denied ever leaving you that message."

A.J. looked grim. "So it was just a ruse someone used to lure me down there. And I walked right into it."

"You're lucky your assistant called McKay this morning looking for you," Madison put in.

She glanced at Dare and then looked away just as quickly. Something about the man reminded her of a human package of dynamite waiting to detonate. Beneath his thin T-shirt every muscle seemed chiseled with tension.

With effort she gathered thoughts that were strangely fragmented. "My guess is that the other one, Randy, was calling the shots. But he was working for someone else. He made the comment that I must have really angered the wrong person."

"And chances are that Randy has already heard what went down and skipped for healthier climates," observed Gabe. "The scumbag we locked up is named Tommy Barnes. He and Randy are cousins. And you're right. Randy's usually the one that arranges their jobs. Tommy's not long on smarts." He cocked his head, studied her. "Any ideas on who might have given the orders?"

Even as she shook her head, Dare spoke. "There doesn't seem to be much question of that, does there? It's got to be connected to the case. Someone wants her out of the way. First she's nearly run over and now this." His voice was flat, his eyes hard. "Most likely it's the same guy with reason to pay for Delgado's defense."

"Mannen," Gabe said grimly, exchanging a look with his partner.

Dare pushed away from the file cabinet. "I think you have enough information for now, don't you, guys?"

Connally glanced at Dare's expression, cleared his throat. "Yeah, sure. A.J. can call us if she thinks of anything else."

"I'll take you home, then." Dare addressed the words to Addie, his tone carefully neutral.

She looked up, hesitated. "I need to call work."

He reached for her elbow and began leading her away. "I already called the courthouse."

It was a measure of her surprise that she didn't protest at being shepherded through the station house and bundled into his car. "When did you do that?"

He closed the passenger door on her question, rounded the vehicle to the other side and got in. "On the way to the station house." Addie had chosen to ride there with the detectives, and he'd followed. It had given him time to tuck away the frustration that still simmered. Time to stop wanting to put a fist through the walls she'd already managed to rebuild.

They were there, shaky but unmistakable. Most women would have collapsed by now. Most men, too, come to that. But Addie couldn't be compared to other people, because of one inescapable fact. She stood alone. And even in her darkest hour, when she'd clung to him for comfort, she hadn't really needed *him*. At least not for long.

So he matched his impassive expression to her own and refused to be moved, even when she became aware of their destination.

"No, you don't, McKay. I'm not going to a hospital."

"You're right," he agreed imperturbably. "You're going to a clinic."

"Same difference." Rather than giving in to the ridiculous fear bubbling to the surface, she reached for anger. "All I need now is food and rest. I don't need a doctor to tell me that."

He pulled to a stop and hardened himself against the flash of sheer panic on her face. It softened something inside him, but he remained implacable. Experience had taught him what to expect when he softened toward Addie.

"Be really good in there. I hear they give lollipops to their most well-behaved patients."

He was out of the car before he could hear her response, but he was imaginative enough to guess its content.

Despite her annoyed protests, Dare pushed in to her house behind her and shut the door. Then he checked all the rooms until he was certain they were empty.

"Well, thank you, Mr. Security."

"You won't be thanking me when you see your kitchen door."

Her brows furrowed. "What?"

There would be time enough later to discuss that subject. "Never mind." He'd had a ridiculous sense of guilt riding him ever since she'd rejoined him at the clinic, pale and caustic. But he'd needed to reassure himself that she'd suffered no real physical harm. "What do you want to do first? Shower or eat?"

Her smile looked forced. "Actually, twelve full hours of sleep sounds good."

He nodded. "First you shower. Then I'll fix you some food. Then sleep." When she would have protested, he cut her off. "While you're in the shower I'll get your briefcase and purse out of my trunk."

He'd succeeded in distracting her. "You have them? That's a relief. Until now, I didn't even think about them."

"Yeah, well, you had a few other things on your mind. I found them in the warehouse. They didn't look as though they'd been disturbed." He strode past her to the bathroom, pulled back the curtain and started the water. When he had it adjusted to the right temperature, he switched on the shower. He went back out into the living room, to find her standing right where he'd left her.

"Go in and take your shower," he directed. It helped to keep his mind on what needed to be done and off the fact that she appeared perfectly capable of handling it all herself. "I'll go out and get your stuff, then get you something to eat. Soup, I think," he said, eyeing her critically. He doubted her appetite was very strong, but she needed fuel.

She took a breath, exhaled slowly. "I appreciate all you've done. Believe me." Her emphasis on the last two words reminded them both just how grateful she'd been earlier. "But there's no reason for you to stay. I'm just going to stagger in to bed in a few more minutes."

He turned away, unwilling to hear the rest of her speech. Her body fairly vibrated with tension. He already knew that she was back at her peak. The weakness that would normally affect anyone after an ordeal like hers had been miraculously short-lived. And it was incredibly telling that she'd looked even more shaken by her trip to the clinic than she had when he'd found her in the warehouse.

After Dare had retrieved Addie's briefcase and purse, he deposited them in her living room on the table that served as her desk. He cocked his head, vaguely pleased to hear the shower still running. Hot water would go a long way in releasing some of the stress she was refusing to admit to.

He rummaged around in her kitchen, found some soup and fixings for salad. While the soup was simmering on the stove, he prepared the rest of the meal. He had the food on the table, accompanied by a glass of milk, before he began to wonder what was keeping her.

Walking back into the living room, he could still hear the shower. Curiosity, and a lingering feeling of protectiveness, had him crossing to the bathroom door and knocking on it. "Dinner's ready. Are you about done in there?" He listened, but there was no answer. There was no sound at all, save for the pounding water.

Easing the door open, his gaze first landed on her ruined clothes lying in a heap on the floor. His jacket was folded neatly on top of the pile. His gaze flickered to the shower. "Addie?"

It was her silence that tipped him off. He'd expected to hear her berate him for invading her privacy. Crossing to the tub in two quick steps, he drew back the curtain. And saw her, finally, sitting on the floor of the tub, head down, arms wrapped tightly around her knees. Her body rocked back and forth, silent sobs shaking her.

Emotion gripped his throat, seized his heart. "Ah, baby." Without a second thought he stepped in, sank down behind her. His arms folded around her and drew her back against his chest. And as the water hammered over them, surrounding them in a world of their own, there was more than comfort offered. More than need returned.

A.J. woke reluctantly, consciousness gradually swimming up to the surface. She opened her eyes, feeling remarkably rested. There had been no dreams to mar her sleep, no remembered terror to haunt. It was more, far more, than she'd hoped for.

Sitting up in bed, she pushed her tousled hair back from her face and squinted at the alarm clock next to the bed. Nine o'clock. She'd slept nearly twelve hours. Yawning, she slipped from bed and was in the bathroom before memory slammed into her.

Dare. He'd stayed. Long after she'd ordered him away. Long after the thin strand of strength she'd clung to had snapped. Thoughts of her vulnerability last night didn't make her squirm, but knowing that he'd witnessed it did. Most men, she imagined, could be excused for making a quick exit in the face of unchecked emotion. He'd done more, far more, than she'd had any right to expect.

A second shock awaited her when she went back to her bedroom and found him there, sitting on the edge of the bed, bare-chested, and sipping a cup of coffee. Upon her entrance he rose, crossed to her, and handed her the cup. Reflexively, her fingers closed around it, her gaze never straying from his.

"I didn't know you were here." She brought the cup to her lips, sipped.

"I've been up for hours. You slept in. That's good. You needed it."

Comprehension punched through her like a quick left jab. Her eyes went to the pillow beside hers. The was no impression left on the pillow, but she knew the truth, anyway. "You stayed here last night?" She voiced the question, but it was something other than words that gave her her answer. The effortless slumber had been his doing. It had been the strength of his arms that had kept the dreams away, the warmth of his body that had warded off the lingering ghosts. She stared at him, with all the confusion she was feeling apparent on her face. "Why?"

Her words would have infuriated him, if he hadn't been so moved by her expression of bafflement. "Why do you look so surprised?" He took the cup from her nerveless fingers and drank, deliberately placing his lips where hers had been. "I suppose I should have asked if there was someone else to be called. Someone else who could have stayed with you." Something in her silence made him edgy. "Was there?"

"No."

Her answer was without emotion, without self-pity. She'd never sought comfort, wouldn't have known where to turn for it. She'd always been the source of strength for her mother, first as a child then as an adult. The fact had never been questioned, never resented. She didn't know how to accept something like this, freely given, without strings. And she didn't know how to counter the effect his act had on her system, tying her heartstrings in nice neat bows.

She set the cup carefully on her bedside table, then closed the distance between them, still marveling. Reaching up, she touched her lips to his. She could feel the heat of him, that wonderful warmth that had chased away the ice in her limbs last night and calmed her raging nerves.

Her mouth moved on his, gently, sweetly. She could taste the coffee on his lips, knew he could taste it on hers. Moving nearer, she increased the pressure, the kiss full of wonder.

Dare was drowning in sensation, battling a need that rose swiftly, was banked ruthlessly. He didn't want thanks and he damned well didn't want pity. A ragged sense of honor kept him motionless, when instinct dictated he haul her into his arms. It was the memory of the bewilderment on her face that kept him from giving in to those urges; that had shouted, clearer than words, her unfamiliarity with a simple gesture of caring. He wondered if there had ever been one person in her life who'd offered it. He suspected he knew the answer.

Her mouth moved to his jaw, and he clenched it, hard, when her lips dragged over the stubble he hadn't bothered to shave that morning. His lungs dragged in the scent of her in a guilty, greedy swallow, and his muscles quivered with the force of his control.

She didn't need this. The thought hammered in his head, keeping rhythm with the pulse in his veins. He didn't know what drove her, but he knew she was vulnerable in a way she'd never allowed herself to be before. Knew that even her well-worn defenses must have limits.

And he was equally certain that given time they'd be firmly back in place. She was still reeling from her recent experience. He tried to remember that, as she caught his bottom lip between her teeth, scored it gently. Sweat beaded on his forehead as she traced his mouth with the tip of her tongue. She needed time and distance to regroup.

Perhaps it would have been easier to withstand if she'd touched him with fire in her blood and no heart at all. But there'd been emotion in her answer, in just that single word. And it was apparent in her kiss. Each touch crumbled his control a bit further.

Her fingers skimmed over his chest. His muscles jumped beneath her touch, quivering like a ready stallion. His hands went to her hips, intending to put her away from him. In a moment. This must be a special kind of hell reserved just for him, for offenses as yet uncommitted. He could almost smell the sulfur, feel the flames of perdition lapping at him.

Because when her mouth returned to his, his arms snaked around her waist, and he kissed her back with a bruising passion that should have alarmed her. Should have had her pulling away. Instead it served to enflame them both.

His fingers tangled in her hair, and he held her head still, devoured her mouth. And he imagined, just for a moment, what it would be like to make love to her without fearing the inevitable moment when her walls would go back up. Locking him out and the memories away.

But there were no barriers between them now. The certainty shimmered between them, beckoned promisingly. And the knowledge was sweet, perhaps made more because he knew how rare the moment was.

Her heart was racing, keeping pace with his. His tongue stabbed at her lips, and they parted in a seductive welcome. He brought her closer, one hand sweeping under her shirt, smoothing over her silky back. She arched against him, and the last vestige of his control gave way under the weight of his need for her.

The freedom to touch her was a sinful pleasure, and best savored slowly. He reached for the hem of her nightgown, drew it over her head. Flesh pressed against flesh, and the sensation of her breasts flattened against his chest whipped his blood to a torrent. He skimmed his lips over the curve of her shoulder, his muscles tense, waiting for the rage of desire to settle again.

The bed was right behind him. He could ease her back just a matter of inches and they'd fall together, every inch of their bodies touching. They could give their passion free rein, forget all thoughts, all doubts. It would be easy and gloriously satisfying. He knew she'd welcome it, return it. Instead he gave her more.

He bent to scoop her up in his arms and laid her on the bed. When he followed her down, it was with passion held in check, and something far more dangerous rising to the surface. He loomed half over her, combed her hair back from her face with his fingers. An aching path of tenderness etched through him. It was an unfamiliar emotion, but not an unwelcome one. Her injuries had bloomed over the hours, ugly reminders of what she'd endured. His lips brushed over the bruise on her jaw and then found another beneath her eye.

A.J. stilled under his lips, recognizing the change in his rhythm, uncertain of her response. She felt his mouth move down her body, tactilely cataloguing each of her injuries, soothing each. His gentleness undid her. Again he was offering her something she didn't know how to accept, or return. She only knew that the foreign experience tangled her emotions. Wreaked havoc on her system. The minutes stretched, dusted with gold.

Dare worked his way back up to her mouth, saw her eyes, glazed but wary. And comprehension slammed into him, so sudden and violent he was nearly rocked with it. Defenses worked both ways. Walls were built as much to protect what was inside as to keep others out. He wondered if she knew which reason kept hers so solid.

Their lips met, tongues tangled. The desire was still present, but contained for the moment. He gave her long, stirring kisses; languid, lazy caresses. And when he felt her body melt against his, heard her breath hitch slightly, he knew this was what he wanted. What he'd always wanted. To feel her go pliant with pleasure. To feel her hands on his flesh. To know that with every gasp and moan he drew from her, she thought of him. Nothing but him.

His hands drifted over her breasts, fingers circling, never settling. Her breath hissed in and she reached for him, her fingers clutching his shoulders, skating over his chest. A thousand points of flame burst beneath his skin. Control wavered, took conscious effort to steady.

To pleasure her, and himself, he dipped his head, drew her nipple into his mouth, savagely satisfied to hear his name tumble from her lips. Cupping her other breast in his hand, he fondled it, until the dual assault had her body twisting against him.

A haze seemed to have formed over all thought, all reason. There was only Addie, her flavor tracing through his system, her scent embedded in his senses. Sunlight slanted through the window, a single ray painting their bodies. Her fingers were fumbling with his jeans, and each slight brush of her knuckles against the front of his fly was the most exquisite form of torture.

Need streaked through him, made a mockery of his intentions. Easing away an inch, he helped her pull the heavy jeans down his legs, and kicked them away. Then he rid them both of the only barrier left between them, and pulled her to face him, until they lay together side to side so that every inch of their bodies touched. Finding the pulse at the base of her throat, he laved it with his tongue. She drew up a leg, not quite innocently, let it glide over his hip.

His breath sawed out of his lungs. There was a reason for taking it slow. But at the moment it was difficult to recall. His hand caressed the satin of her thigh, felt the whisper of muscle beneath the silky skin. It was always an erotic delight to rediscover Addie's softness. His fingers trailed closer to her core of heat, and he thrilled at her quiver.

She forgot to breathe. He gave her no choice but to feel. A.J. gloried in the choice, even realizing it came with risk. But right now there was only his body close to hers, smooth flesh stretched over padded muscle. Her fingers traced over him, where sinew and bone joined to leave intriguing hollows. Each begged to be explored with soft lips and swift hands.

Longing battled with doubt. He traced the crease where her leg met her hip and she stiffened, her lungs clogged. He was moving down her body, painting her flesh with his tongue. Her blood turned hot, molten and chugged through her veins like lava. Her world, her focus, narrowed to include only the two of them.

Need, Dare was finding, was a double-edged sword, one as painful as it was pleasurable. And, poised on that razor-edged peak, he was as primed as she for a fall. He couldn't find it in himself to care. His mouth found her moist warmth and her back arched. He slipped his hands beneath her hips, lifted her to devour. The soft, strangled sounds tumbling from her lips urged him on, to take more. To give more. And when she shot to release in a wild shuddering mass, she cried his name.

A.J. fought to haul breath into her lungs. Her limbs were weak, lax. And for the moment at least, she felt utterly tranquil. She felt the bed move, and her eyelids fluttered open. Tranquility abruptly fled. Here was the danger she'd forgotten, in the primally masculine man bending over her. Her hand raised of its own volition, curved around his neck and brought his mouth to hers.

She'd never known desire to be quenched so violently, to return so quickly. He was hard, intriguingly so, and when her fingers went in exploration, he suffered her touch for only a moment before moving her hand away. Her lips curved. He was determined to maintain control. She was equally determined that he lose it.

She pushed him to his back, surprising him, then went on a journey of discovery. His breath heaved out of his chest as her teeth scored his skin lightly, nipping a path from his shoulder to his belly. His restraint unraveled a bit more with each soft touch.

They rolled across the sheets, into and out of the sunlight spilling on the bed. Dare's gentleness had vanished, hunger raging. His vision misted, but his other senses were alert. Achingly so. The sweet dark flavor of her tongue battling with his. The silkiness of her hair, brushing against his skin, and the sexy tight grasp of her hands as she explored him where he was hot, hard and pulsing.

The teasing was gone. Gentleness was beyond him. His arousal was primal, basic and immediate. His hands battled hers, and he rolled her to his side, drew her leg over his hip. Testing her readiness with one finger, he watched her eyelids droop.

"Look at me, Addie," he demanded, his voice as ragged as his control. "Open your eyes."

He moved into position, his shaft barely parting her warm cleft and stilled. Only when she dragged her eyelids open, eyes dazed and unfocused, did he ease into her, pausing as she twisted and moaned against him. He moved in tiny increments, not satisfied until he was seated deep inside her. Then he took her mouth with his own, savagely aware that they were touching, every inch of their bodies. Inside and out. And still it wasn't enough.

He withdrew from her only to lunge again, each time deeper, harder, faster. They were caught in a vortex, spinning wilder and wilder. Out of control. He saw her face spasm, felt the clench of her inner muscles, swallowed her cry with his mouth. And then, only then, did he let the tide sweep him under and dash him up and over the edge.

Minutes, or hours, later he stroked a hand along the curve of her waist before settling it possessively on her hip. Each beat of her heart was echoed with his. Their breathing slowed, and eventually reason intruded. He started to move away, and her fingers tightened, in an automatic reflexive response. Reluctantly he ignored it. The protection he'd used was fast losing its effectiveness. He took care of it and rolled back to her. To please himself, he pushed the heavy tangle of hair away from her face, and skimmed his fingertips over her shoulder and down her arm.

It would be easy to stay like this. To cuddle and make love, eat, sleep, make love some more. He knew from personal experience that it would be intensely satisfying. He also knew it would be a mistake.

Once before, he'd thought they'd forged a bond, and Addie had been able to draw away, until the distance had yawned between them like an unspannable chasm. He wasn't going to make the mistake again. This time she'd choose.

Picking up her hand, he measured it against his palm. "This wasn't just sex, Addie. At least, it doesn't have to be." Her eyes widened, and the fear he read there tightened his gut. "You need to choose. If sex is all you want, just say the word and I'll be out the door. If I stay, we have more. It's your call."

Without conscious volition, her fingers locked with his. He couldn't know what he was asking. She wanted, badly, to choose sex. To have the strength to watch him leave her bed, dress and walk out of her life. Even as she mourned the choice, she knew it'd be easiest in the long run. Less risky. And considerably less terrifying than the alternative.

She hated this. Trying to quench the lick of panic in her veins, she reached for anger instead. Who was he to make such demands on her? She didn't want to deal with this jumble of emotions, the mingled doubts and fears. Far better to end this now. Again. Before there was a sticky tangle of recriminations and disappointments to assuage.

His eyes were laser blue, focused on hers. They demanded an answer. She gave him the only one she was capable of, certain even as she spoke it that it was a mistake.

"Stay."

Chapter 11

The most intimate thing A.J. could imagine was waking up beside a man. She lay quietly next to Dare, listening to his quiet breathing, watching the even rise and fall of his chest.

Nerves made a frantic little circle in her stomach. In the past she'd taken such care to avoid just this moment. Sex was a natural need, one to be judiciously indulged, quenched and then forgotten. It was simplest that way. Uncomplicated.

The man beside her had been nothing but complications since they'd met.

Muscles tense, she was compelled to move. Slipping from the bed, she walked noiselessly to the bathroom. She wrapped herself in the robe hanging on the door, then tiptoed out to the living room and watched dawn paint the sky in glowing pastels.

The early morning hours had a way of stripping secrets bare, uncovering truths that would be more comfortable to ignore. It wasn't the sex, had never been the act itself that had sent her running from Dare's arms two years ago. It was the bone-jarring connection that had been forged so easily, despite her efforts at distance. That kind of bond, she'd always thought, was to be avoided at all costs. It wouldn't be as devastating to lose a man as it would be to chance losing a piece of herself.

As always when such doubts rose and threatened to swamp her, she thought of her mother. Her life, her happiness had been so entwined with her husband's that each of his betrayals had torn a jagged wound that wouldn't heal.

An abusive drunk with quick fists and a mean tongue, Rich Jacobs had never taken care of anyone but himself. How was it, then, that the man's betrayal had stolen her mother's very sanity? How much more dangerous would be a man who was kind? Compassionate. Witty and warm.

Palms damp, she wiped them on the front of her robe. She'd never been a risk taker. It was doubtful that a lifetime of playing it safe could be overturned by one night. By one man. But she could no longer deny that she dearly wished otherwise.

Dare watched her in dawn's pale glow and could almost hear the thoughts bouncing frenetically about in her practical mind. He was beginning, perhaps, to know her a bit better. And, understanding her, he had an idea how to play this moment so that it would go more smoothly than their last morning after. Or so he hoped.

For whatever reason too much closeness too fast sent her backing away at breakneck speed. The answer could well lie in distraction, an area in which he had a certain expertise. And although he could think of much more pleasurable ways to divert her than with conversation, he tucked his hormones firmly away and concentrated on the matter at hand. The trick was to give her enough distance to allay her fears but not enough to separate them.

Because he was through being held at arm's length.

"Your morning etiquette is definitely lacking. First one up is supposed to put the coffee on." He pretended not to notice the start she gave. Crossing to the kitchen, he set her machine brewing before joining her in the living room, buttoning his shirt.

"How are you feeling?" He dismissed her automatic reassurance and examined her with a critical eye. The bruises on her face were blooming rainbows, but her eyes were clear, if one discounted their faint sheen of panic.

"I'm going to work today."

It was plain from the tinge of belligerence in her tone that she expected an argument. He skirted it, and her, to go to the front door. Retrieving the morning paper, he skimmed the headline. "Good idea. You're going to want to rethink your whole strategy with Delgado. Maybe even consider new charges."

He'd managed, finally, to divert her. "What are you talking about? There's no way we're ever going to prove a connection between my kidnapping and his case."

He looked up then, his brows raised. "No, but we do have a witness willing to testify that Delgado paid him to plant evidence after a homicide." He gave himself a moment to enjoy her dumbfounded expression, then strolled out the kitchen, whistling tunelessly.

"You've been holding out on me?" Incredibly, she sounded indignant. "When did you get this new information? Why haven't you mentioned it before?" Trailing after him, she peppered him with the questions.

"I just found out the day before yesterday. And you'll have to excuse me," his tone was dry, "but I've been a little busy in the time since."

It was a measure of her interest that the reference barely registered. Instead she was busily connecting the pieces. "You followed up on the lead I found, didn't you? You went and talked to Benson." At his nod, she slapped the counter. "I knew it! C'mon, Dare, start at the beginning. What'd you find out?"

There was a certain male satisfaction in knowing that he'd managed to make her completely forget her earlier nerves. But that satisfaction was nothing compared to the pleasure curling low in his belly just at the sound of his name on her lips. Dare. Not McKay. Not any of the other creative variations she'd come up with over the years.

And he needed to wonder just how completely he'd lost it if such a simple thing could mean so much.

Pushing that troublesome thought aside, he sat down and proceeded to fill her in on his visit with Benson. When he finished, she got up and walked into the other room, opened her briefcase and took out a legal pad. Returning to the kitchen, she took the mug of coffee he'd poured for her and sipped. "Did you have a chance to talk to his associate and corroborate his story?"

He nodded, picking up his own mug. "His name is Gellar, and he pretty much repeated what Benson had told me. Both of the men are prepared to talk to Connally, and you."

Jotting some notes, A.J. said, "Even if they'll testify to it, it's not proof that Delgado actually did the murder." She looked up then, a sly gleam in her eye. "But it sure does give us leverage."

She was unable to contain her excitement. Dare fanned it by relating the tale Benson had told him about Delgado's murder of the inmate at Leavenworth. "Think Delgado might start to get shook up if he knew we had some people willing to testify they knew him as Paulie the Knife? And how he actually came to earn the name?"

They grinned at each other. Dare added, "I'm thinking just the smell of this information is going to convince ol Paulie to cut a deal and name names. Would Beardmore be interested?"

A.J. got up, drained her remaining coffee. "There's only one way to find out."

The Cook County Courthouse was a magnificent building. On the national historic registry, it boasted a history dating back almost two centuries, from a time when architects built public buildings designed to impress.

Perhaps its most imposing quality were the two flights of marble steps leading up to its entrance, each set numbering exactly fifty stairs. A.J. had always figured that just going to and from work saved her at least ten minutes a day on the treadmill.

"I don't know what you hope to get accomplished here," she told him as they climbed the steps. "I have meetings to set up with Beardmore and Stanley. Then I have to get in touch with Connally and..."

"And I'm going to be there during it all." His voice brooked no opposition. "I'm the one who interviewed Bensen."

"After I came up with the lead." She made no effort to keep the smugness out of her voice as she trotted lightly up the steps. When he didn't keep pace with her she turned. "You said it was a long shot, remember...." Her voice trailed off when she caught his expression, and she swallowed hard.

She'd seen him angry before...had had that chilling rage turned on her more than once. But she'd never seen him like this. His face was closed, cold, but his eyes...they burned with a loathing so strong it nearly staggered her.

A.J. turned her head in the direction of his gaze and saw a meticulously dressed older man approaching. He drew to a stop before them, a slight smile playing on his thin lips.

"Mr. McKay. How fortuitous to see you today. Might I hope you're here to defend yourself against a well-deserved libel suit?" The man adjusted the cuffs on his immaculate pin-striped suit, his diamond pinky ring flashing in the sunlight. "I admit the idea titillates the imagination."

"*Mannen.*" Ice could have been chipped from the word. "Don't tell me that Justice has caught up with you at last."

Victor Mannen. A.J.'s blood went glacial. This was the man Dare was convinced was behind Delgado's kidnapping attempt of Meghan and ultimately, all that had befallen her, as well. She studied him in the bright sunlight. He was an advertisement for old money and impeccable bloodlines. Whatever else he was didn't show on the surface.

Mannen's brows rose above his chilly gray eyes. "I wouldn't know what you're referring to, I'm sure. I hope I won't be reading such tripe in your column. Slander carries such a nasty penalty these days." He switched his attention to A.J. "Miss Jacobs. I recognize you from television. I'm afraid you look the worse for wear. I hope you haven't been the recipient of McKay's temper. I know for a fact that he doesn't always keep firm control of it."

Dare bared his teeth in what couldn't pass for a smile. "You'd be surprised what I have a firm control over these days. As a matter of fact, you'll probably be finding out for yourself very soon."

There was a flicker in Mannen's eyes, quickly hidden, before he said disdainfully, "Threats, McKay? You should know by now that no one will ever believe your absurd vendetta against me." He began his descent again, started to pass by them. "How is your father, by the way? Still getting a bang out of life?"

One moment Dare was standing rigidly at A.J.'s side, the next he had Mannen by his crisp suit lapels, his face shoved close to the other man's. "Don't think I've forgotten, you bastard. Don't ever make the mistake of believing I've forgotten."

A.J. reached out unconsciously, laid a hand on Dare's arm. She could feel the muscles jumping reflexively beneath her fingers. He appeared impervious to her, his attention focused solely on the man before him. For one tension-charged minute their gazes battled, hatred emanating from them in waves. Then slowly Dare loosened his grip and Mannen pulled away, smoothed his suit front.

"As I said, Ms. Jacobs, his temper is uncertain. I'd advise you to use care around him." He continued down the steps and only then did A.J. feel the tension begin to seep from Dare's body.

It was all she could do to keep up with him as he moved up the stairs. They didn't speak until they were inside the courthouse, its shadowy interior decidedly cooler than the already steamy temperatures outside. When it became obvious that he wasn't going to speak, A.J. did. "Mannen is certainly as unpleasant as you made out."

Dare gave a harsh laugh. "Unpleasant? Yeah, I guess you could call a drug-dealing murderer unpleasant." It was apparent from his bitter tone that his rage still simmered.

"How does he happen to know your father?"

Silence stretched, long enough to convince her that he didn't mean to answer. The certainty was accompanied by an absurd sense of disappointment. She had no right to the feeling, not when the thought of lowering her own defenses with him could still bring her to a state of alarm. Tucking the unfamiliar emotion away, she said evenly, "I'm sorry. I shouldn't…"

Her words seemed to pierce the stillness that had overtaken him. "Yes," he said. "You should." Taking her elbow in his hand, he drew her out of the line of traffic to one of the huge marble columns that dotted the entry. "I'm not shutting you out, Addie." His words were deliberate and reflected her thoughts with embarrassing accuracy.

"About four years ago I was involved in a story on a drug cartel, and I was pretty sure that Mannen was up to his ears in it. He must have known I was getting close, because he came after me.'' His narrative was flat, emotionless, but when his gaze met hers she saw that the earlier rage had only been tucked away, not forgotten. ''He had my car wired with a bomb, rigged to blow as soon as there's any disturbance to the vehicle.

''My dad was at my place. His car was acting up, and he was supposed to go to visit my sister. I'd said he could use mine. About twenty yards from the car he used the automatic lock release I have on my key chain, and everything blew to hell.''

She gasped. His words were all the more devastating for their dispassionate delivery.

''He lost his arm to just above the elbow. The doctors and cops said he was lucky to be alive. He went through three surgeries and I don't know how many skin grafts. And the worst part of the whole thing was knowing he'd been hurt because of me. Because Mannen had wanted me out of the way.''

Now she understood the reason for his palpable hatred of the other man. She also understood, too well, the thread of guilt in his tone.

''The story?''

He seemed to come back to her then, with an almost physical shift. ''Won my first Pulitzer. My dad was at the ceremony, and as soon as I got back to my seat I handed the award to him. He's...'' He shook his head, as if words failed him. ''He's the greatest man I know. I was proud to win for him, but I won't stop until Mannen pays for what he did.''

Unconsciously she reached for his hand, squeezed. ''He really hates you. What's to stop him from trying to kill you again?''

The concern in her voice, in her touch, warmed something inside him. ''When I told the police about the connection between my case and Mannen, they were all over him. Couldn't pin the bomb on him, of course, but he doesn't like the attention. Makes it difficult to conduct his business.'' But he had no doubt that the man was merely biding his time.

"He isn't going to get the chance to hurt anyone again.'' The words were a promise, perhaps the only one she could give him. "This time we'll stop him.''

He threaded his fingers with hers. "Yeah.'' He released an explosive breath and raised her fingers to his lips. "We will.''

When they entered the office, Song looked up, her welcoming smile instantly fading, eyes going wide with concern. "Ms. Jacobs! You look…'' She must have caught the warning shake of Dare's head, because she swallowed the rest of the sentence and said instead, "Are you sure you're well enough to work today?''

A.J. pretended she didn't know exactly how Song had intended to complete her original sentence. "I'm fine.'' She made a credible attempt at a smile. "Rather glad that you had the foresight to start looking for me as soon as you did.'' She gave the woman a heartfelt smile. "Thank you.''

Song swallowed hard and nodded. "I'm glad everything turned out okay.''

"A.J.'' Dennis Beardmore paused theatrically in the office doorway before striding toward her, taking her chin in his hand and turning her face to either side. "I think you understated your injuries. Are you certain you should have returned to work so soon?''

"I'm sure.'' What she was most certain of, however, was how quickly she was becoming tired of the attention. Unobtrusively she freed herself from his grip. "Actually you're just the person I need to see. I want to update you on some new developments in the Delgado case.''

He frowned. "I think we could have spared you for a

few more days. You've been through a terrible ordeal. Simply terrible. I'm going to run a tough-on-crime platform, you can count on that." It was plain his words were more for Dare's benefit than her own.

She managed, barely, to avoid rolling her eyes. Trust Beardmore to take even her circumstances and use them for his own gain. No doubt he was hoping Dare would pounce on his not-quite-accidental slip and provide his possible candidacy some valuable news space.

If that was his hope, he was doomed to disappointment. Dare said only, "Not to worry, Dennis. One perpetrator was arrested on the spot, and it's just a matter of time before his accomplice is picked up." He gave a bland smile at the other man's obviously chagrined expression. "I know you must be worried about one of Addie's attackers still being on the loose."

"Of course." Dennis was nothing if not diplomatic. The expression he turned on A.J. oozed concern. "I hope you'll be very careful until the other man is caught."

It appeared that everyone she came into contact with today was going to drown her in sympathy. She found she didn't care to be the recipient. Crisply she said, "Do you have any time right now? Dare has some information you really should hear."

"McKay?" Beardmore gave the reporter a speculative glance. "Of course. Let's go into my office." Before turning to follow the other attorney out the door, A.J. told Song, "Get hold of Stanley and have him meet us. If he misses this, I'm never going to hear the end of it."

The walls in Beardmore's office were covered with his framed degrees, commendations and pictures of him with various politicians and local leaders. The display was, she thought, an altar to his ambition. She seated herself at the long conference table, and Dare sat beside her, both facing

Dennis. In the next moment there was a knock, and the door opened to reveal Mark Stanley.

He checked himself midstride, gaping at her. "My God…"

"You're just in time, Mark." She was completely out of patience with well-meaning expressions of solicitude. "If you'll take a seat…?"

Encompassing Beardmore and Stanley with her gaze, she said, "The day before yesterday Mr. McKay discovered some information that may well change the direction of the Delgado case. I'd like you to listen to what he has to say, and then we can discuss our next actions."

"Really, A.J." Mark frowned. "This is highly irregular. I don't see what—"

"Let's hear McKay out," Dennis said, cutting the attorney off. "I, for one, am interested in what he's got that's so urgent."

"What I've got is a possibility that Delgado is guilty of far more than he's been charged with. Not to mention a couple of witnesses who will attest to the same." Dare's words seemed to snag both men's attention, so he proceeded to report what he'd learned from Benson and Gellar. When he got to the part about Gellar's girlfriend witnessing Delgado handing the incriminating package to Gellar to plant at Benson's, Beardmore's hand clenched once on the table, then released.

"What about the girlfriend? Is she willing to testify?"

"Connally has already rounded her up, and she corroborates Gellar's story. I think the state would have a good case for homicide charges." Dare watched Beardmore's face carefully. He would be the one, after all, who'd make any decisions.

"So if this lead pans out, we'll press additional charges." Stanley frowned. "I don't understand how this impacts Patterson's case."

A.J. drew a breath. Negotiations had just gotten tricky. "Detective Connally has held from the beginning that Delgado wasn't working on his own. He believes he's a hit man known as Paulie the Knife. Benson says the same thing. If that's true, I'm wondering how interested the state would be in finding out just who he's worked for."

She'd never doubted Beardmore's legal mind. While Mark still looked slightly confused, the other attorney was eyeing her shrewdly. "Mr. McKay, would you mind stepping out for a moment, please?" He never took his gaze from her while Dare moved to comply.

When the door had closed behind Dare, Beardmore said, "I have no intention of jumping on something that turns out to be all accusation and very little solid evidence."

"No, sir." She waited, knowing even as she sat that the man was considering all the possible ramifications. All the ways the possible glory could reflect on him.

"That said," he continued, "I'd be cautiously interested if Delgado could offer something solid. I'd take nothing less than some tangible proof of the people who hired him. If he can provide that..." He shrugged. "Then we might be able to deal."

"A plea bargain?" Mark's voice was incredulous. "Excuse me, sir, but I suggested from the beginning that we could plead the Patterson case down."

"I won't deal on that case." On that point A.J. was adamant. Delgado was going to be held accountable for Meghan Patterson's kidnapping and attempted murder. If anything, her own recent experience strengthened her empathy for the woman. If Meghan was right, she'd lost a sister to the man. Had almost lost her life. Delgado wasn't going to skate away from *all* his deeds free and clear.

Choosing her words carefully, she said, "I think we should still go after Delgado for Meghan Patterson. But what if Connally's right and he's been working for someone all along? Maybe we can convince him to give up that person's name, as well as whoever hired the hit on Dorsey.''

Beardmore leaned back in his chair, his eyes suddenly shuttered. ''If I recall correctly, Connally has a hunch about who had hired Delgado most recently.''

''Yes, sir. Victor Mannen. As a matter of fact, we ran into him just a few minutes ago, leaving the courthouse.''

''Who's that?''

Both of them ignored Mark's question. A.J.'s gaze was fixed unwaveringly on her boss's. The sheen of affability that he affected in public had vanished. His eyes were shrewd, his expression calculating. She imagined he was weighing the options, carefully selecting the one that would best work to his advantage.

So she was completely unprepared to hear him say, ''Actually, Mr. Mannen was in to see me this morning.''

When she could find her tongue again, A.J. strove to keep her voice expressionless. ''What did he want?''

''Will someone please tell me who the hell Victor Mannen is?'' Mark's words were truculent.

Beardmore answered him almost absently. ''He's a wealthy local businessman with a somewhat colorful past.''

''He was charged with murder several years ago,'' A.J. added flatly. ''And I believe Justice has some interest in his business holdings.''

''He'd heard of my possible candidacy for county state attorney.'' Dennis brushed an invisible bit of lint off his sleeve. ''Came to pledge his support. I declined, of course.''

She knew she'd have to proceed with caution. ''Naturally, it must be difficult for you to suspect a supporter of yours.''

Eyes glinting, Dennis leaned forward. ''If he turns out to be dirty the last thing I want is to be affiliated with him, even remotely. If, however, he's being unfairly maligned, I certainly won't advocate ruining his reputation.''

Which was, A.J. thought dryly, a way for the attorney to have it both ways. Do nothing that might offend a potential donor, unless the situation could be turned around to help him another way.

''Delgado has to give us something solid before we deal,'' he went on. ''I want names of who gave the orders in the Patterson and Dorsey cases. Evidence for both will buy him immunity on the Dorsey murder. But we won't deal on the kidnapping charge. That stands.''

Allowing herself a slight smile of satisfaction, she said only, ''I'll take care of it.''

Dare waited in the outer office. Uncertain of how long the meeting would last, he made himself comfortable. He had, after all, gotten very little sleep the last two nights. Slouched in a chair, he tipped his head back to lean it against the wall and stretched his legs out in front of him.

He had a quick catnap before the door opened and Addie walked in. At her entrance he stood lazily, winked. ''I decided to hang around because I have something pressing to discuss with you.''

Her brows arched, but she only walked past him, opened the door. He followed her into her office. ''What is it, exactly, that's so pressing?''

''This.'' He crowded her against the wall and sealed her mouth with his in a quick, hungry kiss that was as unexpected as it was devastating. He'd surprised her with the sudden move. She surprised herself with her reaction to it. Her arms twined around his neck and she kissed him back, with just as much fire. Lips, tongue, teeth…the connection was elemental and all too encompassing.

When he dragged his mouth from hers, something deep

inside her mourned. He rested his forehead against hers. "I have to go."

She seemed to have no control over her hands. They smoothed over his shoulders, to grip his biceps. "You stayed to tell me that?"

"Among other things." He allowed himself one more quick kiss before stepping away from temptation. "I've got some other ideas I want to follow up on." It would be interesting, he thought, to see if a connection could be found between Mannen and Benson, Dorsey or Mulcahy. Some judicious digging was in order. "Unless you're willing to let me tag along with you today?"

She surprised herself with the amount of disappointment she felt in the answer she gave him. "Afraid not. I've got work to do."

"And you have until exactly five o'clock to do it." He ignored her raised eyebrows, kissed the tip of her nose. "You owe me a date, remember?"

She feigned blankness. "I don't recall."

"Liar." Dare slipped his hands in his pocket, rocked back on his heels. It was peculiarly satisfying to banter this way with Addie. It was satisfying to do just about anything with Addie. "I'll pick you up here at five."

She was already shaking her head. "I'll take a cab home."

Considering, he gave in on the issue. "All right, I'll pick you up there at seven. Wear a dress. That was part of the deal, remember?"

She did. "Any other orders before you go?"

His eyes gleamed. "Maybe. Wear those shoes I bought for you."

"I'm not sure they'll match my beige suit."

He leaned in, cupped her nape and drew her to him. His lips a fraction of an inch from hers, he breathed, "A dress.

Not a suit. If you're not sure what to pick out, I can help you select it when I get there.''

"I believe I can handle that myself. What do you have in mind?"

"Dinner. Dancing. Candlelight." He punctuated his words with quick kisses, before easing away. "Don't forget the shoes."

She ignored the quick flutter in her stomach and rolled her eyes. "What is it men have with spiked heels?"

He'd moved away, his hand already on the doorknob. "Wear them tonight, and I'll show you."

The promise in his voice caused her pulse to skip. She waited until he was out of the office before she propped herself against the wall, supporting knees that had gone curiously weak. A month, even a week ago, if someone had told her a man could turn her boneless with a kiss she'd have laughed out loud. However, Dare McKay wasn't just any man. And this wouldn't be just any date.

Her heart spun once in her chest. She'd never been one to run headlong into danger, but she seemed to be galloping toward it now. And she couldn't find it in herself to care.

Chapter 12

"A.J. Stanley." Joel Paquin stood, offered his hand to each of them as they entered the tiny room in the basement of the city jail. His gaze lingered on A.J.'s face. "Souvenirs from your last court battle?" He laughed a little. "I'll try to take it a bit easier on you when we meet." There was a hint of triumph in his gaze. "I can't say I was surprised by your invitation to meet today, although the terms are a bit unusual."

She laid her briefcase on the table, unlocked it. "We'd prefer Delgado to be present when we make our offer. That's not a problem for you, is it?"

There was something shark-like in his smile. "It's never a problem to hear an offer from the state attorney's office for an innocent client."

Mark started to speak, and A.J. nudged him under the table. She smiled serenely at Paquin. "That's exactly what we counted on."

The door opened then, and Delgado was ushered in by

a uniformed policeman. She studied the prisoner while the cop left the room. The man had a decided effect on her each time she saw him, and today was no different. There was something reptilian about him, something cold and empty in the eyes that reminded her of a snake beginning to coil.

She was going to make sure that this snake never struck again.

"Mr. Delgado, we invited you to this meeting so you could judge what we have to say firsthand, instead of having it filtered through your lawyer."

He gave a negligible shrug. "Wasting your time. Whatever you got to say you coulda just said to him."

"All right." Adrenaline spiked, hummed through her veins as she opened her briefcase and withdrew some notes she had Song prepare. She handed one copy to Paquin and retained the other. "I'm sure you'll find this as interesting as we did, Joel."

She waited, hands clasped nervelessly, for the other lawyer to skim the material. His reaction wasn't long in coming.

"What the hell is this!" Paquin dropped the sheets with a disdainful motion. "What kind of game are you playing, Jacobs?"

"No game. It just so happens that we've uncovered some of your client's other...activities." She waited, let her words sink in. "Perhaps he hasn't shared his nickname with you. It's Paulie the Knife, isn't it?" This was directed at Delgado, who stared unflinchingly back at her with an eerie lack of expression.

"I suppose you didn't think it was relevant to the ill-fated love affair you and Miss Patterson were engaged in." Ridicule dripped from her words. "After all, why wouldn't the jury believe a man who has spent the past ten years of his life hiring out as an assassin?"

"I expected better of you." Paquin had recovered his unruffled facade. "Do you really think we're going to be reeled in by this pathetic maneuver?"

"It doesn't really matter what you think of it. Those papers—" she nodded at the sheaf he'd dropped "—document interviews conducted by the CPD of a couple of Mr. Delgado's acquaintances." She shifted her gaze to the silent man at Paquin's side. "Benson and Gellar, by the way, failed to send their regards. I'm sure you'll understand."

Joel shook his head sadly. "I should have figured Beardmore would have come up with some trick like this. You'll have to excuse us. We've got nothing more to talk about."

"Fine. You don't need to talk. Just listen." She leaned forward. "Does this information affect Patterson's case? Maybe not. But it does represent a whole new set of charges that are being drawn up as we speak. So after your client is sentenced for kidnapping and attempted murder, he's going to face yet another trial for the murder of Andrew Dorsey."

She directed her next words at Delgado. "Think you can skate on the Patterson case? That Paquin's going to get you off with a restraining order and a slap on the wrist? I'm going to do my best to prevent that. But even if by some stretch of the imagination he's able to accomplish that, you're going to be facing multiple murder charges, of which Dorsey is only one. Do you have the money to pay him for those defenses, too?" She let a derisive smile curl her lips. "Or do you think your last employer will be willing to keep footing the bill?"

Paquin's face had gone thunderous. "By God, Jacobs, I'll bury you for this. You can't come in here and threaten us."

Satisfied with his reaction, she sat back calmly. "Threaten? I came to offer a deal, just like I told you on the phone."

"You ain't mentioned a deal." Delgado stared at her expressionlessly. "What've you got?"

"We're not going to waste any more of our time, Paul." Paquin rose, directing his client to do the same. Delgado remained seated, gazing at A.J. with his peculiarly emotionless eyes.

"It seems as though your client is a bit more interested than you are, Joel." A.J. made the observation with no little satisfaction.

Paquin sat back down, put his head close to Delgado's and began whispering furiously. There was a short, vehement discussion, and she knew what the outcome would be before the other lawyer ever raised his head again.

"My client wants to indulge you, so we'll let you spin out this fairy tale you've concocted before we leave. But the first phone call I make when we leave here will be to Judge Holley."

Brows arching, she invited, "By all means, go ahead. By that time she should be able to contact the state office and get all the details." Fuming, the defense attorney folded his arms, deliberately not attempting to take notes. A.J. began, anyway.

"Nothing we suggest will impact the Patterson case. Your client still faces those charges, and I'll push for the maximum sentence."

"If you win," Paquin inserted.

A.J. ignored him. "Charges are currently being filed charging your client with murder and conspiracy to conceal in the Dorsey case. We've got two witnesses who can testify that he gave Gellar the murder weapon and bloody shirt for the purpose of incriminating Benson. And Benson also gave us eyewitness testimony about the murder of another inmate in Leavenworth."

There was a flicker of expression in Delgado's eyes before they went blank again.

"Our investigators will round the other eyewitnesses to that homicide, and once they do, your client will face those charges, as well." She shifted her attention to Delgado. "You're going away, Mr. Delgado. It's up to you for how long. We know you've hired out as an assassin for the past ten years. We figure Benson and Patterson were only two among your many targets. I want names and evidence. We're not interested unless you have proof incriminating your employers. Paquin just might get you off the kidnapping charges." She said the words, all the while swearing to herself she'd never allow that to happen. "Can he help you dodge these additional murder charges, as well?" Tossing her notebook in her open briefcase, she stood and locked it. "Think about it, gentlemen."

"This is outrageous!" Paquin's face was turning a curious shade of purple. "I'll have you disbarred for this, Jacobs."

She laughed; she couldn't help it. "For what, doing my job? You're welcome to try." Stanley rose and they prepared to leave. Once they reached the door. she turned back to the two men. "Oh, and Joel. These bruises?" She pointed to the colorful marks on her face. "You're right. They're from my last battle. And that guy's in jail, too. I hear he needs a good lawyer." She closed the door on whatever comment he would have made.

For the first time Mark spoke. "Are you sure that wasn't premature, A.J.? New charges haven't been filed yet. The Dorsey thing may well yet fall apart under further investigation."

She refused to let his warnings bother her. She was just feeling too darn good. "You heard Beardmore this morning. He okayed everything I presented today. Connally is preparing his report even as we speak." Together they walked down the hallway, away from the cells.

"It doesn't look too promising," Mark observed. "Paquin didn't seem willing to deal."

"It may not be up to him." She certainly hoped that was true. "Delgado is the one facing charges. He'll be the one ultimately making the decision." She could only wonder whether Mannen would be involved in the decision-making process, as well.

Anticipation ran parallel to nerves when her doorbell rang that night. The second emotion was expected; the first was not. One would think she had never gone on a date before. Had never spent extra time getting ready for a special evening. The truth was, if she had, it had been too long ago to recall clearly.

Her doubts were somewhat allayed by the satisfying look of male appreciation on Dare's face as he painted her with a slow gaze.

"Honey, you do wonders for that dress."

It was his tone as much as his words that sent a warm glow jittering through her. She didn't socialize much. That fact had been borne home when she'd contemplated the dismal contents of her closet earlier. But there was the annual Bar Association banquet, and the odd museum exhibit or play she attended. And every woman, despite her social calendar, knew the value of a having a little black dress on hand.

While liquid warmth shot through her, she assessed him critically. "Well, well. There is something in your wardrobe besides Hawaiian shirts and jeans. I'm...surprised."

"And I'm glad I won that bet." He winked at her, a vision of masculinity in dark trousers, a charcoal suit coat and a collarless, light-colored shirt. "You look a heckuva lot better in that dress than I would have."

His nonsense soothed, as it was meant to. Her stomach was still jittering, but her earlier misgivings were allayed for the moment. As she closed and locked the door behind her, she could feel his gaze sweeping over her, and it seemed to leave a trail of heat in its wake.

"The shoes complement the dress."

More from necessity than habit she tucked her hand in the arm he offered and made her way carefully down the steps. "These shoes are an open invitation to a sprained ankle."

"That's where I come in. You can lean on me all you want. Take shameless advantage. Please."

She was still chuckling when he got in the car on the other side and pulled away from the curb.

"What did you do all afternoon?" The question that had played at the back of her mind all day fell off her tongue without her conscious permission. She wasn't used to wondering about a man; his whereabouts, his actions. She wasn't used to missing one, nor to looking forward to seeing him hours later. The experience had been unfamiliar but not altogether unpleasant.

He took the exit ramp onto the freeway as he answered. "Talked to my editor. Did some research. Made some notes for my next column." Mostly, though, he'd thought of her. Images had filtered across his mind despite the task or level of concentration required. Visual pictures of Addie, her beautiful face twisted with the desire they ignited in each other. That catch in her breath when he'd mounted her, found again the sweet moist clench of pleasure as she closed around him.

With some effort he returned to the original thread of conversation. "It's a long shot, but I'm following up on the rest of that list we started on. We got lucky once, we might again. How about you?"

"Oh, I offered a deal to Paquin and his slimy client." Her voice held a hint of smugness. "Immunity from the Dorsey murder charges in return for the proof of who ordered it, as well as whoever hired him in the Patterson case.''

Dare was jolted by the enormity of her words. Not the implications for nailing Mannen, although that would register later. But the matter-of-fact way she'd shared the information with him, in an easy manner that suggested confidence. Trust. Two qualities that had always been noticeably absent from their relationship.

It hit him like a blow to the chest, landing somewhere in the vicinity of his heart. It was such a little thing, really. The kind of how-was-your-day-dear conversation shared between two lovers. It shouldn't have meant so much. And it wouldn't have if it had been anyone other than Addie. She didn't slip and hand out confidential information to anyone, regardless of the relationship. Two years ago— even two weeks ago—she would have been afraid he'd take the information and print it.

He reached for her hand, sent his thumb skating over her knuckles. ''There's a whole avenue of leads that Connally and Madison alone aren't going to be able to follow up on. Be interesting to find out if the other eyewitnesses to that prison murder will finger Delgado for it, and if they've had any contact with him since his release.''

Her pulse was jumping, but her hand remained in his. ''I'm not sure this case will cover that broad an investigation. More than likely we'll hand our information over to the various law enforcement agencies across the nation affiliated with those unsolved knife killings we compiled. Then we'll turn those leads over to the original officers to follow.''

Concentrating on her voice as much as her words, he nodded, and they drove in silence for a while. Despite the way the case was coming together, despite the fact that his long pursuit of Mannen seemed to be paying off, finally, it was the woman beside him who claimed his attention. His focus was spending time with her. And making it count.

"What are we doing?"

"We have to stop at my place first." He kept a casual grip of her hand as they took the elevator to the apartments and then to his floor. He didn't release it as they strolled down the hallway, as he distracted her with an amusing anecdote about his landlord. He unlocked the door, then ushered her in, watching her face carefully.

She stopped just inside the door and took a deep breath. "Something tells me we've arrived at our destination for the evening."

Taking a quick glance around, he let the door close behind him. The place was just as he'd left it. Candles flickered on a cozy table for two he'd set up in the living room before the sliding glass doors. He'd had some romantic notion of a roomful of candles—women liked that sort of thing, didn't they?—but since he'd had none himself, he'd been reduced to borrowing two elegant tapers and holders from his neighbor next door.

But the music playing softly through the stereo speakers was his own, classical pieces that were at once elegant and seductive. The catered dinner he'd had specially prepared was aromatic, just waiting to be warmed up for serving. Rarely had he gone to such lengths for a woman. But this was for Addie. All of it.

It occurred to him then, in a blind moment of panic, that she might not regard his preparations in the same light he did. That she might consider it a jaded stage set for seduction. An unusual sense of uncertainty speared through him. "We could go out, if you'd rather."

His doubts were soothed a moment later, when she looked at him, her eyes soft. "I'd rather spend our date here."

Lungs easing, he led her to the kitchen and set her to

work pouring the wine while he placed the food in the oven to warm. It was all too alluring to watch her there, performing the routine task, and to pretend that this was where she belonged. Where she would stay. He already knew that once she was gone, her image would linger. It was an image guaranteed to give him many sleepless nights.

The black dress she wore clung to her curves and was held in place by two tiny straps on her otherwise bare shoulders. Those straps crossed in back, and were the only things holding the dress together around her narrow spine. The sheer creativity of the thing gave a man a renewed interest in the laws of physics and gravitational pull.

He accepted the flute of wine she handed him, giving her long bare legs an appreciative glance. Wearing the sandals he'd given her, her shining blond head was only a couple of inches shorter than his own.

She was, quite simply, stunning. That golden hair and creamy skin against the sleek black fabric of her dress was a guaranteed fantasy. The swelling on her bruises had perhaps receded a bit, but their colors were even more brilliant than before. Rather than being self-conscious about them, as another woman might have been, she seemed bothered by them only when other people expressed sympathy.

He'd never met anyone in less need of it.

"From the look of those cartons I'm not going to be at the mercy of your dubious culinary talents."

"I could have made something," he protested. He took a swallow of wine, his gaze meeting hers across the rim. "If you don't mind egg sandwiches and soup."

Her nose wrinkled, although she smiled. "Your skills match my own."

"I think *we* match, Addie, in more ways than you'd like to think." He watched as she digested his meaningful phrase and then switched subjects before it could alarm her. "Shall we take our wine out on the terrace?"

He was gentlemanly enough to allow her to precede him, male enough to appreciate the view when she did. She sat gracefully in the chair he offered. "Your view is spectacular."

He would have agreed, but he doubted they were talking about the same thing. The skyline couldn't begin to compare with the breathtaking woman before him. "If I remember correctly your old apartment had a view to match it." It still puzzled him that she'd chosen to move. Her new place couldn't be nearly as convenient to her work.

Her fingers tightened just slightly on the globe of her wine glass. "My mother's care is very expensive. My new home is adequate, and a great deal cheaper." She gave a shrug. "I'm rarely there, anyway. I spend most of my time at work or at her hospital."

Although her unusual candor surprised him, he made sure it didn't show. "Your mother is lucky to have you."

"She's mentally ill." He could tell what the admission cost her. "Doctors, medication, therapy...it all adds up."

"And how much can Leo be depended on to help?"

"Leo is...unpredictable. I'm happy that he's managed to hold on to a job this long. Continuous employment was a condition of his release."

He could read her answer in the one she hadn't given. Her brother contributed nothing to their mother's care, and since a father hadn't been mentioned, it had all fallen on A.J.'s slender shoulders.

Recognizing the flicker of discomfort in her expression, he sought a topic guaranteed to relax her. "Where did you go to school?"

"Various places. We moved around a lot. I've always lived in Chicago, though. Attended a lot of inner-city schools."

"Ah, that's right." He raised his glass, drank. "You mentioned tough neighborhoods."

"War zones would be a better word for some."

"Learn to roll your own cigarettes?"

She accepted the hint of challenge in his voice, topped it. "We learned to cure our own tobacco." She enjoyed the sound of his laugh, low and husky. He laughed and smiled easily, but he wasn't nearly as uncomplicated as she'd once thought. There was a layer of toughness beneath, and the affability disguised it much as she disguised parts of herself from the world. The similarity was disturbing to contemplate.

"Is the wine all right?"

Self-consciously her gaze dropped to the untouched glass in her hand. "I don't drink much. I'm sure it's fine." As if to emphasize her words, she brought it to her lips, sipped.

Still studying her, he observed, "I've seen you order at Brewster's."

"Tonic water." Her lips curved. "It shouldn't surprise you that I don't like having my senses dulled by alcohol."

Realization flashed through him. No, she wouldn't be one to give up control so easily, and by not letting anyone besides the bartender handle her glass, she could ensure that her drink remained exactly as ordered. The level of control she demanded of herself was daunting.

She shifted a bit under his perusal. "You're staring."

"Because you fascinate me."

She flicked a long nail at the glass she held. "I'm not particularly intriguing."

Giving a short laugh, he rose, waited for her to stand and guided her inside again. "You have no idea."

For a few moments she watched him carry dishes from the kitchen to the table before she asked, "Shall I get silverware?"

He gave her an easy smile. "We won't need any."

And they didn't. He'd chosen finger food, whether for ease or for the seductive pleasure, she wasn't certain. There was broiled shrimp, tiny hard rolls, seasoned scallops. Whether it was the food or the atmosphere, she didn't think she'd ever tasted anything so heavenly.

"Try a scallop," he urged.

She reached for the morsel he was holding out to her, but he moved forward, brought it to her mouth. Hesitantly her teeth closed over the succulent piece. The sudden gleam that leaped to his eyes made it difficult to swallow.

Several times during the course of the meal she lost track of the thread of their conversation. They talked of mundane things, the very ordinariness contrasting to the intimate meal. One time she reached for a shrimp to bring to her lips and he closed his hand over her wrist, steering it to his mouth instead.

The sensuousness of the act torched her blood and flushed her cheeks. She was uneasily aware that her reaction was too apparent to him. But disguising her response seemed beyond her.

Once they'd finished the meal, Dare went to the stereo. After adjusting it to something moody and sultry, he crossed to her again, held out a hand. "Dance with me."

It was more an invitation than a demand, one she was helpless to deny. She put her hand in his, allowed him to help her rise, and stepped into his arms. When they closed around her, she was enclosed in a world that held only the two of them.

He danced as he did everything else, with an almost effortless ease. Their bodies brushed with every movement, making her supremely aware of him. There was nothing to set her nerves to alarm. He was holding her close, but not uncomfortably so. Just near enough that she could smell the soap he'd used that evening, the scent of his aftershave. She thought of that with a sense of wonder—of Dare spending as much time getting ready tonight as she had, and the thought was appealing. He'd gone to a lot of effort, and she found herself curiously touched. She didn't remember anyone going to such trouble for her before.

There was danger in that way of thinking, and she mentally veered to avoid it. It would be a mistake to read too much into their relationship. A mistake to depend on him too much. Logically she knew that. Accepted it. Emotionally she was wrapped up in the moment.

His mouth went to her throat and she arched her neck, allowing him access. She could hear his heart thudding close and realized with faint surprise that it echoed her own. She'd never experienced this: a deliberately gradual rise of simmering arousal, with no hurry to get to the final act. One of his hands touched her bare back, the other cupped her bottom, pulled her infinitesimally closer.

"Are you cold?" His lips brushed her ear, and she realized with a start that she was trembling. She shook her head, fascinated by the curl of male satisfaction on his lips. He would know, of course, that he was responsible for her reaction. The thought dissipated in the next moment when her hips grazed his and she felt the unmistakable hardness there.

Heat surged through her veins, fueled by an innate womanly satisfaction. If she was affected by Dare's nearness, he was just as affected by hers. Closing the small distance between them, she rested her head on his chest, felt the hammering of his heart beneath tightly drawn muscles. His fingers dipped below the fabric at her back and skimmed over her tailbone. Her next act wasn't conscious; it was instinctive.

She unfastened his shirt, one button at a time, pressing

a warm kiss to each inch of golden skin she bared. When she had a smooth wedge of flesh bared, she rubbed her cheek against it once, her eyes sliding shut even as she pulled the shirt tails from his waistband. His hand tightened on her hips, brought her closer against him.

Pushing the shirt over his arms forced him to release her, but not for long. She stepped into his arms again, tested a firm pectoral muscle with her teeth.

His mouth found hers with evidence of a keen edged need that was reciprocated. This time would be different from a few nights ago. She wanted to unleash the animal that lurked just beneath the surface. Tonight she'd have it all.

The air crackled with the electricity they created. His mouth went in search of hers, and their tongues tangled. He pushed the straps from her shoulders, and shock arced through her when it pooled around her feet. She hadn't felt him release it.

She was grateful for the candlelight. The dress hadn't allowed for a bra, and all she was left wearing was a wisp of black lace panties and her sandals, while he...he was definitely overdressed.

For the moment, at least, it appeared he intended to stay that way. He bent his head to catch her nipple in his lips and sucked strongly from her. Her knees buckled in sudden violent response. Her fingers went to his hair, unconsciously drawing him closer as the sensations crashed over her, one wave after another.

She released his pants and found him, cupping his heavy masculinity. He surged into her hands. It was shockingly arousing to be nearly naked in his arms when he was partially clothed. And as much as she wanted to equalize the situation, she didn't want to stop touching him.

He reached beneath the elastic of her panties, found her

warm wet heat and stroked a finger inside her. She cried out reflexively, her fingers tightening around him. His mouth went to her other breast and the dual assault was more than she could bear.

His voice was ragged, muffled against her skin. "Let's go into the bedroom."

Her touch grew more deliberate. "I want you inside me. Now."

His breathing ragged, he gave her a long, deep kiss, and began to move her toward the bedroom. She had no intention of cooperating. She didn't want to give him time to regain his flagging control, to set limits on his own passion, while provoking an aching response from her. She wanted, quite simply, to destroy him, as completely as their love-making destroyed her, before the shattering explosion completed her again.

"The bedroom," he panted, his mouth moving to her jaw, her ear, her throat. "Now, Addie."

Instead she went to her knees before him, pressed her lips against his hardness. It was gratifying to feel his body quake against her, to feel his shuddering response. She traced her tongue down the length of him, exploring him with lips and tongue, until he hauled her to her feet and into his arms.

His mouth covered hers fiercely. His kiss evoked a similarly violent response in her. She responded to his violence with more of the same, demanding a response. He backed her up against the wall, then reached down, shredded the panties that shielded her from him.

The savagery of the action shocked and aroused her. "Dare." He pressed his mouth to hers and swallowed the sound, while cupping her bottom and lifting her to impale her with one long stroke.

The sweet velvet slide on his shaft, the delicate pulsations as her body adjusted to his invasion, was almost more than he could bear. He didn't think about the need for protection, didn't consider anything but this moment. This woman.

Surging forward, he heard her moan and went in search of her mouth. Sealing it with his, he pistoned his hips, thrusting hard and deep, wringing wild cries from her. Her legs were wrapped around him, her arms clinging to his shoulders. Each savage thrust flattened her breasts against him and the exquisite sensations threatened to send him over the edge.

Fingers digging into her bottom, he held her steady as he pounded into her, his vision graying, beginning to blur. He dimly felt her heels pressing into his back, her body tensing then clenching around him. He was blind, deaf to all but this woman.

When he felt her release, he lunged harder, buried himself inside her to the hilt and followed her into oblivion.

They made it, eventually, to the bed. Night fell, passion rose again, was satiated with clever mouths, pleasuring hands. The hours spun into an endless cloak of pleasure. One neither of them wanted to relinquish.

She came out of the bathroom the next morning wearing one towel and drying her hair with another. "Where do you hide your blow dryer?"

He decided then and there that she was the only woman alive who could look elegantly sexy even wrapped in terry cloth. She would look even better in nothing at all.

He reached out and gripped the edge of the towel, gave a tug. "Come over here, and I'll tell you."

She pulled away, then stopped when her action nearly succeeded in loosening the precarious knot holding up her covering. Dropping the towel she'd used on her hair, she used both hands to secure the one that was rapidly slipping. "Behave yourself. I don't have time to wrestle this morning."

He cocked an eyebrow. "No? Then maybe you should throw in the towel." He gave a yank, and she hit the bed at approximately the same time her covering dropped to the floor. They rolled across the bed, and she laughed, struggling in vain to evade him.

"You have a one-track mind. I know your type, McKay."

"You're my type, Jacobs." He wrestled her to her back, stretched out on top of her, holding both her wrists above her head with maddening ease.

There was a feminine curl of excitement at the sight of him leaning over her, his face stamped with primal male appreciation. Her voice was more breathless than she would have liked when she asked, "What type is that?"

"Tall, blond and *naked.*" He kissed the smile from her lips, turned it much too easily to need. He let go of her hands to cup her face, and she promptly twined her arms around his neck, fingers raking into his hair.

The ringing of her cell phone seemed to come from a great distance. When it became apparent that Dare would ignore it, she wiggled free to pick it up from the bedside table where she'd left it. Her voice was breathless when she answered, made more so when his arms suddenly snaked around her. Flipping her to her back, his mouth did sneaky sexy things to the cord along her throat.

It was an effort to make sense of Song's message. Once she did, she pressed one palm against Dare's chest to stop his distractions and straightened slowly.

"I'll get there as soon as I can. No, don't expect me. I'll drive directly to lockup. Do we know who his public defender is yet? Find out. And when you do, set up a time for him to meet me at the jail in two hours. Give the same message to Stanley.''

Dare had raised his head, was studying her carefully. She listened for another moment, then said, ''I'll let you know when I'm on my way. Thanks for tipping me off, Song.''

She ended the conversation and flipped the phone closed.

''Sounds serious.'' Dare's expression was quizzical.

''I think it is.'' Excitement of a different sort sizzled through her veins. ''Delgado fired Paquin last night. Sounds like he's ready to deal.''

Chapter 13

A.J. had never met Hank Rambo, Delgado's new public defender before, and she took the time to update him on the recent offer her office had made to his client.

"I think you should know, Ms. Jacobs, that I've cautioned my client not to rush into any sort of agreement with you until we see something in writing."

Without a word Mark Stanley handed the written agreement to the man, who skimmed it rapidly. When he'd finished with it, he said, "Mr. Delgado is willing to speak to you, only as a matter of supposition at this point, admitting to no wrongdoing in his current case or in his past."

She nodded her agreement.

Delgado took over then. It was obvious he and his attorney had worked out their roles earlier. "Let's say maybe you're right, and maybe I did some work for some people. I give you names, and then what?"

"Then nothing," she told him bluntly. "Names are worthless if you can't back them up with irrefutable proof."

"Irrefutable." He turned the word over, smiled chillingly. "How 'bout tape recordings of the transactions? Would that be irrefutable enough for you?"

"He's bluffing," Mark put in. "If he had that kind of evidence, it would have been found when the cops seized his possessions in Ohio."

Delgado never even spared him a glance. His gaze was fixed on A.J. "What do you say? I've got the guys on tape, describing the job, giving me my orders and promising me cash. Half on acceptance of the assignment and half on completion."

Assignment. Completion. He made the topic sound like they were discussing schoolwork. Determined to disguise the revulsion she felt, she gave him a short nod. "Upon delivery of the tapes, and upon our satisfaction that the voices match the names you give us, then you'll have your immunity granted for the Dorsey homicide."

"What about this crap you're trying to pull on me committing some hit in prison?"

Her smile was cold, ruthless. "One thing at a time, Paulie. This deal is for the Dorsey hit only."

"Alleged hit," his attorney put in. The other people in the room ignored him.

Delgado leaned back in his chair, studied her. "And if I can come up with more than just those two tapes?"

"Then we'll discuss the matter further. Right now I want the name of the man who ordered Dorsey killed."

Delgado was still playing it cagey. "Suppose I could guess…"

"Yeah, why don't you do that." Suddenly she was out of patience with the whole thing. "Guess who might have given the order to have Dorsey murdered."

He pursed his lips, gave the appearance of a man deep in thought. "If I was to guess I'd say Mulcahy."

Releasing a breath she hadn't been aware of holding, she

nodded. The name matched the one Benson had given her. But this interview wasn't done yet. "And who would you guess wanted Patterson and Connally dead?"

His eyes went sly, and his mouth twisted into a parody of a smile. "My guess would be Mannen. Victor Mannen."

"He named Mannen," A.J. informed Beardmore an hour later in his office. "Now we wait and see if he can deliver the tapes he claims he has."

"We still have to match the voices on it," Stanley reminded them. "That's not going to be easy. With the technology available today there must be a dozen ways to alter tape recordings."

"And just as many ways to detect such alterations. We'll have his testimony, too," she reminded him. "I have the feeling this thing is just starting to unravel. Delgado must feel the same way, or he wouldn't have unleashed Paquin and gone off on his own." She had no doubt that the defense attorney had tried to talk Delgado out of the action he'd taken, resulting in his firing. Since it was certain he hadn't acted in his client's best interests, he must have been protecting someone else. Mannen?

"We'll have to proceed with caution." Dennis wore a ponderous expression. "There's the potential for a huge success here if this thing pans out. If it blows up in our faces, however, the embarrassment to the office would be devastating."

And, she thought, put the kiss of death on his candidacy. "We'll take it one step at a time," she promised. "Delgado's new PD is already making noises about filing for a delay, with the excuse that he's new to the case. Do you want me to counter if he does?"

Beardmore shook his head. "No, let it play out. More time can only aid our investigators in their task." He stood, indicating the meeting was over. "Good work, A.J., Mark.

If this proceeds the way we hope, our office will receive national exposure.''

For once A.J. didn't let his ambitions mar her mood. They were close to nailing Delgado, and with him, Mannen. Nothing could ruin her satisfaction at the prospect of putting the pair of men away for good.

Dare hung up the phone, excitement spiking. He rolled his chair to his computer, typed in the name he'd just acquired and waited impatiently for his personal files to unfold. He scrolled from one to the other, skimming. He was already fairly certain that his supposition was correct, but when he found the information he was seeking, the jolt of realization was still sharp. ''My God,'' he muttered, shoving his wheeled chair away from his desk. ''All this time, and we've had a prime lead right under our noses.'' He picked up the phone again, this time to dial Connally's number. ''Where are you?'' he asked, wasting no time on preliminaries when the detective answered. ''At your desk? Well, put down your coffee, quit trying to sneak that cigarette and get to the computer.'' He grinned at the other man's suggestion. ''Still testy, Connally? Nicotine withdrawal is hell, isn't it? Punch this name in and see what you get—Peter Rollins.''

He waited, not quite patiently. It was a measure of their growing friendship that the detective didn't balk, although his cooperation wasn't accomplished without griping.

Gabe's voice came on the line again. ''I've got three hits—two currently in prison and one aggravated assault, pleaded out two years ago. What am I supposed to be looking for here?''

''Try the assault. Does he match this social security number?'' He recited a string of numbers, and Connally affirmed them. Dare's grin grew wider. The picture was so sweet when the pieces fell together.

There was a hint of grudging admiration in the other man's voice. "McKay, how the hell do you get your hands on that kind of information?"

"Trade secret, m'boy. Peter Rollins used to be Peter Randolf until he changed his name nine years ago. Did it all nice and legal. His employer is the careful type. But while he was Peter Randolf he served time in Leavenworth. Bet if you enter that name into the computer you'll get a whole list of hits." He waited, until the name he'd mentioned rang a bell in Connally's memory. He didn't have too wait for long.

"Son of a—Randolf is one of the names Benson mentioned as witness to the knifing at Leavenworth."

"You get ten points for putting it together, son, but I gotta deduct a few for lack of speed." He chuckled at the detective's expletive. "You want me to tell you where you can find that fellow now?"

"I have a feeling you will anyway."

"You're right." Dare felt undeniably cheerful. "I'll save you the trouble of tracking this one down on your own, and we can talk about what you owe me later. Peter Randolf has been working in Chicago for the past nine years. He's Victor Mannen's right-hand man."

Mannen's office had the artwork of a museum and the opulence of a palace. He sat behind an acre of burnished cherry, both curator and king. When his visitor was shown into the area, he had his hands folded serenely, his face arranged in an expressionless mask.

"Mr. McKay." He arched one slim brow. "I wish I could say it was a pleasure."

"Mannen." Dare cast a derisive eye on the glittering surroundings. "Crime seems to be paying off well for you."

Mannen's diamond pinkie ring caught the light, shards

of brilliance reflecting from its surface. "I'm sure I don't know what you're referring to. Please state your business before I lose patience and call security." He allowed himself a small smile as he contemplated the possibility. "I'm afraid you wouldn't care for their methods for your removal."

Ignoring the office chairs spaced around the room, Dare pulled up a scrolled ornamental piece that was obviously an antique. The flicker of alarm on Mannen's face when he dropped his weight into it was worth the trip over. "Threats? After all we've been to each other? Gee, Vic, I'm hurt. After I came here to do you a favor, too."

The man made a show of checking the slim gold watch on his wrist. "I really am pressed for time."

"Yeah, I could see out front that this place is a real bustle of activity." There was no denying it, Dare was enjoying himself. He'd worked too long for this moment for it to be any other way. "But I won't keep you. I just wanted to ask a couple questions about one of your employees. Peter Rollins. Used to call himself Peter Randolf."

With meticulous precision, Mannen adjusted the cuffs of his suit. "Peter is out of the city at the moment. What possible interest could you have in him?"

"I suppose I have the same interest in him that the CPD is beginning to show." The stillness that came over Mannen's features was fiercely satisfying. "See, they know about the connection he has to Delgado. And that connection leads right to you, too. You realize that, don't you?"

Having accomplished what he came for, Dare stood. Pulling out his wallet, he extracted a business card, dropped it on Mannen's desk. "When Rollins gets back, have him call me. After he's done with the police, of course." His smile was hard. "I never pass up a chance at an exclusive."

Being a cautious man, Victor waited until the front desk

had called to affirm McKay was out of the building before speaking again. "You may come out, Peter."

An adjoining door opened, and the huge man who'd served him faithfully, if somewhat unimaginatively, for the past nine years, stepped out. There was a look of worry on his usually impassive face. "You think there's anything to what McKay said, sir?"

He hadn't hired the man for his brains, but his dullness could be trying at times. "Of course there is." His voice was patient, as if addressing a small child. "I'm very certain that you can expect a visit from the police shortly. Come." He waved the man to a seat. "I can hold them off with tales of your travels on my behalf until we've finished with our current business."

The other man set himself down gingerly on the chair. One hand went to his neckline, as if it had suddenly grown too tight. "Do you think this calls for a change of plans?"

Mannen cocked his head, as if considering the possibility. "That wouldn't be prudent. We've already set them in motion, after all. But perhaps it would be best if you went on a vacation when we finish. The French Riviera is exquisite at any time of year, with enough gambling to keep even a man of your appetites happy. All expenses paid, of course."

The advantage of employing the terminally dull, Mannen thought, was the certainty that man wouldn't suspect he would never return to Chicago. Or, for that matter, be given long to enjoy his vacation. "Let's focus on the matter at hand. Is everything in place for phase two of my plan?"

"Yessir. It's set for tonight, just like you ordered."

"And you remember the points you're to follow?" It was tedious, really, to have to deal with these mental plodders, but he'd always thought a brighter, more ambitious associate could pose another sort of threat. He listened with a long-suffering air while Peter ponderously listed the points in their strategy. When he'd finished, Mannen praised him like a well-performing pet. "Excellent. Now if all goes well, we'll have this whole nasty mess behind us by tomorrow."

Dismissing his employee, he went behind his desk, pressed a spot on an almost invisible seam in the wall, and a safe swung open. From it he extricated a gun and an extra cartridge. He hadn't taken the risk of becoming personally involved for many years now. It was safer that way, if less fulfilling.

He snapped the cartridge into place, enjoying the weight of the gun in his palm. It was a beautiful piece—a German-made Lugar Special with a hand-crafted silencer. He wasn't totally displeased that the plan called for his personal supervision. There were loose ends to be taken care of. And the best thing to do with loose ends—he hefted the piece, took imaginary aim—was to snip them off. One thread at a time.

Dare figured Addie had had enough time to deal with Delgado and Beardmore so he called her as he was leaving Mannen's office. It was a letdown to hear Song explain that she'd left the building on a personal matter.

"What kind of personal matter?"

The woman hesitated, and his voice went persuasive. "Now, Song, if you don't tell me, you know I'm just gonna have to come on in there and wait for her. You don't want to be tripping over me for the next few hours, do you?"

"Actually, Mr. McKay," the woman lowered her voice conspiratorially. "It was her mother's hospital calling. I think there was some kind of emergency."

His previous good mood suddenly evaporated. "What's the name of the hospital?"

"St. Anne's. It's on the corner of Fifth and West, across from the park."

* * *

Dare made it to the hospital in record time, but he still figured his arrival had to have been a good forty-five minutes behind Addie's. He stopped by the front desk, where a plain-faced nun was writing up some charts. "I'm looking for Addie Jacobs."

The woman looked up. "Addie?" Then she smiled. "You must mean A.J. Yes, she's here, but I'm afraid she's busy with her mother at the moment."

"What room are they in?"

Her face closed. "I'm afraid I can't divulge that information. But if you'd like to wait in the visitors' area right around the corner, I'll be sure and let her know you're here."

Dare nodded, smiled. "I'll do that." He dawdled until the phone rang, and when she went to answer it he checked the chart on the woman's desk. By the time she'd turned around he was already out of sight.

It wasn't difficult to figure out which room he was heading for. The keening sounds coming from room 118 mingled with low, comforting tones that he immediately recognized. Pausing in the doorway, he took in the scene, felt it grab him hard in the chest.

An older woman with hair a shade lighter than Addie's was rocking back and forth in a wooden rocker, clutching a doll to her chest. Addie was kneeling in front of her, her quiet voice having little effect on the woman's mournful wails.

He was sure he made no sound. Certainly the other woman seemed unaware of his presence. But Addie looked up and for a moment he thought, he hoped, he saw relief.

The next instant her face went expressionless, and he knew if he gave her the opportunity, she'd throw up her damnable defenses, effectively locking him out.

He didn't intend to let that happen. "I called your office. Song said you were here."

She rose from her position on the floor. "You didn't need to come. Mama just had an upset." It was easier, she thought, than to say *setback*. Easier and oh, so much more optimistic.

"Is she all right?"

She forced a brisk tone. "She'll be fine. She's had a sedative, and she'll sleep soon." As if to deny her words, the woman grasped her hand, clung tightly.

"It was Rich, A.J., come back for me."

"No, Mama." It was harder, far harder than it should have been to keep the bleakness out of her tone. "You're imagining things."

"He had his gun. Remember? He had his gun and was going to shoot us both." Her face crumpled and she wrapped both arms around her middle. "Make him stop, A.J. Make him go away."

The past slapped her with a malevolent force. This time she was aware of the quaver in her voice. "He's gone, Mama. I took care of it, remember? He can't hurt you again."

"He's gone." Her mother repeated the words in sing-song, in rhythm to her rocking. "He's gone. A.J. made him go away. And he never can come back, can he?" Her eyes filled with tears, and her tone turned wistful. "You made him go away and never come back. He'll be better next time. He loves us, I know he does."

Dare watched the scene narrowly, noting Addie's reaction. She jerked a little. Then, in a familiar move, she straightened her shoulders. "You should try and sleep now." He could almost believe the even tone, devoid of anything but concern, if he hadn't seen her eyes.

He recognized the look he saw in them, was certain he'd worn it himself when he'd stood by his father's hospital bed and railed at the randomness of fate. And he wondered what had happened to put that load of guilt on Addie.

A nurse appeared in the doorway in response to the lit button Addie had pushed. "Would you help her to bed, please?" The nurse hustled to comply, and Addie bent, kissed her mother on the forehead. "I'll be back tomorrow, Mama."

"And Rich will come, too." The hopeful tone in her mother's voice had fangs and stabbed deep. A.J. walked swiftly from the room, holding tenuously to control.

Dare followed her out, put his hands on her too-stiff shoulders, drew her to rest against his chest. She was rigid for a moment before the fight streamed out of her and she allowed herself to lean against him. For just a moment. It really wasn't that difficult, she discovered, to lean on a strong shoulder if she tried hard enough.

"It never changes," she murmured. His arms closed around her, and she leaned even more heavily on him. "My father drank. Beat all of us. Threatened to kill her more than once. Came damn close a time or two." A bitter laugh escaped her. "And still she calls for him. Still she has some sick need for a man who was never any kind of husband, any kind of father."

He tucked his chin on top of her head, tightened his arms and wished he could vanquish the past. "It sounded like she was having some kind of flashback."

Exhaustion washed through her, a bone-deep weariness that had more to do with the soul than with the physical. "That last night, he threatened us with a gun. Actually shot her, grazed her in the arm. I don't know if he meant to or not, but I honestly thought he'd kill us all. That was the night I made her leave for good."

She closed her eyes against the memories she was too weak to fight off. "Even then I had to bribe her, to keep her from going back. I told her that the only way I wasn't going to turn him in to the police was if she promised to move away from him for good this time. That's the only reason she left. To protect him." She gave a bitter laugh. "She agreed, so I took her to the hospital one more time. Lied to the doctors and the social workers one more time. Because I thought it would be over then, you see. I thought at last it would be over. I was fifteen. I still believed in, if not happy endings, at least peace."

Her gaze was sightless, blind to the nurse leaving her mother's room and discreetly slipping away. "But it wasn't over. Because she never stopped loving him. Never stopped needing him in some perverted way. He stole her sanity. Most of the time I really believe that. But then there are times," her voice dropped to a whisper, "when I think maybe I'm the one at fault. Because I took her away from the thing she needed the most. He was her lifeline, and I removed it. And no matter how much I tried, I could never take his place."

Comprehension swept through Dare in a brutal wash, and he brushed her hair with his lips. He thought he understood her now, far better than she would have liked, and the knowledge was bittersweet. It was all too easy to see where her distrust had sprung from. "You probably saved her life, baby. And that wasn't love your mother felt. At least not a healthy kind. Love doesn't have to be like that."

"I wish I could believe that," she whispered, her voice so soft he could barely make out the words. But he did hear them, and they clawed a hollow furrow deep in his chest. Because God only knew, he wished she could believe it, too.

Chapter 14

The call came as they were walking through the hospital doors. A.J. reached for her cell phone to answer. As she listened to the person on the other end of the line, her movements slowed, until she finally halted. "How long ago?" The words were terse, forced out a throat that had suddenly clenched. "Where?" She was aware that Dare was watching her, his expression alert. "You tell him I'm going to want some answers before he goes home tonight. We're on our way."

She flipped the phone closed, the action imbued with frustration. "That was Connally." Her gaze met Dare's, held. "He wants to meet us at the police morgue." She forced the next words out, wishing futilely that there had been some mistake. "Delgado's dead."

Dare swore quietly, with a great deal of inventiveness. "How?"

"If the medical examiner sticks around like I ordered, we may be able to get the answers to that question very shortly.'' With grim purpose in her voice, in her step, she headed outside. "This is just too damn coincidental, isn't it? The day after he fires Paquin? Just when he decided to flip on Mannen?"

His tone matched hers. "I have the feeling we're going to find that coincidence had nothing to do with it."

From her first look at Gabe's face, A.J. knew she wasn't going to like the news he had for them.

"The medical examiner, Doug Trump, is in there working on the body now." He jerked his head toward the door. "I gave him your message, but he was none too happy about sliding Delgado to the top of his priority list."

"Well, I'm not particularly happy, either, so that makes two of us." She looked at the door. "How long's he been working on him? Does he have any ideas yet?"

"It's been a little over an hour, and if Connally hadn't ticked him off and gotten us thrown out of there, we might have had a little more information by now."

Gabe threw his partner a dark look. "Doug was being touchy. I just made a few suggestions."

Madison rolled his eyes. "Yeah, like how to do his job."

"What do we know? When did this happen?" she asked.

"Midafternoon. The security camera showed a commotion in Delgado's cell. The jailer went in there, and Delgado was lying on the floor. He called for backup before going in, and they couldn't find a pulse. Medics tried to bring him to, but he was already gone."

She shook her head in disbelief. "Just like that?" Then her eyes narrowed. "Has anyone checked the food to see if it had been tampered with?"

Gabe nodded. "We've got a technician on it. But I'm afraid there's a chance this is due to plain bad luck. Delgado had a heart condition he was being treated for."

"So you're telling me it's possible he died of a heart attack?" She couldn't believe her cosmic bad luck.

"Hard to believe he had a heart," Dare muttered.

Rubbing her brow, she considered the news. Delgado had given verbal agreement to his attorney, instructing him to retrieve supposed evidence to turn over to her. Evidentiary rules plainly indicated grounds for her to utilize that evidence as she saw fit. But there was no doubt that by losing Delgado as a witness against Mannen, they'd lost a valuable piece of any case they would build against the man.

Her gaze flicked to Gabe. "At least it's over for Meghan. She won't have to go through the trial."

He nodded. "She'll probably be relieved. Me, though..." His eyes hardened. "I would have just as soon seen him live out his days in maximum security."

A.J. seconded that emotion. She couldn't help feeling that, by his death, Delgado had somehow escaped justice.

Her thoughts were interrupted when the morgue door opened. A tall dark-haired man with deep-set eyes approached. "Assistant State Attorney Jacobs? I'm Doug Trump, medical examiner. I understand this corpse is one of yours."

"I'm working the case, yes."

"Get to it, already, will you, Trump?"

The coroner made a point of ignoring Gabe. "You know your guy had heart problems, right?"

"So I've heard."

Doug went on. "The organ shows signs of older, moderate damage, but nothing that would suggest any massive infarction that would have killed him."

"So you're saying he didn't die of a heart attack?" Dare said. "Can you say with any certainty at this point what he did die of?"

The man stalled. "It will be a day or so before I can be sure. I need to run several more tests, and the technicians have left for the day already. But I did do a preliminary screen on the blood and found something disturbing. His records indicate he was being treated with digitalis. He had three times the normal level in his blood.''

There was a moment of silence. ''What's that mean?'' A.J. asked.

''You're saying that it wasn't a heart attack that killed him,'' Dare said slowly. ''He OD'd on the medication.''

''Which means someone got to him,'' Connally put in bitterly. ''And I think we can all guess who.''

She still couldn't quite believe it. ''Could there be some other explanation? A blood disease, or...'' Her imagination failed her. ''Something else?''

Trump rubbed the back of his neck. ''At this point I wouldn't rule out other possibilities.'' He paused for just a moment. ''But I'd suggest you get your hands on the medication that was being given to him and have some tests run on it. Because right now I'm leaning toward overdose as cause of death.''

A.J. was barely aware of the medical examiner's departure. She slumped against the wall, still reeling from the ramifications. ''How is this even possible?'' she demanded of the detectives. ''Is Mannen's reach so long he even has contacts in the jail?''

''He was able to pierce a protective custody arrangement for the witnesses who were going to testify against him six years ago,'' Gabe reminded her grimly. ''If he has contacts in the U.S. Marshal's Department, it's not too hard to believe he's got someone in the jail, too. C'mon, Cal.'' He was already striding away. ''We'll seize the medication and then start listing everyone who would have had access to it.''

Dare and A.J. trailed the detectives out of the morgue and up the stairs. She rubbed her forehead tiredly. She didn't even want to guess Beardmore's reaction when he heard that the high-profile trial he was counting on to give him a political boost was never going to transpire.

Slipping his arm around her waist, Dare said, "It's been a long day. Why don't we grab dinner and relax for a while?"

Considering his suggestion wistfully, she said, "I'm going to have to let Dennis know about this."

"He'll go ballistic."

"Definitely."

"All the more reason to put the conversation off until tomorrow." Dare's voice was coaxing and much too persuasive.

"I can call him from the restaurant," she decided. She'd wait until after they'd eaten. Something told her that the upcoming conversation would kill any appetite she might have.

By the time they reached her home there was a dull throb in A.J.'s temples. Any pleasure she'd taken in the meal she'd shared with Dare had been marred by Beardmore's reaction. Not surprisingly, he'd been more concerned about the loss of the exposure the trial would have afforded his campaign than by the murder itself.

"Are you still brooding about Beardmore?" Dare fitted her key into the lock and opened the door.

"Not really. I'm sure by tomorrow he'll have come up with a way to spin this whole thing so that his candidacy gets a boost."

"That shouldn't be difficult once Delgado's PD turns over the tapes he promised." There was a clicking sound as Dare attempted to turn on the lights. "What'd you do, forget to pay your electricity bill?"

"Funny." She pushed him aside, reached for the switch and flipped it. The house remained dark. "I must have blown a fuse."

"Where are they?" Dare's arms came around her, swept her figure, as he nuzzled her neck. "I can change them for you."

Laughter sounded in her voice. "Well, you won't find them in there." Pushing his wandering hands away, she placed her purse and briefcase on the floor. "The fuse box is downstairs."

Not having been blessed with night vision, she made her way through the living room and to the kitchen more by feel than sight. She found the flashlight she kept under the kitchen sink and switched it on.

"Do we have to take that?" Dare's voice was disappointed. "I was looking forward to getting you alone in the dark."

"Later," she promised, leading him to the basement door and opening it. "We're going to need this to change the fuse." Carefully she descended the steep steps. Although the basement ran the length and width of the house, it was little more than a cellar, with as many twists and turns as a rabbit hole. Because her former apartment had afforded her much more space than this house did, she'd been forced to box many of her belongings and store them down here.

With the beam lighting their way, she wound her way through the rows of boxes and showed him to the small back area of the basement. Selecting one of the fuses from the neat row atop the fuse box, she handed it to him.

"Ah, Addie." Laughter sounded in Dare's voice. "Well prepared in case of an emergency. Why am I not surprised?"

Jabbing her elbow into his ribs, she said, "At times like these, being well prepared is—" She stopped, his hand against her lips unnecessary. She'd heard the noise, too.

Goose bumps broke out over her skin. "Probably a mouse," she breathed.

"Vermin, maybe." His voice was merely a breath of sound in her ear. He reached for the flashlight, switched it off. "But bigger than a mouse."

The slight creak that sounded then was unmistakable. Someone was on the stairs.

"Is there another exit out of the basement?"

She shook her head in response to his whisper, and he crowded her against the far wall. Icebergs formed in her veins, owing nothing to the chilliness of the area. The footsteps were coming closer, heralded by a beam of light. As it swept back and forth it highlighted the gun held in the outstretched gloved hand.

"Where are you, A.J.?" Shock rendered her motionless for an instant. She wondered if Dare had recognized the voice, but didn't waste time asking.

"We have to split up." She barely breathed the words.

He shook his head violently. "Don't even think about it." His voice was no less lethal for being nearly soundless. "You stay here. I'll cause a distraction."

When she didn't answer right away, he reached for her hand, squeezed warningly. "Okay," she whispered, and waited for him to relax a fraction, release her.

Then she bolted away, scurrying as quickly as she could, slipping through a space between the wall and the furnace. Dare would be furious, but she couldn't regret her action. She wasn't going to stay there while he put himself in danger on her behalf. It wasn't Dare's battle to fight, and she wasn't going to allow him to get hurt. It had been her job that had swept them both into danger.

And it was her brother who'd been sent to kill them.

"Funny, I don't remember inviting you, Leo." She used the cover of her words to mask the sound of her movements, as she crept further away. "Don't tell me you're lost."

"It's a long story." She could hear him moving to where

he'd last heard her voice, and she used his movements to disguise her own. "If you come out I'll tell you about it."

"I was never the brainless one. But you must be, if you think I don't have this all figured out."

"You never suspected a thing." The sneer was apparent in his voice, and despite the blanket of darkness, she could picture his face, lip curled derisively. She'd seen the look numerous times. "Bet you didn't know I was in your house almost every night, did you?"

He'd managed to shock her yet again. In her house? She heard his stealthy movements come nearer, and she stilled, holding her breath.

"Why'd you think I stopped by that first time, to chat about old times? I made a wax mold of your key, had one made, and I was in and out of here as often as I liked. Some of my old skills really come in handy."

She'd taken advantage of his speech to inch further around a corner. "Why?"

"For your notes on the case, of course. Every night while you slept peacefully in the other room, I was in your brief-case. I knew everything you discovered, every action you were going to take. I was paid handsomely for passing that information on."

"Who was paying you?" It was Dare who asked the question, and A.J. could feel herself tense. He was follow-ing her original suggestion, splitting up from her, so Leo would have two directions to contend with. She knew it was their only chance out of there. But fear for him was sending splinters of ice through her heart.

"It doesn't matter." For the first time she heard a note of uncertainty lace her brother's voice. She knew in that instant that he'd been drinking. The false bravado, the cour-age he could only ever seem to gain with a liquor crutch, were dead giveaways.

"How much did you have to drink to convince yourself

to go through with this?'' she asked in a conversational voice, scooting along a wall and around another corner. ''What'd it take? One bottle? More?''

''Shut up.''

She proceeded as if she hadn't heard the venom-laced word. Maybe if she kept him diverted, Dare could find a way to safety. Their best chance was to coax Leo further into the basement, allowing them a chance at the stairs. ''I know you couldn't do it on your own.'' She allowed a tinge of amused pity to enter her voice. ''You never did have any guts.''

''Shut up!'' The shout was punctuated with a deafening blast, and she pressed her face against the floor. He'd fired the gun. The knowledge was mind numbing. Even learning what he'd been involved in, she was still astonished. Still heart torn.

''Addie!''

Hearing the terror in Dare's voice, she swallowed hard and answered. ''I'm fine. My brother's no better at shooting than he was at anything else in his pathetic life. What's the matter, Leo? Didn't get enough practice?''

''Hard to get any practice when I had the gun stashed in the old lady's room.''

She stopped, in the middle of ducking down another row of boxes. ''What?''

''You heard me.'' He was back on top of his game, certain he had the upper hand. The beam of the flashlight he carried swept the rows as he stalked her. ''Kept it safely above one of the ceiling panels. Gave her quite a start when I retrieved it today.'' There was a shrug in his voice.

''You bastard.'' Cold-blooded fury was pounding through her veins, melting the ice there. The scene in her mother's room that afternoon took on a new meaning. She hadn't slipped into one of her mental fugues—she'd been shoved, sadistically, by seeing a gun in Leo's hand. ''Did you ever once consider the memories that would hold for her?''

''She won't even remember it tomorrow.''

A.J. held her breath when a beam played over the next row. It was probably her imagination that there was a hint of regret in his words. Leo, she well knew, felt sorry for no one but himself.

''Let's stop this.'' His voice was coaxing, the sound of his footsteps as he walked along in the row beside hers plainly audible. ''You can't believe I'm going to hurt you.''

She huddled on the floor, much too close to him to try answering.

''I didn't let anything happen to you when you were kidnapped, did I? You weren't hurt. Not really.''

Bile rose as she listened to him rationalize her kidnapping, attempted rape. Knowing that her brother had been behind that was something she doubted she'd ever get over.

He'd moved beyond her. She crawled in the opposite direction. ''Maybe your buddies didn't understand your directions well enough.''

''Tommy got out of hand. I heard that. But you came out of it okay, and you will this time, too. My orders are just to keep you and your boyfriend confined for a while. Nothing more.''

Did he really expect her to believe that? Did he believe it himself? She heard a slight noise, was desperately afraid it was Dare. To cover for him she spoke, deliberately sounding uneasy. ''Are you sure?''

''I wouldn't lie to you, A.J. I'm not going to hurt you.''

She heard a sound nearby. Terror clutched her heart when she realized it was Dare. Time was running out. She knew him well enough to be certain he'd try to overpower Leo, and she wasn't going to allow him to endanger himself for her. Without questioning where the fierce feeling of protectiveness welled from, she took a deep breath, prayed that he'd follow her lead. "Okay. I'm coming out." Slowly she rose, stood still, as the light swung across her, then back to steady on her. The glare blinded her for a second, and then the light went flying away in the midst of a crash.

Listening to the sounds of the struggle, A.J. ran for the light and turned it in the direction of the two men locked in battle. They rolled into and out of its beam. Dare smashed his fist against Leo's jaw, and then the other man reached for his throat. She used the light to search frantically for the gun. If she could just get her hands on it, she could put an end to the scene.

The men broke apart for an instant, and she located the weapon. It had slid across the floor a ways, halfway between the two men and her. She prepared to spring for it when another voice sounded from the stairs.

"For God's sakes, you fool. Shoot her!" For an instant there wasn't a breath of movement. It was as if they were trapped in a frozen tableau. "Then get out of the way so I can finish McKay."

She flinched as the bright beam spotlighted them, leaving the stranger shrouded in darkness. There was no time to wonder at the man's identity. No time to wonder how he'd gotten there. Only one thing filtered to her brain. Dare was in imminent peril.

"I said shoot her, man! Or step aside and I'll do it myself."

As if the words shattered their inaction, Leo, Dare and A.J. simultaneously dove for the gun. Her brother got to it first. Time slowed to a crawl. His arm raised...he aimed...Dare grabbed him...

And a shot blasted through the room. A.J. watched as Leo staggered, clutched his chest. Dare dived for the gun, but her eyes were glued, horror-stricken, to her brother. His gaze locked with hers, blood seeping through his fingers. For an instant the rest of room faded away. She was by his side as he dropped to the floor, shrugging out of her jacket to press it futilely to the gaping wound.

"Addie, get down!"

Dare's warning had her attention shifting. Two more shots split the silence, deafening in the small area. A tearing pain sliced through her shoulder. A moment later a weight hit her, rolled her across the floor in a dizzying arc. More shots sounded. Dare uttered a curse. Then she came to a sudden stop, her head slamming into something solid. She had a flare of panic for Dare's safety before everything went black.

"You have no idea how happy I am to get out of that place."

Dare figured he had a pretty good idea, given the pace Addie had set. She'd all but run to the car once they'd gotten outdoors.

"I hate hospitals!"

Recognizing the panic beneath her vehemence, he kept his voice soothing. "I know, honey. Here, let me." He opened the passenger door of the car and helped her inside. Then, rounding the hood, he opened the opposite door and slid in beside her, reaching over to secure her seat belt.

"I'm not an invalid."

"I don't want you reinjuring your shoulder. You're supposed to go right home and get some rest. The doctor was clear about that."

Her lip curled. "He was a quack."

"He was head of the trauma department, honey. You're just holding a grudge because he made you spend the night there."

She didn't quite manage to hide her shudder. "The longest night of my life."

His lips quirked. Most of the night she hadn't even been conscious, due to the sedative they'd managed to slip her.

He sobered quickly, remembering how she'd looked crumpled on the floor, still and bloody. The instant it had taken him to find her pulse had been the worst moment of his life.

He started the car and pulled from the hospital parking lot. He had no intention of taking her back to her place. Not after last night. Not yet. To distract her from the direction they were heading, he said, "What'd Beardmore want this morning?"

She gave a humorless laugh. "Despite his dismay at my near-death experience, he wanted to congratulate me on the case. You may now address me as Chief Deputy Assistant Attorney of the Felony Division."

"You got promoted?" Keeping one eye on the traffic, he leaned over, placed a delighted kiss on her cheek. "Something must have changed his mood since you talked to him last night."

At that moment A.J. couldn't work up an answering enthusiasm. She, better than anyone, knew just how easily this case could have turned out to be totally different. There was, however, satisfaction to be had in thinking about Stanley's reaction to the news. He wouldn't relish having A.J. as his superior. The thought was cheering.

Belatedly she returned to her explanation. "What changed Beardmore's mood was the tapes Delgado's PD delivered today. Justice is showing definite interest in them, and he's elated to be working closely with that department. It seems that a voice sounding suspiciously like Victor Mannen's is heard ordering hits on Patterson and Connally."

"Son of a—" Dare said, pounding the steering wheel lightly with one fist. "We finally got him."

She slid a glance at him. "Not yet, but he must be running scared. He's already retained legal counsel."

"Paquin?"

Thinking of her nemesis, a small smile settled on her lips. "No, Paquin is going to be kept busy for a while defending himself from charges of suborning perjury. The testimony of those two witnesses he introduced at the prelim aren't going to stand up to close scrutiny. We're not going to drop that part of the investigation, even if Delgado is dead."

She made no protest when he turned in to his apartment's parking garage. Just the thought of returning home had her shuddering. She wondered if she'd be able to live in the house again after what had happened there.

Maddeningly, just the walk from the car to his apartment was enough to exhaust her. She sank into a chair as soon as they entered the apartment, despising the weakness she felt. "I need to call St. Anne's."

"I called this morning and explained to a Sister Katherine that you wouldn't be by today."

She opened her mouth to contradict him, but her protest was quelled by the look on his face. Arguing with him in this mood would be futile.

"Your mother had a good night and was in the recreation room with the other patients when I called."

She looked at him sharply. "In the recreation room? She hasn't joined the other patients in weeks."

His brows lifted. "Then I take it this is good news?"

For the first time that day a real smile curved her lips. "Very good news."

Sitting on the arm of her chair, he reached over, toyed with a strand of her hair. "You haven't mentioned Leo."

"I spoke to his doctor. He came through the surgery all right and his condition is guarded."

Once that carefully empty voice would have maddened him. But he knew just how deep the emotional wounds went, knew just how difficult they would be to heal. Taking her hand in his, he toyed with her fingers. "I'm not sure how much you remember about those last few minutes that night."

"I remember the stranger telling Leo to shoot me." He hated the flat, emotionless tone she used. "I remember Leo going for the gun."

"He got to it a split second before I did, but he didn't aim it at you, Addie." His gaze probed hers. It was important that she believe him. "He was pointing it at the man threatening you. That's why he was shot."

There was a dart of pain directly under her heart. She wasn't certain it would ever go away. "I wish I could be sure of that."

"I'm sure." His voice was firm. He brought her hand to his lips, pressed a kiss on her knuckles. "I'm sure, Addie." She gazed at him searchingly, a flicker of hope mingling with the despair in her eyes. "Despite everything else he did, I really don't think he meant for you to be harmed."

"Whoever he was working for had other plans."

Dare's face went grim. "Connally was able to talk to Leo this morning. I don't think there's any question who your brother was working for. He made an effort to disguise his voice, but it was Mannen, I'd stake my life on it. He never actually saw the man who was paying him, but he was ordered several times to divert you from the case. Last night he was supposed to keep us confined." His jaw went tight. He wouldn't share with her the conclusion he and Gabe had drawn, that Mannen had intended to dispose of all three of them once Leo had followed orders. Addie's injury was the latest in a long list of grievances that Mannen needed to pay for.

She drew in a deep breath, released it. Immediately his gaze went to her face, examining it critically for any hint of pain. When he didn't find any, he relaxed minusculely.

"Did Connally have any answer on Delgado's medication?"

Dare nodded. "It had been tampered with, just like we figured. Mannen must have been playing it cool, as long as Delgado believed Paquin would get him off. But the moment you went in there and blew his nice little plan all to hell, he revised his strategy and got rid of him altogether."

People were expendable to Mannen, A.J. thought bitterly. Leo, Delgado…anyone who stood in his way. She and Dare had very nearly figured among his victims.

"How about if I fix you something to eat?" he offered. She'd fallen into a brooding silence that made him uneasy. "Or we could order out if you don't trust my cooking. I have it on good authority that we can order a year's worth of Chinese food at a time, to be delivered daily. You never have to worry about going hungry."

"As enticing as that sounds, you'd better forgo the plan. I can't stay here forever."

"You could. If you wanted to." Her gaze jerked to his. "When I saw you lying there, bleeding, I couldn't think of anything but getting help for you. I didn't consider chasing Mannen, all I could focus on was getting you help. There's no way I'm going to let you out of my sight again. I want you here with me tonight. And tomorrow. And every day after that."

He felt the gradual stillness that crept over her and almost wished he could retract the words. He knew too well what happened when Addie felt threatened. But his feelings were out in the open now, and he'd force her to deal with them. "You can have all the time you need to get used to the idea. But you need to know what I'm hoping for."

There was a measure of anxiety in the way she was trying to free her hand from his. The sign of her nerves had talons clawing in his gut. "Are you sure you're not feeling tired? Because I'm thinking maybe you ought to lie down for a while."

It was as if she didn't hear him. "I don't need time to think about what you said."

Panic tap-danced across his chest. "Shoot, honey, of course you do. Don't rush into a decision." The words tumbled out of his mouth in a mad rush. "Take all the time you need. A few months...years if you want."

She was shaking her head. "I've already come to a conclusion. I've been afraid, forever it seems. That if I really cared for someone, gave them that kind of power over me, I'd be left defenseless." Her gaze met his, sought understanding. "That terrifies me."

Unable to answer, he gave a terse nod.

She frowned a little, seemed to search for words. "You could walk out right now, and I'd survive. I'm convinced of that."

"I know," he said bleakly. Rising, he jammed his hands in his pockets to keep from reaching for her.

"I'm doing this badly. It's just that...I've never really needed anybody. I've never let myself. And I got so wrapped up in running from the emotion that it took a while to understand that needing and wanting are two different things. I don't need you in my life to complete it. But I do want you there."

He stilled, his gaze cutting to hers.

"Do you understand the difference?" At his stupefied silence, her lips curved slightly. "Or do you still want me to take some more time to think about it? I think you mentioned years?"

"Not a chance." He was back at her side, in two quick steps his mouth taking hers in a kiss that was half desperation, half relief. "You've taken a couple of years off my life in the last few minutes alone." He cupped her jaw, his forehead resting against hers, a shudder working through him. "I guess as long as you've come this far, I won't scare you off by telling you I love you, will I?"

She turned her head, pressed a kiss into his palm. "You'd better."

"I love you, Addie." He drew back, watched the wonder on her face, found himself reaching for more. "I can wait for the words. Give you some time. If we're talking years again, though, it just might kill me."

She smiled, shook her head. "I love you, too. I can't say it doesn't scare me to death, but I'm willing to work through that."

Nuzzling her neck, he murmured, "We've got the time to work through it together. Decades. A lifetime."

A trail of flames lit beneath her skin, fired by his touch. A lifetime. It sounded about right to her.

*   *   *   *   *

Don't miss the third story in the
CHARMED AND DANGEROUS series,
HARD TO TAME,
available in October 2002
from Silhouette Sensation.

SILHOUETTE®
SENSATION™

AVAILABLE FROM 20TH SEPTEMBER 2002

HARD TO TAME Kylie Brant

Charmed and Dangerous

Cynical and untouchable undercover agent Nick Doucet had to find Sara, a runaway witness, for a killer's trial. But then he did something he thought he'd never do—he caught her...in his arms!

THE RENEGADE AND THE HEIRESS Judith Duncan

Finn Donovan was hard and unyielding but he had sworn to keep wealthy Mallory O'Brien safe. But Mallory ached to know the secrets of Finn's past— even as she longed to share his future.

BY HONOUR BOUND Ruth Langan

The Lassiter Law

Micah Lassiter had to protect heiress Prudence Street from a crazed killer. But watching over this beautiful woman was sweet torture especially when Micah wanted Prudence to be his.

BORN BRAVE Ruth Wind

First-Born Sons

When Hawk Stone and Laurie Lewis had to go undercover, they never expected to feel such heat between them. Could they deny their attraction long enough complete their mission?

ONCE FORBIDDEN... Carla Cassidy

The Delaney Heirs

Johnna Delaney's hectic world stood still the moment she laid eyes on Jerrod McCain again. Seeing him had awakened passionate memories that couldn't be ignored.

BABY, BABY, BABY Mary McBride

Melanie Spears had a date with a sperm bank! Then she bumped into her new neighbour—her drop-dead gorgeous ex, Sonny Randle—who had his own plan to do things the old-fashioned way!

THE STANISLASKI

Sisters

NORA ROBERTS

From the bestselling author of the Stanislaski Brothers, Nora Roberts brings you the spirited, sexy Stanislaksi Sisters.

Bestselling author of Night Tales

Available from 19th July 2002

SILHOUETTE®
INTRIGUE™

wants to play

HIDE and SEEK

with bestselling author

Susan Kearney

*For years a deadly secret kept a family apart,
but now it's out... Suddenly, Jake, Alexandra
and Melinda have to* hide *from mortal danger
and* seek *passionate love along the way!*

THE HIDDEN YEARS
August 2002

HIDDEN HEARTS
September 2002

LOVERS IN HIDING
October 2002

0802/SH/LC41

SPECIAL EDITION™

SENSATION™

DESIRE™ 2 IN 1

SUPERROMANCE™

INTRIGUE™

*REVEALING OUR FANTASTIC
NEW LOOK SILHOUETTE...*

FROM
18TH OCTOBER 2002

 **SILHOUETTE®**

FREE

2 BOOKS
AND A SURPRISE GIFT!

We would like to take this opportunity to thank you for reading this Silhouette® book by offering you the chance to take TWO more specially selected titles from the Sensation™ series absolutely FREE! We're also making this offer to introduce you to the benefits of the Reader Service™ —

★ FREE home delivery
★ FREE monthly Newsletter
★ FREE gifts and competitions
★ Exclusive Reader Service discount
★ Books available before they're in the shops

Accepting these FREE books and gift places you under no obligation to buy; you may cancel at any time, even after receiving your free shipment. Simply complete your details below and return the entire page to the address below. **You don't even need a stamp!**

YES! Please send me 2 free Sensation books and a surprise gift. I understand that unless you hear from me, I will receive 4 superb new titles every month for just £2.85 each, postage and packing free. I am under no obligation to purchase any books and may cancel my subscription at any time. The free books and gift will be mine to keep in any case.

S2ZEC

Ms/Mrs/Miss/Mr ....Initials...
BLOCK CAPITALS PLEASE

Surname...

Address...

....

....Postcode ....

Send this whole page to:
UK: FREEPOST CN81, Croydon, CR9 3WZ
EIRE: PO Box 4546, Kilcock, County Kildare (stamp required)

Offer valid in UK and Eire only and not available to current Reader Service subscribers to this series. We reserve the right to refuse an application and applicants must be aged 18 years or over. Only one application per household. Terms and prices subject to change without notice. Offer expires 31st December 2002. As a result of this application, you may receive offers from other carefully selected companies. If you would prefer not to share in this opportunity please write to The Data Manager at the address above.

Silhouette® is a registered trademark used under licence.
Sensation™ is being used as a trademark.